WALK OUT THE DOOR

WALK OUT THE DOOR

PEARL WOLFE and EVELYN ANDERTON

atmosphere press

EVELYN ANDERTON:
For my wife, Janet Anderson
For my sisters, Mary and Joan Anderton
In memory of Kit Anderton

PEARL WOLFE:
Especially for my husband, Bill Goldsmith
For our children,
Chris Goldsmith and Rachel Wolfe-Goldsmith
For my sister, Eleanor Wolfe
In Memory of Mary Wolfe Hewitt

CHAPTER 1

Becca found the road. She looked over at Emily and could tell from her stiff posture and grim expression that she also knew how risky this was. "Is it a go?" Becca asked, thinking how lucky she was to have such a smart, experienced intern like Emily. She was small, but she had the toughness of her hometown, New York City.

"We have to," Emily replied without hesitation. "It's Molly's only chance before the worst happens."

"O.K. But if either of us wants to leave, we say so and get into the van as fast as we can." As the shelter supervisor, Becca was ultimately responsible for what happened. They didn't normally go to a woman's home. This was a major break in protocol. They were trained to always meet women in a public place, like a 24-hour restaurant where it would be safer to decide if a situation required the confidential location.

Emily nodded. "I'm glad you trust me enough to join you. I can't stand to let another batterer commit another murder."

"My first week of work, a woman left the shelter one morning to pick up her things. Her husband shot her in their driveway."

Emily groaned.

"I'll never forget the pall that hung over the shelter for months. After that, it was almost paralyzing when we got crisis calls where weapons were involved."

Becca tightened her grip on the wheel and Emily took a deep breath. They were only a half-hour from Eugene, but they had hardly seen any other cars for miles, none since turning off the highway. At a row of three mailboxes, Becca slowed and wheeled into a long driveway. The headlights and nearly full moon illuminated sparse gravel and potholes; a canopy of trees shadowed drainage ditches with high grass and thistles. It all reminded her of the road to her sister Anne's house in Wisconsin. She had the same sick feeling whenever she visited Anne in that place, always hoping that Matt, Anne's husband, wouldn't be there. It had been three years since Anne left him, Becca thought. Will these feelings ever go away?

After a quarter of a mile, Becca reached a small, single-story, green clapboard house tucked in among the Douglas fir trees and covered in wisteria. Although it needed a paint job and the railing along the front steps had fallen to the ground, some charm remained. Best of all, it looked like they had made it in time. There was no pickup truck in sight. A good sign.

Becca pulled up and turned the van around, nose pointing toward the way they came in. When she and Emily approached, the front door swung open and a diminutive woman looked out. She had short blonde hair and wore jeans and a yellow rain jacket. Dogs barked

WALK OUT THE DOOR

nearby when she walked onto the porch. The woman's right arm dangled at a strange angle, her left eye swollen shut. Were they too late after all?

"Hi, Molly. I'm Becca from Jill's Place. We talked on the phone. This is Emily," Becca said with an encouraging smile. She was glad that Molly was on the porch, so she didn't have to stoop to greet her. Becca's 5'11" height and athletic body had sometimes intimidated the women and children in the shelter when they first met her.

"Hi. I'm so glad you're here," Molly replied, wincing as she moved her arm slightly. "Danny doesn't usually come back until really late or early the next morning after he does this. He figures I can't get away. No vehicle, I'm stranded."

"Let's prove him wrong," Becca said, walking up the porch stairs to follow Molly back inside.

Before joining them, Emily poked around the side of the house and was startled by two dogs charging at her, barking furiously. She screamed and jumped back but the dogs fell short, banging against the chain-link fence of their run. They kept lunging and snapping while she moved quickly to check the backyard. She saw only a dense forest with ferns and vine maple encircling the house. Six-foot-tall Himalayan blackberries were out of control and impenetrable. No one was there. Satisfied, she edged past the dogs and returned to the porch where she stopped to listen for incoming sounds of cars or motorcycles. Nothing. Relieved, she entered the house.

Past Becca and Molly, Emily saw a small boy sitting on the living room couch with a baby in his lap.

"This is my son, Jason, and my six-month-old, Jenny," Molly said. "Jason, meet Becca and Emily."

Jason looked at them.

Molly nodded at him like she wanted him to speak.

The boy finally said, "I'm scared." His shaky voice was convincing.

"I believe it, Jason," Emily said, kneeling down to get to his level. "Let's get going to a safe place."

Becca turned to Emily, "I'll help Molly. You take Jason and the baby."

Emily nodded and got busy with the children. Becca noted her can-do attitude and flexibility, once again grateful for such a competent intern at her side.

Molly interrupted Becca's thoughts. "I think we're almost ready. I tried to pull together the things you suggested on the phone."

Becca reviewed the list of essentials with Molly: I. D. documents, any money in the house, keepsakes, a few changes of clothes, toiletries, coats, and medications. Meanwhile, Emily sat down on the couch. "Jason, you're so good with your sister."

Jason turned to look at her directly, probably to see if she meant it. He was tall for a seven-year-old, his wavy blonde hair disheveled, his clothes rumpled, like he'd dressed in a hurry. He told Emily that his Mom had asked him to sit with Jennifer while she packed. He shifted the baby on his lap to a more secure position. "I'm holding her because Mom can't. It's her arm this time."

Emily put a hand gently on his shoulder. He winced before she said, "I'm sorry. We'll make sure she sees a doctor to fix it."

Jason watched her intently. She was a stranger. Who knew what she would do next?

Emily leaned back, hoping to make him more comfortable. "Do you have all the stuff you want to take? Your favorite toys?"

He took her to his room carrying Jennifer carefully. Pausing at the door, he seemed undecided. After a moment, he handed Jennifer to Emily and began gathering his toys and clothes into a heavy black trash bag. He stopped again, this time turning a full circle, locating a vinyl diaper bag at the foot of his bed. He dragged two things back to Emily, left them at her feet, and reached up for his sister. When he had her head supported and her body secure in his arms, he looked up at Emily. "You're nice," he said with a hint of surprise in his voice.

Emily knelt once more and lightly ruffled his hair. "So are you! But are you quick?"

Jason nodded, eyes locked on Emily's face.

"Let's see how fast we can get this stuff into the van." She hoisted the bags and led him outside.

Becca and Emily tried not to show their growing concern but the danger was increasing with every passing minute. It would take the Lane County sheriff at least an hour to respond to this rural area if they had to call 911. Useless in an emergency.

Jason put Jenny into a car seat so he and Emily could carry the bags out to the van. Jenny whimpered but stopped when Jason squeezed her tiny hand and said, "Shhh, Jenny. I'll be right back." He laid a fleecy yellow blanket over her and tucked it around her chin.

Becca and Molly followed them out to the porch and stood looking around as if trying to think of anything they'd forgotten. Neither seemed to notice the racket the dogs were making until Jason ran up.

"What about Lobo and Cassie?" Jason was crying, looking from Becca to his mother and back. "Danny will kill them for sure this time."

Becca started to respond, but Emily beat her to it. Stooping down next to him, Emily said, "Your Mom told us about the dogs when she called. We have a place for them until you have a new home."

"I want them with us," Jason whined, sounding more like the seven-year-old he was.

"Of course, you do. But they'd be all cooped up where you're going. They're country dogs. Becca has a friend who has a farm with lots of horses and places for dogs to run and play. After we get you and your Mom settled at the shelter, we'll make sure they're safe too. I promise. But now, let's get out of here."

Jason dropped the bag. Toys rolled down the porch steps. Startled, he brushed at his tears with an angry swipe and stomped back to the van. Emily quickly scooped up the toys and hustled to stuff them into the back of the van. Becca made sure the door was locked and Molly retrieved the dogs. In less than a minute, the dogs were next to the bags in a secure crate. Emily climbed into the back seat with Jenny and Jason. Becca got behind the wheel and Molly settled into the passenger seat where her damaged arm might not get as jostled.

Becca frantically shoved the key into the ignition. The dash clock showed they'd made this rescue in under fifteen minutes.

As they started to pull away from the house, a pickup rattled up the driveway. "Everyone quiet," Becca whispered, looking into the backseat at Emily, Jason, and Jenny. "Once he pulls in, I'll step on it and get past him." This situation is exactly why they met women in public places. Now everyone was in extreme danger, including the kids.

Emily pulled Jason closer and whispered, "It'll be okay. Don't worry." Becca caught her eye in the rear view mirror and knew that she wasn't convinced.

"It's just Mike, my neighbor," Molly shouted over the barking dogs, as she opened the van door and stumbled out.

Mike jumped out of the truck with agility. Shock washed over Becca, thinking she was seeing Matt, her sister's abusive husband. The same height and shaggy beard. When he got to the front of his truck and stepped into the headlights, she could see a strong resemblance, but it wasn't Matt.

As soon as the dogs saw Mike, they stopped barking and started wagging their tails.

"I saw the van come up the road so late at night and heard the dogs," Mike said, scanning the area around them. "Damn late. What the hell is going on?"

Molly said, "It's alright, Mike. We're leaving. These women are here to help us. Don't tell Danny."

"You can't just walk away." Mike was shaking his head. From the driver's seat, Becca could see how hard the man was breathing. "Your dad left the place to you, not Danny. He has no right to it!"

"I have to leave," Molly said, looking back at the house.

"That bastard! I'll kill him," Mike said, noticing Molly's arm.

"Stop it!" Molly's voice was rising toward hysteria. "What is it with you guys?"

"I'm sorry. I care about you and the kids. I know your father would want me to do something. I just don't know what."

"I'll call you when I get settled. I'll need help then," Molly said, climbing back into the van, wincing as she hit her arm on the armrest.

"I'm here. Whatever you need," Mike said and did his best to smile. "I'm glad you're getting away from that son of a bitch!"

Becca pulled out and headed down the road, watching in her rear-view mirror to see what Mike would do. He stood there for a moment and was slowly getting into his truck as she turned the first curve.

"Danny's gotten more and more jealous of Mike ever since I got pregnant with Jennifer. There's nothing going on between us. I swear! He's a family friend. Our neighbor for years."

"I'm glad you have a friend close by," Becca said, never taking her eyes off the road. "Many women are totally isolated."

They hit the outskirts of Cottage Grove amidst a misty rain smearing the windshield. It made the visibility worse than a real rainstorm.

"Watch for Danny's truck," Becca said to Molly. "If you see it, let me know and duck down. We've gotten this far, so let's not take any chances."

They drove through Cottage Grove. Passing a parking lot outside the Tap-N-Keg, Jason suddenly ducked. "There's his truck! Mom, get down! He'll kill you. He said so."

A green, ¾-ton Chevy pickup was parked near the bar door. It had obviously seen a lot of use, muddy, rusty, and banged up. Molly just stared at it as they drove by. Becca was busy remembering the location of the Cottage Grove police station. Main Street, she thought, across from the Centennial Covered Bridge.

In a few seconds, Emily gave the all-clear. "He never came out," she said, helping Jason to sit upright again.

"It'll take us about half an hour to get to Emerald Hospital in Eugene," Becca said. "Everyone, rest up. It's going to be a long night."

As they pulled onto I-5 a few minutes later, all breathed a collective sigh of relief. Becca and Emily knew the next danger point would be at the emergency room if Danny came home and figured out where Molly had gone. No matter how drunk, he would set out to find her.

Becca asked Emily to call both the Cottage Grove and the Emerald Hospital emergency rooms to give a description of Danny and warn them he was dangerous and might come looking for Molly and the kids.

As they approached the hospital, Emily pointed to a building, "There's the Shady Grove Cafe where I work. I'm supposed to open up in the morning. Think I'll make it?"

"You will," Becca replied, nodding to her in the mirror. She frowned remembering that she needed to tell Emily soon about her connection to the Cafe. Becca wanted to keep tabs on Matt Foley, Shady Grove's co-owner and her sister's abusive ex-husband. She knew secrets had a way of popping up at the worst possible time and ruining everything. She didn't want Emily to get caught up in the Foley family mess and risk losing her job.

When they arrived at the hospital parking lot, Becca carefully helped Molly out of the van. The children remained in the back seat and Emily got behind the steering wheel. Molly came to the side door, gave Jenny a kiss, and reached over and stroked Jason's hair. "Stay with Emily and be good." Jason seemed like he wanted to argue but was too exhausted.

"This won't be too long," Emily said. "Your mom needs to get her arm fixed. We'll just go to the shelter and get ready for her to join us." She could see the tears in his eyes and felt the pain of all the children whose lives got turned upside down. Her eyes began to well up before she put the vehicle in gear and drove away.

Once inside, Molly and Becca headed to the admitting station. Before they could speak, the heavy-set nurse behind the counter stood up when she saw Molly's injured arm and black eye. She said, "Let's take a better look at this arm." She grabbed a fold-up wheelchair on her way around the plexiglass shield.

"Just down the hall." She helped Molly get seated and began wheeling her toward a series of numbered cubicles on both sides of the long corridor.

Molly held her hand up to stop the woman. "Wait. Can Becca come with us?"

"Of course. Is she your sister? A neighbor?"

"Shelter counselor," Molly said, her voice sounding weaker by the moment.

"Say no more," the nurse motioned Becca to come along.

"My name is Cynthia," the nurse said, scanning each tiny room as she walked past. "That arm looks painful. Let's talk and then hopefully I can give you something for the pain."

"How long will this take?" Molly asked as Becca caught up with them. "My children—"

"The doctor will be in as quickly as possible. Let's start with your name and birthday," Cynthia asked as she pushed Molly into an empty cubicle.

Molly responded and said, "Please hurry. My arm is killing me!"

"I'll be quick," she said. "Tell me what happened."

Molly described Danny's latest explosion, her rescue by Becca and Emily, and the danger she was in. When she finished, Molly closed her eyes and let her chin drop to her chest. She reached toward Becca for help.

"Hi, Becca." Cynthia glanced up at Becca but she continued charting. "I recognize you from Jill's Place. We've worked together before."

"More than once. Just so you know, we've called the Cottage Grove Hospital as well as this hospital's security to warn that an irate batterer might come tonight. When he doesn't find Molly in Cottage Grove, you all would probably be next. That's assuming he isn't too drunk to think."

"I have a picture of Danny on my phone if that would help," Molly said, fumbling in her purse.

"Good thinking," Cynthia responded. "Let's forward it to the front desk to alert security. I'm almost done with this paperwork, and then we'll get an x-ray and look at that eye."

Nearly an hour later, as Molly and Becca were waiting for test results, they heard an ambulance siren in the parking lot. Becca stepped out of the cubicle in time to see the double doors at the end of the hall open. Two EMTs pushed a stretcher down the hallway. She thought she also saw a man step quickly into the lobby, just as the doors started to close.

Two nurses came out of the office to take the patient from the EMTs. One of the nurses looked questioningly at a man walking quickly down the hall and nodded at Becca. They both recognized Danny from Molly's photo. "Yes, it's him," mouthed Becca.

"Excuse me, sir. May I help you?" the nurse asked.

"My wife and kids beat me here. I'm just looking for them," Danny answered calmly, smiling. Becca never ceased to be amazed by how quickly these guys could pull themselves together in front of witnesses and turn on the charm when the situation demanded it.

The nurse looked down at the burned patient on the stretcher and hesitated. As Becca ducked back into the cubicle, she heard the nurse say to Danny, "Please wait here while I find out where your wife is. What's her name?"

"It's Danny," Molly whispered, ducking under the sheets.

Becca stepped through the curtains again. The nurse was gone. Danny was coming toward her, sweeping the curtains open as he passed each cubicle. When he got to Molly's cubicle, Becca stood in his way.

"My mother just died. Please, don't disturb us," Becca said with tears suddenly running down her cheeks.

Danny hardly hesitated before pushing aside the curtain. When he saw a body covered with a sheet, he shoved Becca back into the cubicle and moved on. He left a trailing odor of alcohol and sweat.

Becca peeked out and saw two Eugene police officers moving down the corridor. Danny saw them and ran down a side hallway. Within seconds, Becca heard sounds of a scuffle and figured they'd caught him.

There was a cracking sound and a thud, then Danny shouting, "Get the hell off me... my family... You got no right—"

Becca realized she was hyperventilating and ducked back into the cubicle. "Sounds like they have him," she told

WALK OUT THE DOOR

Molly, hoping it was true.

"How could you be so brave?" Molly asked, breathlessly. "How did you think so fast?"

"You were just as quick, pretending to be a dead body."

They looked at each other and burst into semi-hysterical laughter. Molly reached up and threw her good arm around Becca's shoulder. They held each other until they stopped laughing and shaking.

Before the doctor came in to set Molly's arm, one of the police officers stuck her head through the curtain. "Excuse me. I'm Officer Susan Brody. You must be Molly."

"That's me. Did you arrest Danny?" Molly asked, voice still unsteady.

"He's in custody." The police woman stepped inside and closed the curtain behind her. "He did quite a bit of damage at the Cottage Grove Emergency Room, so hopefully we can keep him for a few days. But, we never know if we'll have enough jail beds. It just depends how many felons we arrest."

"He'll kill me and the kids if you let him out and he finds us."

"I know it's scary. But if you feel up to it, you should go to court tomorrow and get a restraining order against him. Becca or other staff at the shelter will help you. It could help keep you safe."

"Right," Molly said, rolling her eyes. "Like a piece of paper will stop him!"

Sarcasm. Becca was surprised to see a side of Molly she hadn't expected.

"It gives us more power to hold him if he breaks it. And it sounds like you know him well enough to think he will." The officer frowned, obviously frustrated. "I know. It's the best the system can do at this point. Can I document your injuries with some photos? We may need them in court as evidence." Molly nodded.

The doctor came in a few minutes later to check for signs of a concussion and write down instructions for how to set Molly's arm. While the orthopedic technician came in to apply the cast, Officer Brody popped in for one last question, "Danny's not talking. He has no ID and won't tell us who he is. Does he have a driver's license or state ID?"

Molly shook her head. "No driver's license because of DUIs. But he does have a state ID. His name is Daniel O'Hara. He has several arrests on his record for assault."

The officer made note of that, stepping closer to Molly. "One more thing. Even if we have available cells, we may not be able to keep him long. Men like Danny get out of jail too quickly. Friends or family post bail. Are you going to the shelter when you leave here?"

Becca gave a thumbs up.

As the tech put the final touches to Molly's cast, Susan Brody and Becca went into the waiting area and exchanged business cards. Susan showed Becca the photos of Molly's injuries and said, "Now that I have these, I think the D.A. might prosecute." She spoke softly to avoid being overheard.

"And Molly?" Becca asked.

"At this point, she seems willing to assist in the investigation and testify."

"Hope so," Becca said.

"I'll request that the Custody Referee inform me when Danny's going to be released."

"I appreciate that. I'll let Molly know you'll be doing that."

As she turned to leave, Susan said, "Hopefully our next meeting will be in court at Danny's trial."

✗

After stopping to drop off the dogs, Emily and the children got to the shelter near midnight. Emily parked in the alley around back and carried Jenny up the stairs to the rear entrance. Jason dragged himself out of the van, squirming like he needed to pee, and followed them, lugging their overnight bag.

Once inside Emily showed Jason the bathroom and took Jenny to change her diaper on the changing table in the kids' playroom. Then she moved into the kitchen to heat up a bottle for Jenny, who had awakened and started to cry. Holding Jennifer in one arm, she poured a bowl of cereal with bananas for Jason.

When Jason came out of the bathroom, he turned round and round, scanning every room he could see. On the way over, Emily had told him that as many as five families lived together for up to six weeks in the shelter. Some of the women had children and others did not.

"Where is everybody?" he asked, alarmed when he couldn't see Emily.

"I'm in the kitchen," she said, smiling and peeking around the corner. "Everybody else is upstairs asleep." She paused to let him digest the information. "How about cereal before we go up?"

"Uh," he said, entering the kitchen. He walked slowly, wearily, taking everything in.

Once he finished eating, Emily lifted Jenny and pointed

to the stairs while putting a finger to her lips to let Jason know he needed to be quiet. At the top of the stairs, they went down the hall and into the last room on the right. Emily laid Jenny gently in the crib without waking her.

"Is Mom...um. When's Mom coming?" Jason asked.

"As soon as she can. It'll be okay," Emily whispered, pulling his pajamas out of the bag. "I'm here with you." Once he was ready for bed, she arranged his blankets and asked, "Can I give you a good night hug?"

Jason held out his arms as Emily embraced him and said, "The doctors are taking good care of her. You know your mom is lucky to have a smart boy like you. Most kids your age wouldn't understand that coming to the shelter makes it easier for her to get the help she needs."

Jason tugged his covers up to his nose, looked around and whispered, "I'm not sure I'm so smart. I usually just make Danny mad. Will he come here?"

"This house is a secret. We don't give anyone the address. Only families like yours are brought here," Emily said. "Nobody else knows where it is." She leaned over for another quick hug before standing. "And, by the way, everyone makes Danny mad. It isn't your fault."

Jason watched her face for another moment, then yawned and closed his eyes. In less than a minute, he was asleep. Across the room, Jenny made a gurgling sound from the crib.

Emily found a fold-up chair by the door, reached into her purse, took out her Kindle to finish *Nine Parts of Desire* for her Women, Gender and Sexuality Studies course. She felt the irony of reading about oppressed Islamic women while sitting in a shelter with oppressed American women. She imagined women all over the world. Educating each other, uniting, gaining strength. Moments later when her eyelids drooped, she wondered if the kitchen pot had any coffee. She had to stay up long enough to read her assignment.

CHAPTER 2

Emily arrived promptly at 7:00 am for her shift at the Cafe. As she got out of her car, she watched Liz flip the sign by the front door to "OPEN."

"Hey, Liz. How's it going? You're early. Didn't expect you until our 10 o'clock meeting."

"I was up late last night. The band had a meal after the show and we talked way too long. Matt should be in soon. You look a little ragged. What's up?"

"My shift went long at the shelter because of a late-night assessment. A mom and two kids. One was a baby. A lot to handle."

"I don't know how you manage it all. School, an internship and working here. Seems like a lot to me!"

"Two cups of mocha java should take care of the droops. Then, back to being a hyper-functioning restaurant manager." She gave Liz a thumbs up as she walked back to the kitchen to make sure everyone was ready to open.

Liz moved to a table near the office door to review yesterday's food receipts and music ticket totals on her laptop. As the first group of customers came in, she watched Emily warmly greet them by their first names, much like she and Sophie, her old business partner used to do. Liz glanced outside towards Willamette Street. She loved the view of Japanese maples in the center divide. Their colors never failed to impress her.

Even though she was tempted to chat with the regulars, she stayed at her table to compare how the Cafe was doing this month compared to last year. The breakfast and dinner totals for March were holding steady but lunch business was down by 15%. Not to worry. Since she'd opened the Cafe six years ago, she'd become well aware that small businesses have their ups and downs.

Running a restaurant and a music club in the same building was not simple. Liz and Sophie had originally wanted to open a cafe with only music, coffee and desserts. During their early planning, it became evident that a restaurant needed to be part of the equation to survive. After running the numbers, Liz reflected on the business changes through the years, especially after she fell in love with one of her customers.

X

On a cold and rainy January day, Matt Foley had rushed into the Cafe to escape an intense downpour. Liz couldn't help but notice the curly-haired, bearded man in his early 30's, dripping onto her purple and white tiled floor. He stopped just inside the front door. She later learned he had just completed a four-day drive from Madison, Wisconsin. No wonder he looked road-weary. Liz ran her hand through her shoulder-length, auburn hair. The gesture calmed the nervousness caused by this attractive man who caught her eye.

She was sipping a steaming cup of coffee from a lavender mug with a tree motif. The words "Shady Grove" encircled the graphic. Her obsession with purple was obvious in the branding of the Cafe. Even her Prius was a dark shade of purple. Custom painted, no less.

"Welcome to the Shady Grove Café. Hi, I'm Liz. We're still serving breakfast. Can I seat you?" Liz was a striking woman. Her hair was parted down the middle, wavy, just touching her shoulders, and shifted enticingly when she laughed. Her deep hazel eyes jumped out at first glance along with a ridiculous amount of freckles covering her face. When she walked into a party, she often drew a crowd. Everyone had something to say to Liz, especially here at the Cafe. Customers always wanted to catch her read on the best music for the month. Her energy was magnetic.

Liz had laughed when she saw him sniff the air. "I think your nose is crying out for our breakfast special. Hot and just out of the oven, cinnamon streusel muffins. How about I get you a free sample? Some say it's life-changing."

"I think something already did," Matt gazed intently into her eyes. "It's nice to meet you, Liz. I'm Matt Foley. You must be the owner."

"Yep. I own the business and it kind of owns me. Sometimes I feel like I live here."

Liz returned his warmth as she seated him at a table next to where she had been working. The way Matt had looked at her just moments before made her tingle. She placed the menu before him but lingered. It had been a while since someone had piqued Liz's interest and she found herself wanting a longer conversation.

"Bet it's hard work and long days. You know, I think I've been here before. It was a toy store then."

Liz nodded. "Not many people remember that."

"When I was growing up, I spent summers visiting my grandparents in Cottage Grove. We came here all the time. It's a longer story. Come sit with me if you have time."

"I'd love to." She slipped into the seat across the table from him, restraining herself from fiddling with the napkin in front of her.

He began, "Our Saturday routine started with Gramps, me, and my cousins heading to downtown Eugene. Our first stop was always Saturday Market."

He described their Saturdays in detail. The 50-year-old outdoor market featured handcrafted wares by 400 vendors covering two park blocks. The maker of the craft was in each booth, which made for rich conversations, buyer and creator talking face to face. His Gramps would chat with numerous vendors that he knew from the 1970s when he and Grandma Vivie sold fresh raspberry and strawberry lemonade at their own booth.

Gramps and the cousins always made a stop at the food court for hot chocolate at Willa's Famous Cheesecake, then sat at tables in front of the stage to hear live music. They heard everything from cigar box guitarists to marimba bands to Cajun music. Matt's oldest cousin often struck up a dance routine near the stage. He'd spin his cousins into a frenzy until they fell on the ground, laughing from the dizziness.

Next, they'd always head to this very location, Lola's Toy and Hobby Shop, to browse. They knew Gramps would get a small toy, book or puzzle for each of them. Then they'd stop to get double fudge brownies at Elsie's Bakery. They counted on this weekly ritual.

"What sweet childhood memories. Sounds like your family was really close."

"Some parts of it close, some distant. Those summers were an important part of my life. This building seems so much smaller to me now than when I was a child. I guess most things seem that way when we're all grown up and go back to what we only knew as kids."

"Definitely. It's a small space, my cozy cafe," replied Liz. "Honestly, small was my intention. Customers tell me the Cafe feels like their kitchen and the stage in the next room is like their living room. Kind of the way you describe the old toy store."

"I wonder how you do enough business in this sized space to survive."

Liz gave him an exasperated look. "It's not about money. I'm proud of what I've built here. I make a simple living doing what I want. The business is profitable enough so the people who work here make a decent living. Full-timers get health insurance. I operate with a social conscience. We serve organic and locally grown foods. The music we present makes you think and feel." Liz clearly had explained her business philosophy numerous times to the press and new customers.

Matt was watching her face. They were both exchanging brief glances and then looking away. He impulsively asked if she might be hungry.

"Sure. I need to eat before my monthly finance meeting.

You'll give me a reason to postpone facing the numbers."

As he sipped his second cup of coffee, Matt began scraping the cinnamon streusel crumbs off his plate, licking his fingertips. "What would it take to get the recipe? I'll do anything!"

"What a flirt," thought Liz. She laughed and responded, "Our first kitchen manager, Hannah, deserves all the credit. She was really a baker at heart and responsible for those muffins being a fixture on the menu. She learned the tasty recipe when she worked in the kitchen at the Manzanita Hot Springs Center during a summer break in college. It was an intentional community, with vegetarian food, meditation, yoga, and massage. A place to get your life back in balance. Hannah pulled a coup by getting permission to use their recipe here. The muffins have become a staple."

"Good story. Quite an operation you have going here," Matt said, taking it all in.

"French jazz playing in the background and all the amazing artwork sets the right mood."

A wide variety of customers inhabited the room. Some college students at one table, a family with a toddler at another. Three middle-aged women were caught up in a spirited conversation. Two men in suits sat at the counter, drinking coffee, reading the *New York Times* and making occasional remarks. They created a buzz and brought life to the restaurant that morning.

A group of six bicyclists came up to pay their bill. Matt had helped Liz push two tables together to accommodate them. You had to be creative in a 70-seat cafe. When the group approached the front counter to pay, one asked Liz where they could refill their water bottles. She graciously offered to do it for them.

"What's the quickest way to get back on the South Riverfront Bike Path?" asked a bicyclist wearing tiger-print leggings as she pulled her rain pants out of her pack. Liz pointed her to the Lane County Bicycle Map on the wall and went over to show her the shortest route.

While Liz was helping the bicyclists, Matt walked around the Cafe. After she was done, Liz watched Matt carefully check out the art on the walls, as though walking through a gallery. She imagined him getting some insight into how she viewed the world. He paused to look at the colorful framed posters of musical, political, and literary events of the last four decades. Political posters with anti-Iraq war sentiments covered the east wall. He stood for a while in front of a 1960's movie poster, 'Wasn't That A Time,' with Pete Seeger and the Weavers. He saw the hip-hop and reggae posters as well. Liz heard a deep sigh as Matt lingered at the large mural painted by a well-known Bay Area artist, Leah Jesse Mandel. The mural's intensity seemed to draw him in.

When Liz came up to him, Matt smiled and said, "We must be kindred spirits. Your decor tells me a lot about you."

"What did you learn?"

"Just guessing here. You lean left of center for sure. At the least, liberal."

"You're on the right track."

"Isn't Leah Jesse Mandel kind of famous? Didn't she get an arts award from Barack Obama?"

"Yeah, she's been in the news a lot. She got national attention about her work in the *New York Times*. This mural is 'Lioness Rising'. See the strong images of an

African woman superimposed over a lioness? It was on the cover of *Emerging Culture*, a big deal arts magazine. The article mentioned the Shady Grove Cafe as the mural's home. I'm reminded of Leah's friendship every time I look at it. Even with all her fame, she shared some of the limelight with me."

"So, you do it all. You offer great music, local food and art. Good combination."

"Thanks. Leah and I stayed in touch after college. She was excited to support my small business by painting a mural for the Cafe's opening."

"Pretty generous gift."

Next, Matt stopped to look at old labor organizing posters on the west wall.

"I've been interested in the labor movement since my Dad started out as a labor lawyer. He spent lots of his time in factories and breweries in Milwaukee."

"Funny. I was into the *Sociology of Work* when I was in college. I did an internship with the local head of the Teamsters. We definitely have some things in common. Is your father still doing labor law?" Matt was standing close to her as they walked together through the room.

"No, he's a judge now, Judge Quinn Foley. He became well known for civil rights litigation and defending anti-Vietnam War resisters in Madison. I got a little bit of pressure from the family to follow Dad's career path. Only I dropped out after two years at the UW Law School."

"Why did you leave? Disillusioned with the system?"

"No, it was more complicated." Matt moved away from her, pointing at the tables. "Tell me about them. This place is filled with stories."

Liz looked at him quizzically and wondered why he

dodged the question. "Oh, the tables. I love these tables. Kind of a labor of love. I made them with Sophie, my best friend and business partner. All sixteen of them are handmade."

"Are the strips redwood? Those tiles in the center of the table are a work of art."

"Good eye. Sophie and I figured those blue and orange flowers contrasted perfectly with the wood."

"Impressive."

"Thanks. We took pride in the final product. Neither of us could saw a piece of wood without chopping off a limb before the Cafe. We picked up these tiles traveling in Ensenada, Mexico and knew we'd put them to good use one day."

Liz was watching Matt's hands as he slowly stroked the tiles, running his fingers along the glossy, wooden strips. She felt self-conscious when he caught her gaze.

"It seems that you can do anything you put your mind to."

A party of four walked in the door. Liz went to seat them and Matt resumed his tour. He noticed there were some beat-up instruments hanging in a line across the wall, each held up precariously by a nail and a string. He walked up to look more closely at an Appalachian mountain dulcimer, a funky three-quarter sized Martin guitar and a bluegrass banjo minus a string. A washtub bass stood near the stage. All the instruments looked well used.

When Liz rejoined Matt, she learned that Gramps had taught Matt and his cousin to play guitar, fiddle and washtub bass. Matt continued to play guitar in high school and college. He even wrote songs.

He turned to her and said, "I wish I could write a love song like the one your cafe is named after. It's one of my favorite old folk songs."

"My Mom sang it to my brother and me at bedtime. We'd fall asleep hearing the line:

Shady Grove, my little love
Shady Grove, my darlin'
Shady Grove my little love,
I'm going back to Harlan."

"Nice memory," said Matt. "Maybe you need an old mandolin to add to your collection. I happen to have one that's still fully strung and has a decent sound. It would fit right in on this wall. Another piece of history."

"Do you have one in your little house on wheels?" joked Liz, pointing to his refurbished postal van parked by the front door.

"No, it's at my grandparents' house in Cottage Grove, along with a tambourine, fiddle and fretless banjo. I'll be staying out there. I'm just here to clean things up and put the family house on the market. My Dad asked me to take on this project. I was happy to do it. Now that I'm here, I feel sad, too."

"I get it. Kind of the end of a chapter?"

"Yeah, but it could be the start of something new."

Returning his gentle smile, Liz said, "You know, I'd love to see those instruments. If you're in town, you could bring them here. Or, I could come down there... I mean, if you're serious."

"Absolutely. Come on over. I'll even make you a hefty Midwestern breakfast."

Laughing, she threw back her head and said, "Just try and top my muffins."

"So, where exactly is your grandparents' house?" Liz asked after agreeing to come out on Monday, the one day a week the Cafe was closed. Matt gave her directions and warned her that Google Maps wouldn't get her there.

As Matt was getting ready to leave, Emily came up to Liz. "Fran is here and ready to go over the financials." She smiled at Matt and asked Liz, "Hey, who is this guy taking up your morning? A musician looking for a gig?"

"No, he's a new friend, Em. Emily Palmer meet Matt Foley. He's just got to town. He'll be staying in Cottage Grove for a while."

"Good to meet you, Emily. I should head out and let you get to your meeting."

"You too, Matt. I bet that I'll be seeing you again." Liz and Matt looked at each other and laughed. Matt grabbed Liz's hand and gently squeezed it. She impulsively hugged him goodbye.

The accountant interrupted the farewells as she walked up.

"See you Monday," Matt said, walking out the door.

"Interesting, Liz. Tell me more about your new friend," Emily said.

"Maybe, I will," Liz said. While she was taken with Matt, she was puzzled by his dodging her question about leaving law school. Was he hiding something?

CHAPTER 3

As Matt left the Cafe, he began thinking about his past. He had just returned from Costa Rica where he had gone for two years to distance himself from the trauma of the end of his marriage to Anne. Now, his project in Cottage Grove would give him a month or two to contemplate his future. He could return to law school or find a new career direction. When Matt had loaded his van and headed out of Madison on Interstate 90, it felt like a positive step. Leaving the Shady Grove Cafe, it felt even more so.

When Matt first arrived in Cottage Grove, he assessed the situation and texted his father that he needed to do more than clear out the contents. The place required a renovation before it could go on the market. And he needed a personal renovation, too. Even with time away in Costa Rica, he still felt lost. His psychologist, Dr. Fitzgerald, told Matt that while it was alright to leave Wisconsin, whether to Costa Rica or Cottage Grove, his internal struggles would go with him. Matt and Dr.

Fitzgerald had also spent time working through the domestic violence Matt had experienced growing up.

Right after Matt's ex-wife left, his father began to speak so negatively about her that Matt wondered if he was somehow involved in Anne's abrupt exit and complete disappearance. His father denied the suspicions. "You just need to move on, Matt. It wasn't a healthy marriage. We all knew it!"

When Matt thought about his relationship with Anne, he remembered how loving and exciting it had been at first. He met Anne at the University of Wisconsin when he was still an undergraduate. They discovered their Wisconsin-Oregon connection right at the start. Matt noticed a strikingly tall woman with straight, jet black hair halfway down her back, wearing a bright yellow and green Oregon Ducks sweatshirt. She stood ahead of him in the cafeteria line at his co-ed dorm. As Anne served herself a heaping spoonful of mac and cheese, some fell onto Matt's shoe. She looked over at him and burst out laughing. "Is your toe OK? This food is pretty heavy."

"No, it's not okay. Might be badly hurt. Sure hope my toe isn't broken!" Matt laughed. "Hey, where'd you get that sweatshirt?"

"My uncle and aunt live on the coast in Florence, Oregon. This was a gift from them."

"That's weird. I grew up spending summers in Cottage Grove, Oregon with my grandparents and cousins. Do you know it? It can't be more than an hour and a half from Florence. Hate to be competitive, but I own a Ducks hoodie, a dark green cap and an obnoxiously bright yellow T-shirt."

As they scanned their meal cards for the cashier, Matt

pointed to an empty table. "Want to sit?" She nodded and followed him.

"Of course, I know Cottage Grove. We used to picnic at Dorena Lake. My aunt and uncle loved the covered bridges there. We'd do the loop and hit all six of them."

During their first lunch, Matt learned they were both close to their Oregon cousins. She and her family traditionally spent Thanksgiving and spring breaks in Florence. She learned how to fly fish on the Siltcoos River and Matt got hooked on bicycling in rural Lane County. They both liked the idea of being in a place where they could be outdoors year-round.

Anne jumped up suddenly and said, "Shoot. I'm late for French class. My professor wants me to do junior year abroad in Paris. I've got to stay in her good graces. Let's exchange phone numbers. We're not quite done yet, are we?"

"I'm not," Matt said with a grin. "I better brush up on my high school French before we talk again!"

When Matt returned to the dorm, he told his roommate, Bobby, about meeting Anne and how they were going to walk to campus together in the morning. Her French class was in the building next to his first class. He hoped to catch her afterward too.

"Does this mean you'll ditch all your other girlfriends?" Bobby asked. Matt was annoyed by his badgering.

"No way!"

It turned out that despite Matt's denial, he saw Anne exclusively for the first couple of months. After that, things began to change.

"Anne, I'm meeting tonight with my computer lab partner, Cindy. She's been having problems with a new programming sequence we're supposed to know for the exam on Tuesday."

"Really, Matt? Again? I feel like I'm single again. I've barely seen you. Is there something else going on?" Anne asked with an exasperated look.

"Remember I told you in the beginning that I wanted a unique relationship with you, not a traditional one? You agreed."

"That's not how I remember it. I wanted an equal relationship."

"I meant an open relationship. I mainly want to be with you, but I still want intimate relationships with other women. I thought you wanted that, too."

"No way. I don't know where you got that from. That's not what I signed up for."

"Monogamous relationships don't work. It certainly didn't for my parents. They had an ugly divorce when I was in high school. I'm fighting for something different."

Anne blamed this "innovative idea" on their Political Science class. Anne and Matt were in a study group debating this very issue after reading Karl Marx's essay "On Marriage." She wrote a compelling paper arguing that women didn't benefit from Marx's position on having multiple partners since women were primarily responsible for pregnancies and child-rearing. Women didn't bode well under the looser new world order on love, marriage, and commitment. Matt's paper argued for the success of a revolutionary model. The teaching assistant found Anne's feminist perspective more compelling and she got the higher grade, making it a sore point between them.

In addition, Anne had a traumatic experience growing up, making commitment a hot topic for her. Her father had a long-term affair with a married colleague during his 20-year marriage to her mom. Her mom had suspected for years, but it was Anne who discovered it by accident and exposed her Dad's other life. She passed a bustling cafe that she had always wanted to try. She looked in for a moment and did a double-take. When she saw her father passionately kissing a woman at a corner table, she stormed in and confronted him. At her insistence, he later confessed his long-kept secret.

On having her worst fears confirmed, Anne's mother promptly filed for divorce. Devastated, her marriage felt like a lie.

Anne was a sophomore in high school at the time and her older sister, Becca, had just begun college about four hours away. It was hard having Becca away at school during the upheaval. All their lives, Anne and Becca had idolized their father. For years after, they often reviewed this time as "the end of our family as we once knew it." Their father spent years working to regain his daughters' trust. He was even willing to go into therapy with them which was not exactly a Dad thing to do. Now, both Anne and Becca had relationships with their father, but it took them a long time to forgive him and let him back into their lives. It helped, they both agreed, that he never married the "other woman."

During their first year, Matt and Anne broke up a couple of times over the multiple partner issue. Interestingly, the precipitating event that resolved this conflict was Anne's attraction to Matt's housemate, Evan. She first got to know Evan after Matt moved out of the dorms and into a house with some friends. Since she spent so much time there, she began to have long political conversations with Evan. The two got extra time without Matt when they both registered for a European Social History class. After class, they began going out for coffee and their friendship deepened. Anne told Evan she hated Matt being with other women and felt like a low priority. It pushed a lot of buttons from her past. When Matt heard from a mutual friend about how close the two were getting, he guessed Anne might leave him.

He had to act fast. So, he asked Anne to dinner. After they finished dessert at their favorite Italian restaurant, he looked her in the eye and demanded, "Tell me the truth! Are you more than friends with Evan?"

"Well, in the spirit of open relationships that you clearly live by, we're thinking about something more," Anne replied.

"You can't be serious. How could you even consider it? What about us?" Matt said, loud enough for the people at the next table to take notice.

"That is the question, isn't it. What about us? Can't you see what a hypocrite you are?"

"How could you go after Evan? I've always been careful to go out with someone you don't know. Those were our rules!"

Anne grabbed her purse. "I refuse to have this conversation. I'm out of here." As she stormed out, she warned him, "Here's something for you to think about. All Evan wants is me. No one else. Mull that over."

Matt was stunned and waited a week before calling. He asked her to meet him on campus, at the top of Bascom Hill for lunch.

When Anne arrived, Matt jumped right in. "I thought about what you said and you're right. I was being a hypocrite. I can't imagine you being with someone else. I've been a fool. I don't want to lose you to Evan or anyone else."

"Seriously? What happened to you over the past week? Did your last fling dump you?"

"Whoa! That's harsh. From all this experimenting, I now realize that you're the one who matters most to me. Let's move in together." Matt was no fool. He knew exactly what Anne wanted to hear and went with his instincts. Those instincts told him that he needed Anne.

"I sure wasn't expecting that. I don't know what to say. I need time to think it over."

Anne needed to discuss this with her sister, Becca. They spoke every Sunday and texted often. That Sunday, she told her about Matt's move-in proposal.

"I know you have questions about him, but I am in love with Matt. Never met anyone like him. I can see myself marrying him," Anne said.

Becca hesitated. "Don't rush into it. One minute Matt's picking up any hot woman he lays his eyes on and now he suddenly wants you to move in with him. Obviously, your relationship with Evan was too threatening for him. Sounds manipulative! Maybe you should take more time to decide."

"I know this is fast, but it just feels right. Matt has come around since I walked out on him in that restaurant. He came to his senses and suddenly woke up. I don't want to miss this chance."

"But how long will this last? When Evan came on the scene, I had high hopes for him. Not as exciting as Matt, but your relationship was easy and not filled with drama. He was almost too good to you."

"Why don't you say it, Becca? End it with Matt!"

"You're right. I don't trust him. He has two sides. A magnetic personality and also a manipulator. Sort of a Dr. Jekyll and Mr. Hyde."

"Give me an example."

"When you first met, you described him as kind, loving and attentive. Then during our weekly calls you said he felt distant at times. Edgy. Angry over small things. You never knew what would set him off."

"You know how it is early on. Couples try to figure each other out. How much space each person needs. Now things have evened out."

And so, Anne moved in with Matt. As Becca predicted, it wasn't too long before Anne found herself frustrated with the return of Matt's unpredictable behavior. Anne ignored Becca's insistence that she call him on it.

When Anne had finally had enough, she complained to Matt. "You do this crazy-making thing with me."

"This kind of talk is not like you. Sure sounds like your sister. Don't you think she's too involved in your love life?"

"Not really. I count on my sister. Since you never had a sibling, you can't imagine how important she is to me. But I do have my own mind. Living with you was my choice. Definitely not hers!" Immediately after saying it, she wished she hadn't.

Since they were living together, Matt had arranged their lives so they spent little time with Becca or her mom. He surprised Anne with hiking trips and ski adventures during school breaks and holidays. Anne complained, "I want more time to myself and to hang out with my family."

His response was compelling. "I love you. I want to be

with you as much as I can when I'm not studying or working. How about we invite your mom and Becca to stay with us at Lake Tahoe next month? They already know about our seventy-two-mile bicycle ride there. They were impressed with three thousand cyclists joining us from all over the world. They should come and cheer us on."

So, the trip was planned, but at the finish line, the unexpected happened. With the other members of the Madison team cheering him on, Matt got down on one knee to propose. As he slipped the ring on her finger, he asked, "Will you bicycle with me forever?"

Between the exhilaration of completing the ride and being surrounded by family and friends, Anne didn't hesitate for a moment. "Do you mean will I marry you? Hell, yes!"

Since the media was there for the event, it got picked up and went viral on social media. Becca put her arm around her mother, Debra and said, "That guy sure knows how to put on a show doesn't he?"

"No way she could say no, was there?" Debra noted.

Anne and Matt had a busy first year of marriage. With graduation and Matt adjusting to his first year of law school, it was exciting. They moved into a bigger, two-bedroom house and settled in. They went to parties with law students and faculty. Matt regaled them with stories about his Dad's civil rights work. Anne's first job after college as a French teacher created another community of like-minded people. Monthly, Anne and Matt hosted a French cuisine foodie group. They both felt like everything was falling into place.

Halfway through the second year of law school, their idyllic life began to change. Matt, who had been at the top of his class the first year and made the law review, seemed distracted and moody. His grades dropped. He came home late from classes and his study group. Periodically, he even came home drunk and stoned on a week night.

"What's going on with you, Matt?"

"I wonder if law school is for me or if I'm here because it's what Dad wants."

"If you're unhappy with law school, why not take a leave of absence?"

"Not an option. My father would kill me," he said as he stumbled up the stairs.

A couple of weeks later, looking up a contact she needed, Anne found a disturbing text on Matt's phone. Laura, one of his law school friends messaged: "Can't wait to see you Friday." Heart and kiss emojis followed. When confronted, Matt said they always kidded around like that. It was nothing.

At the same time, Matt was jealous of Ed, one of the teachers Anne taught with at the French Immersion School. Things escalated. He badgered her about the friendship, and then even went so far as to call and tell Ed to stay away from her. A week later when Matt came to pick up Anne from work, he saw her talking to Ed. He jumped out of the car and ran towards them shouting, "Get away from her. 1 already warned you." Yanking Anne's arm, he dragged her to the car.

The ride home was silent. Replaying the scene outside the school all the way home, she was furious. When Matt pulled into the driveway, Anne exploded. "Matt, you humiliated yourself and me in front of everyone!"

Once she entered the house, she fled into the kitchen. Matt was right behind her. Anne stepped behind the butcher block table and said firmly, "Stay away from me. You've done enough for one day."

"Don't you dare talk to me that way!"

Matt marched around the table and shoved Anne against the stove. All the hanging pots and pans crashed to the floor around her. Anne began sobbing and her whole body shook.

"What happened was your fault!" He stormed out of the house, slamming the front door behind him.

The next day after word got back to the principal, he met with Anne to tell her that her job could be in jeopardy if Matt came on the grounds again and made the school unsafe.

"We won't tolerate domestic violence in the workplace. Your safety is our concern, too. Please come to me if you need help."

She nodded. "Trust me. I'll take care of it."

Anne didn't think she needed help. What she needed was to get out. What happened at school was a clear indicator that their marriage was unraveling. She knew Matt had no idea how unhappy she was. After he returned from a law conference in Chicago, she abruptly told him she needed a break to sort things out. Matt tracked Anne down at a friend's apartment and tried to convince her to come home. "I'll back off from trying to run everything in our lives. I can change," Matt begged.

"Our marriage was a mistake. I'm never coming back." Anne stood her ground.

After Matt began showing up at her workplace repeatedly, the principal warned Anne that it had to stop. She filed a restraining order. It was never issued because Matt's father, Quinn, asked a favor from the presiding judge who denied the order. This was a huge relief to Quinn largely because of his ambition to become a judge. He was concerned Matt's domestic problems would reflect badly on his reputation.

And then, Anne disappeared. None of their mutual friends could say where she had gone.

CHAPTER 4

Two years after Anne left, Matt and Liz fell in love hard and fast. While Matt was renovating his grandparents' farmhouse in Cottage Grove during those first months, he came to Eugene as often as possible to spend time with Liz. One morning he had arranged to meet Liz for an early breakfast so he could shop for supplies in town before starting the day's work. When he arrived at the Cafe, she was sitting at their favorite table, the one where they had met. Unabashedly Liz planted a passionate kiss on Matt's lips followed by a long embrace before handing him a menu.

Just as Liz flagged Emily down to take their orders, she noticed her brother, Drew, come in from the deck. She waved him over and said, "Come meet Matt, the one I told you about. He's even old enough to remember Lola's toy store."

Matt stood up and shook Drew's hand. "Nice to meet you, Drew. You hungry? Want to join us?"

"Hi, Matt. Good to finally meet you too. Yeah, I just got off a ten-hour shift at the hospital. I'm starving."

"Great." Matt motioned to a seat next to him.

When Emily stepped forward to take his order, Drew teased, "Can you anticipate my every need, as usual, Em?"

"Always at your beck and call, Drew. The usual?" Emily said, throwing her arm around his waist and laughing.

After Emily went back to the kitchen, Matt turned to Drew and asked, "So what do you do after your horrendous shifts at the hospital?"

"Getting out in nature helps me clear my addled brain." As Liz and Matt laughed, Drew continued, "I've become addicted to fly fishing. Especially on the Metolius River. If I don't have time to go that far, the Row River outside Cottage Grove is my second choice."

"My grandfather took us fly fishing to both those spots when we visited in the summers. I haven't done it for quite a while. Wonder if I've lost my touch."

"When's your next day off, Drew?" Liz asked. "If you two go fishing together and catch enough, I'll make my famous Mediterranean Trout. Why don't you invite Elise to join us? I haven't seen her since your fishing trip to Colorado last month."

"Good idea. I'll call her before I go to work tonight."

Matt rolled his eyes and asked, "Does this have something to do with your pep talk about me needing to find some guy friends, Liz?"

"Was I too obvious?" Liz and Drew laughed.

"You've been spending a lot of time with this guy, Liz. Maybe I should check him out."

"He's all yours."

Drew turned to Matt. "There's a fly fisher saying by Tom Brokaw: 'If fishing is a religion, then fly fishing is high church.' Want to go to church with me?"

"You're on. I knew something was missing in my life," Matt responded quickly. "How about the Row River? I'm staying at my grandparents' place in Cottage Grove."

"If Friday works for you, we could meet at the crack of dawn at Schwarz Campground."

"I know, I know. Gramps always said to get rolling between dawn and two hours after sunrise."

"Your gramps was a pro. He's right. Let's meet at 6:00 am."

"It's a deal."

"I'll call and we can talk about what gear and food we'll need. I'm sure I have stuff you can borrow and I pack a mean after-hatch lunch," Drew said.

"Good! I'll check out Gramp's barn to see if he left anything I could use."

After breakfast, Drew left to get some sleep. Matt turned to Liz with a broad smile. "Your brother seems like a good guy. From the way you talk about him, he's pretty much the most important man in your life."

"Actually, now there are two!" Liz declared. Matt breathed a sigh of relief.

A couple of weeks later, Liz called Drew. "I have an idea to run by you. I know you and Matt have been fishing a couple of times. He'll be finishing up the renovation soon and putting the house on the market. What do you think about me offering him a job at the Cafe?"

"Well, Liz, while he's a good fishing buddy, don't you think it might be a little soon to bring him into our business? How much do you really know about him?"

"You know, since Sophie got married and went into the Peace Corps with Pete, I've been working too many hours. I'd like to ask Matt to work half-time to take some of the load off. Just a temporary thing if you're okay with it. He's been spending a lot of time at the Cafe and gets along with customers and staff."

"Hmm. You never ask me about hirings. I'm your strong but silent partner. What's up? Is there more to this?"

"Kind of hoping he'll stay in town longer. I'm getting a little attached to him and I want to see where this goes."

"I figured it may be something like that. Take it slow, Lizzie. I'm not ready for a third partner. It was hard enough getting used to the huge change after Sophie left."

"Got it. Taking it slow."

"Alright, then. Let's give it a try for a month or two and see if he fits in. Especially if he stops catching more fish than I do," Drew said.

That evening, Matt described the failing septic system at his grandparents' house. He couldn't finish the renovation until it was replaced. "I'm thinking of moving into town temporarily until the work is done. I contacted short-term rental agencies today."

"Oh, that's funny. I was just thinking of asking if you'd help me out part-time at the Cafe. I'm short-staffed."

"I wouldn't mind doing that. I'd like to see you more."

"I'd love that."

"Here's a crazy idea. How about I stay with you temporarily until I find my own place?"

Liz paused, thinking that this was just what Drew had warned her about. Moving too fast with Matt. But I'm my own woman, she thought. If it feels right, I should do it.

"Let's just go for it." She was into Matt as much as he was into her.

After a couple of weeks at Liz's, Matt discovered that he felt better about his life than he had since Anne left. Spending time with Liz, Drew and Elise was one of the reasons. A weekend camping trip to Mary's Peak and lots of dinners and movies together made him feel at home in Eugene. It reminded him of when he was first married to Anne.

One afternoon when Matt and Drew were driving back from a fishing trip on the McKenzie River, Matt asked him, "So, what's with you and Elise? Do you ever talk about getting married?"

Drew looked uncomfortable, but answered, "We've been together long enough that I've talked to her about it. She reminds me every time that she has no interest in having children, so why get married? Her father was a brute so she's afraid to be a parent."

"Is that a deal-breaker?"

"She knows it's a big deal to me. She can see how important family is to me. Look how close I am with my sister. I keep hoping Elise will change her mind but hasn't so far. Two years later and I keep trying."

"Too bad. She's a catch."

Drew laughed and said, "Like that twenty-four inch steel-head you caught today?"

"Good one!"

When they arrived at the Cafe a few minutes later, Matt said, "Thanks to you I'm addicted to fly fishing. We'll see you two here for dinner on Thursday."

"See you later." He hesitated and watched Matt go inside, wondering if it was a mistake to confide about

Elise. While he had a good time with Matt, he realized how little he knew about his new friend's private life.

A few weeks later, Drew stopped by the Cafe when Liz was working and he knew that Matt was out bicycling with his cousin. After they settled down with coffee and chatted for a bit, he said, "You know it's strange that as much time as I've spent with Matt, I don't feel like I know him very well. Of course, fly fishers don't talk much because we don't want to scare off the fish. And as men, we're taught not to get too personal."

"I remember how long it took Dad to teach me to shut up when he took me out fly fishing." They both laughed.

"True. But as friendly as Matt is, he's never told me anything about his life before he landed here. Even after I've told him something personal."

"I think he's at one of those points in his life when he's trying to figure out what he wants to do next. So, he stays in the present. The past is off-limits."

"But don't you wonder what stopped him from the path he was on? Wasn't he close to becoming a lawyer?"

"Yes, he was. He's a bit of a mystery to me too. Look, I'm really into this guy. He gets me. I don't want to scare him off. I doubt there's anything dark behind his mystery."

"I just don't want you to get hurt while he's figuring things out."

"Whichever way this Mystery Man goes, you won't have to help me pick up the pieces this time. I've grown up."

"Got it, Lizzie."

X

Matt and Liz got married in a small ceremony on the banks of the Metolius River, a favorite spot of theirs. They wanted it simple, inviting a handful of family and close friends. It was just ten months after they met and were expecting a baby in the summer.

By the time of the wedding, Matt had finished the remodel of his grandparent's farmhouse and had moved the rest of his belongings into Liz's. It was no surprise when Liz asked Matt to co-manage the Shady Grove with her. She had convinced Drew that as a silent partner he would continue to weigh in on the big decisions about the Cafe's direction. In spite of his doubts, Drew went along with it.

The next few months were a bit of an adjustment for Liz. She was sharing the operation of the Cafe with her new husband. But Matt was so energized by running the music club, his enthusiasm made Liz let go of any qualms she had.

One day Drew and Ira, the head chef at the Cafe, were taking a hike up Spencer Butte. Drew mentioned his uneasiness about Matt. "There's more to Matt than he's letting on."

Ira nodded. "I've noticed things that bother me too. Like he's positive and high energy when Liz is around, being super friendly to customers. Mr. Charisma. Then minutes later, he comes back into the kitchen and talks trash about some of them. Sometimes it's regulars, folks we've known and liked for years."

Drew brought up his newest concern. "Matt has ambitious plans to expand the music club. It makes Liz and me nervous. We made it clear to him that we're against it because of the financial risk. Since I'm not on site much, could you keep an eye on him? If you see him doing anything you think I should know about, let me know."

"Good thinking. Will do."

A few weeks later, their banker called. Liz learned that Matt had made a loan request to purchase the two small buildings next door. The banker was concerned that the request came from Matt and not the legal owners. Liz and Drew were furious. When confronted, Matt argued the Cafe needed to expand to attract bigger named performers. He said he hadn't applied for a loan, just asked if the bank would even consider them for a loan of that size. Once he got all the details organized, he planned to run it by them to see if they were on board.

After much debate, Drew and Liz decided to purchase the buildings. They reminded Matt that he should have approached them first, not the bank. According to the prenuptial agreement that Drew had insisted on, Matt did not co-own the business or the building. All major decisions had to be approved by them.

Later, Matt would take complete credit for turning the Shady Grove into what he viewed as a premier West Coast music club. The truth was that national touring musicians frequently performed there before Matt came on the scene. Now, with the performance space tripled in size, even bigger acts joined the lineup. Matt quickly found a way to get himself in the public eye by becoming a board member of the Chamber of Commerce. He used it as a soapbox for his accomplishments.

When talking to his father, Matt bragged about his successful expansion.

"It's still a small operation where you're waiting on tables and doing dishes," his father chided. "It's never too late to go back to law school and transfer your two years of credits from Wisconsin to the University of Oregon. I know the Dean of the UO Law School. You'd have no trouble transferring there."

Matt rejected his father's offer.

The Cafe was on an upward trajectory and working smoothly. Liz came in late mornings when she was hyper and ready to go and didn't start to drag until later in the day. Matt preferred to work when the crowds dined and waited for the show to begin. Coordinating the performers' set up and paying them at the end of the night were his responsibilities.

"I'd love for you to work less, Liz. Maybe do your administrative work from home. I'm willing to carry more of the load around here." Their daughter would be born at the end of the summer.

"I'm pregnant, not an invalid. What century are you from?"

"You need to let go of always being in charge of the Cafe. I'm not your apprentice. I'm your equal." Matt grumbled and walked away.

While Matt mostly liked his new life, it wasn't perfect. In addition to Liz's unwillingness to take his advice, he had recently learned that Anne's sister, Becca, had moved to Eugene. A mutual friend shared that Anne and Becca's aunt had serious complications after a knee replacement. She needed more care than her husband could handle. He sent out a family email asking for help. While on a train in Athens, Becca responded that she would fly to the Oregon coast to help, ending her European trip. Within six weeks, her aunt was on the mend.

When he ran into Becca one day at the Café, he was

shocked. Just seeing Becca made him flash back to Anne since they both were tall and shared the same broad forehead and piercing blue eyes. Will his nightmare ever end? he wondered.

Matt and Becca looked at each other. They simultaneously searched for the closest exit. All they could do was laugh and hug awkwardly. They proceeded to have an uncomfortable conversation for ten minutes, standing near the front counter of the Cafe. It was like a bad blind date, but so much worse.

Matt blurted out, "Hey Becca, what's up? Long time."

"Hi, Matt. I'm good. I heard from your old law school friend, Barry, that you were here to close down Camp Gramps. I thought you'd be long gone by now," Becca replied in the same dismissive tone that Anne had used towards the end of their marriage.

"Actually, I'm living here. I just married Liz, the owner of this cafe."

"Whoa! I hadn't heard that news. Big life change for you, huh?"

When Matt didn't quickly respond, Becca changed the subject. She told him she'd been working at Jill's Place for the past three months. Matt knew she had become a social worker after getting her Master's degree at Ohio State.

The fact that she'd work in a women's shelter, he digested with an internal grimace, but smiled and said, "I know Katrina Strauss, the executive director of the shelter. We held one of our monthly non-profit fundraisers here for Jill's Place. One of your social work interns, Emily Palmer, suggested it was a good cause."

"Emily is great. I work with her alot. I do love the job so I'll be around for a while."

Matt was dying to ask Becca about Anne, but knew better. "I guess I'll be seeing you around, Becca. Enjoy our cafe."

She quickly turned her back on him and headed out to the deck. Matt felt shaken. Everything had been going so well. He had fallen in love again and was getting ready to have a family. He was no longer depressed all the time. Seeing Becca was too much. He needed to talk to someone about the run-in and decided to call his closest friends, Natalie and Marcus Bernstein. Since they knew how his marriage to Anne ended, they would understand his reaction to Becca living nearby.

Matt's old life and new were intersecting. Or were they clashing? His father had recently asked Matt if he'd heard from Anne at all. Matt wondered if he should contact Lyle Oliver, his father's attorney and "fixer," and ask him to find her. Would that help? He began to panic. How would Becca's presence affect his new life?

CHAPTER 5

"What are you up to today?" Matt asked as he grabbed his water bottle and his bike helmet, headed to work.

"Not much," Liz replied. "I plan to stop in later to finish interviewing new servers for the morning shift."

"No need. I have it all under control."

There he goes again, pushing me away from my own business, Liz thought. She'd hoped he would be glad she was coming by. She was growing more and more annoyed by Matt hovering over her pregnancy.

She decided to go ahead with the interviews. She certainly didn't need Matt's permission. Rather than push back, she would talk to Sophie about her growing irritation before talking with him.

Matt gave her a quick kiss on the cheek. "I'll call when I know what time I'll be home."

Liz finished her tea and left the dishes in the sink. The housewife role wasn't what she signed up for and pregnancy wasn't going to change that.

When Liz called to arrange a visit, Sophie invited her over the next afternoon for British tea cakes, a light yeast-based sweet bun with pecans, an old family recipe.

As Liz walked into Sophie's, she gave her friend a long hug while grabbing a luscious tea cake off the serving plate.

"Why the sudden visit? Is something wrong? Let me guess. You want me back as a partner because I have such a great sense of humor?"

Liz tugged on her scarf, nervously adjusting it.

"You're not even close, Sophie. I'm pregnant! Just finished the first trimester. You're the first besides Drew that I've told. Dr. Samuels, my OB-GYN, is the best according to Drew. She's no-nonsense, but caring. The baby is due August 15th." Liz took a sip of tea and a bite of another tea cake.

"Whoa! Lots of information. That's great news," Sophie replied with a flat tone as she ever so slightly looked away.

"Is it? Not so sure from your response. Actually, I may partially agree with you."

"How so?" Sophie asked, looking surprised.

Liz fumbled for words. "This pregnancy came too soon. I bet you think so, too. Something about Matt has changed. He's stressed out all the time and sometimes raises his voice at me. He told me last night that while I'm pregnant, he wants me to mainly work from home, not at the Cafe. Isn't that ridiculous?"

"Kind of. But what do you think is behind it?"

"Let's face it. You never liked him, which makes me a little hesitant to answer. Yet, I just loved your Pete and welcomed him into my life right away."

"All true."

"Come on, Sophie. I know that you have something more to say."

"I'm not going to lie. I had a hard time warming up to Matt. I can't put my finger on why. He just doesn't seem to be what he claims. It's that weird, intuitive thing I do that drives you crazy."

"Give me some examples of what bothers you. Not just your gut feeling," Liz said, annoyed.

"Okay. The first time we met, the three of us took a walk up Skinner's Butte. No matter what I said I felt like he was competing with me. I'd talk about traveling with Pete in Guadalajara and he'd tell a treacherous story to top mine. How he and his friend were nearly beaten up by a gang in Guatemala City on their way to the bus station and on and on. He kept it up for the entire hike. It was exhausting."

"He was just trying to find common ground with you. He knew how important you are to me."

"You asked, Liz. I gave you an example of what turned me off at first. What bothers me now is how overbearing Matt is during your pregnancy."

"He's worried the physical work is too hard for me now. I'm considered an older mom at 35!" defended an exasperated Liz.

"Still, I think you know what you can handle at work. Don't defend him."

"This conversation is hard for a million reasons. I generally trust your advice because you know me so well. But, I also know you thought marrying Matt was a big mistake."

"Liz, you rushed into the marriage. You've always been

cautious in relationships, even indecisive. It bothered me how little you knew about him."

"I know. I know. My therapist said I was ambivalent about commitment because my parents died when I was so young. So the one time I don't sit on the fence...." Her words trailed off and she again tugged nervously at her scarf. "Is he the wrong person for me?"

"You don't need my approval, Liz. You just need to know I'm here for you no matter what."

"I need your friendship now, more than ever."

"Remember our friend, Amanda, from our senior year? She was dating a guy who made her end her friendships, one by one. And it rubbed me the wrong way. When I pointed it out, she stopped talking to me, too. Later, she dropped out of school and a mutual friend said her boyfriend had gotten pretty rough with her and she became even more withdrawn. Neither of us ever saw her again. I've often wondered what happened to her. I wish I had done something more to help her."

"I'm not Amanda."

"Liz, I wonder if Matt acts this way because of his family or something else from his past?"

"Maybe. I made it my business to learn more about his family the first time I met his mother, Joanne. I got a chance to talk with her a month before the wedding. We hit it off immediately. She's bright and funny and spent time with me at the Cafe. For a couple of days, she helped in the kitchen and even hung out with the musicians while they were setting up. We had plenty of time to talk."

"Did she tell you anything about Matt you didn't already know?"

"Well, I did ask her about Matt's marriage to Anne."

"You already told me that Joanne didn't completely understand why it ended so suddenly."

"That's right. She just repeated Matt's rendition about them being young and quickly realizing it was a mistake."

"What else did she say?"

"That their visits were infrequent since they lived in Madison and Joanne often worked weekends in Chicago with her busy practice. When they were together for holidays, Anne was quiet which she attributed to Matt dominating the conversation like his father."

"So, Joanne didn't have any solid ideas about what broke them up?"

"Matt told her Anne struggled with depression but refused to tell her any more than that. Honestly, I don't blame her for not pushing him more. I'm learning what a short fuse he has. When he doesn't want to talk about something, I leave it alone."

"I know. And that's surprising. You typically push if you're not getting an answer. When I decided to leave the Cafe and go to the Peace Corps with Pete, you grilled me until I gave you every single reason why my big life change made sense."

"Your leaving was about the future. This is about a mistake he made right out of college," Liz said defensively.

"Still, I could never understand why you didn't demand the details of his divorce when you were considering marrying him. I just don't get it."

"I don't push him. You know I don't like conflict." Liz sighed deeply.

"But, he's your husband. What could possibly hold you back?"

"My parents never raised their voices, not once. And

now, I have Matt lashing out at me, screaming over little things. When I came home late from my book group, he was annoyed that I hadn't called. So, he grabbed my novel and threw it against the wall, just missing me."

"What? You must have been terrified!"

"I was startled and then shocked more than anything. It was so out of character for Matt."

"Wish you had called me right away. I'm your BFF. I need to know this stuff. It's just not normal. What else has he been doing that's so unusual?"

"I've had complaints from Emily and Ira about his tirades at them. Emily says she can't understand why he does it and Ira claims it's mostly put-downs. No one else from the rest of the kitchen crew or wait staff has spoken up, but they must notice. I've seen it happen a few times in front of customers which can't be good for business."

"Now, you've got me worried. Throwing a book? Talking trash in front of customers?"

"I have to admit that he's scared me more than once. He's losing control."

"How long has this been going on?"

"Pretty much since I got pregnant. But it seems to be getting worse."

"I'm not sure I would count on him stopping after the baby is born."

Liz began tearing up and turned away. "I don't know what to count on."

Sophie put her arms around Liz. "We'll figure this out."

"Don't forget, Soph, Matt isn't all bad. He tells me how much he loves me and how beautiful I am every day. He can be so charming with people at the Cafe and around town. He's welcoming as he seats people, making a comment that makes them laugh and setting the tone for the night. He remembers their interests so he can kid around with them about how the Ducks' women's basketball team is the best in the country or praise the recent performance of *Tosca* by the Eugene Opera."

"What a list!" Sophie tried not to sound sarcastic.

"His greatest strength is connecting with the regulars. Remember Kevin and Stacy? Since Matt started working at the Cafe, they come more often."

"Yeah. Sweet couple. They always came to the best shows. We used to swap travel stories and have long talks with them about hiking off the beaten path."

"Matt once teased them about not being able to resist our homestyle cooking. Stacy actually said that it was Matt that keeps them coming back so often."

"He is likable when he wants to be. I know Matt has a caring and warm side, Liz. It's the other side that concerns me. It clearly bothers you too."

"So... How can I get Matt to stop being so volatile?"

"I don't know, Liz. I think he's the only one who can. What do you need?"

"I honestly don't know and I've had enough 'Matt talk' today. But telling you this has helped."

"Anytime. If you need a break from him, you're always welcome here."

"I needed your honesty and I got it. Let's talk more on our walk up Mount Pisgah on Saturday," Liz said as she got up to leave.

"I'll pick you up at nine o'clock," Sophie replied, giving Liz a long hug.

After the door closed, Sophie called the crisis line at

Jill's Place for advice.

"Jill's Place. This is Becca. How can I help you?"

"Uh, I'm not in crisis," Sophie said haltingly. "So, I don't know if I should use this number."

"We're a crisis line and an info line. If you have questions or just need to talk, that's what I'm here for." Becca's warmth and openness came through.

"Okay. This is the story. I have a friend. Bet you hear that all the time, don't you? Women who don't want to admit that it's really them?"

"Yes and no. We get lots of calls from friends who want to help someone they think is in trouble."

"Sorry. I tend to go off track when I'm nervous. Anyway, my best friend had a whirlwind romance and married the guy after just ten months. I've never liked or trusted him. Just a gut feeling. Today she told me that because she's pregnant he wants her to stop working at their business. Also, that he's been lashing out at her. Bursts of anger."

"Often when a woman becomes pregnant, her partner feels the need to assert more control over her. He's threatened that her being a mother will take attention away from him," Becca explained.

"That makes perfect sense since he's so insecure. What can I do to help her?"

"It's tricky. When friends or family jump in to try to fix things, the woman often takes her partner's side. Especially when pregnant. She likely feels more vulnerable and unable to think about another huge life change. So, tread carefully and try not to alienate her. Does she have anyone else close to her who can help?"

"She's close to her brother but he has begun to have

misgivings about her husband, too," Sophie replied.

"The fact that your friend confided in you about her fears is a good sign. If you can trust her brother not to do or say things to drive her away, talk to him about keeping an eye out for signs the abuse is escalating. I can send you information about what to look for or you can find it on our website."

"I'll go to the website right now. Can I call back and talk to you when I have more questions?" Sophie asked, feeling some relief.

"Well, you may not get me since our crisis line is 24/7," Becca said with a laugh. "When you call back, tell the crisis line volunteer about our conversation. She can answer any questions as well as I can. Maybe better. One last question. Any guns or other weapons in the house? It's important to think about how much danger she may be in."

"No. Her husband is a liberal, anti-gun type. It's odd because I agree with him on most political issues. The way he acts toward her contradicts them. Now, he's using old-fashioned expectations of pregnant women with him being in charge and her becoming invisible. My friend is a feminist so I don't get why she's putting up with it."

"I'm afraid battering has no particular party or class connection. Always trust your intuition. At worst, you misread him. At best, you save the life of a friend who's at risk."

"Thanks, Becca. You've been incredibly helpful. I'll be calling back, I'm sure." Sophie hung up and wondered if it was a bit melodramatic to think about saving Liz's life. She shuddered at the thought that Liz might be in that much danger.

CHAPTER 6

Matt looked anxiously at the time on his cell, worried about the 7:30 show starting on time. Rob, Kofi Harper's manager, called to alert Matt the band would be a half-hour late for the sound check. Since there were a number of new event promoters to meet, Rob had joined the band on the northwest segment of the national tour. When it came to long-term business relationships, he preferred the old-school way. He liked to meet people face-to-face at least once to make a stronger connection.

"I'm sorry about this, Matt. I can't believe that Mountain Airlines scrambled to search so long for Kofi's Weissenborn slide guitar. It's a collector's item with a great sound so we had to wait for them to find it," explained Rob. "We didn't fly into Eugene because instruments and baggage often get damaged or lost at smaller airports. By flying into Portland, we hoped to avoid that. Not true. Now that they've finally found it, we'll head out. I'll call again when we hit I-5."

"We have two sold-out shows tonight which makes it a mild nightmare," Matt said. He held back his anger so he wouldn't get on Rob's bad side. By doing so, he'd alienate Kofi Harper, a multiple Grammy winner. Normally, Kofi played at venues triple the Shady Grove's size. He could play anything – blues, rock, funk, soul. The Cafe had gotten enormous media coverage on the event. It was Thanksgiving eve and the shows had sold out five days before. *Shady Grove Features Grammy Winner!* was the lead story in the Entertainment section of the local paper. The Cafe was attracting major acts that seldom played locally unless presented by the University of Oregon.

Showing Emily the headlines a couple of days before the show, Matt bragged, "I guess my connections are paying off."

Emily rolled her eyes and countered, "Wait a minute, Matt. Liz has been doing all the talent buying for the Cafe until recently. She was the one who got Kofi to add this gig on their way to Seattle."

He often bantered with Emily or at least let her sarcasm go unchecked because she was a long-term employee and close friend of Liz's. Most importantly, Emily was an asset to the business. She had the respect of the kitchen and wait staff. Turnover was low as a result of her management style. But he wasn't going to let her get away with insulting him this time. Matt threw the newspaper down on the front counter.

"You're so aggravating. Just because Liz and Kofi lived in the same dorm in college, she could call in favors. He's here because we run a popular music club, not just because of Liz. Don't you have something better to do?"

"Whatever, Matt." Emily turned and walked away.

As he looked around the room on the night of the show, Matt saw that everyone had been served dinner. Some tables were reserved for people coming for drinks and the show only. He wondered if the band would have to do a rolling sound check where the sound technician made adjustments during the first couple of songs.

An hour later, Matt's cell phone rang. It was Rob again. "You're not going to like this, but we're deep in standstill traffic on I-5, near the Salem exit. I think there's been an accident. We'll probably get there an hour past show time."

"Okay. Keep me informed. We'll try to glue the customers to their seats until you get here," kidded Matt, hiding his increasing frustration. While this could easily turn into a disaster, no point in sharing his anxiety.

Just then, Liz walked out of the kitchen chuckling with Ira, who had concocted a dessert special in honor of Kofi Harper. Making a chocolate molten cake in the shape of Kofi's steel guitar would amuse the lead singer. Liz named it the "Hot Melting Strings Delight." She was still laughing about it as she joined Matt in front.

"I'm so glad that you and Ira are having such a great time with your clever menu ideas while I'm dealing with a late band and irate customers," Matt said in too loud a voice. Liz saw how uncomfortable Matt's comments made the party waiting to be seated. Matt needed to know he had crossed a line.

After Matt seated the group, Liz stepped closer to him and whispered, "Hey, Matt. Back off. Our customers can handle a late show. Let's give them an extra glass of wine or another scoop of French vanilla ice cream on their dessert. That'll do it! Take a deep breath."

"Don't tell me what to do and what our customers can handle. This show is a big deal," Matt seethed.

"Trust me this business has survived much worse than this."

Matt turned to glare at Liz. "You promised me you'd stay home tonight and get off your feet. I thought we'd agreed that you'd start working less, especially on nights like this."

"Remember, I'm pregnant, not chronically ill or near death."

"Never said you were," Matt snapped back.

"If I want to work, I will. I never agreed to work less. You asked me to. No, you demanded it."

Liz wondered if Matt actually believed that she couldn't take care of herself. He seemed compelled to micro-manage her life. It was ridiculous for her not to come in on such a hectic night. Especially when her old friend, Kofi, was performing.

Suddenly Matt was blinded by headlights from a royal blue Nissan van through the window. He recognized Alex and Rose Fox with two other couples as they walked toward the door. Wanting to get back to the front counter to greet them, Matt pushed Liz out of the way.

Emily looked up from a nearby table just as it happened. She saw Matt shove Liz who landed against the wall, crying out as she fell to the floor. A framed poster from an old Beatles concert crashed around her and shards of broken glass dug into her arm. Emily saw Liz panic and try to get up. She couldn't. Liz was sweaty and began to breathe irregularly.

Matt ignored the commotion behind him, even the sound of breaking glass. Later, Liz would describe the incident to Sophie including the irony of the "All You Need is Love" poster shattering due to Matt's violence.

Emily darted over and asked, "Hey, what's going on up here?" She knelt down next to her friend who was lying in the corner. Liz was holding her right arm close to her, trembling, face red and eyes filled with tears. Emily carefully helped her up off the floor.

When Matt turned around, he caught the pained look on his wife's face. "Cover the front, Emily. I'll take it from here. Get someone from the kitchen to clean up this mess."

"Stay away from me. Emily will take me home," Liz fumed.

"Be reasonable. Let's get you to the couch in our office. You'll feel better there."

Matt moved toward Liz, reaching out to comfort her. She was gingerly protecting her wrist by covering it with her other hand. When he touched her, she let out a painful cry.

"Wait, Liz. I want to make sure you're okay."

"I'm not okay!" Liz said as she staggered toward the door, leaning on Emily.

Matt glanced up at the clock above the entryway. It was 8:20 p.m. The band had just pulled up and Kofi Harper was already out of the vehicle, heading toward the front door. He waved at Liz and Matt. As he approached, Emily led Liz past Matt, out to the parking lot. Liz stopped to greet Kofi and her old friend, Noah, the bass player.

"I just slipped on the floor and fell. I've hurt my wrist badly and need to head home, guys," Liz said, forcing a smile.

"I'm so sorry," Kofi said, gently touching her left shoulder.

"We'll do our best show for you tonight. Healing music coming your way!" chimed in Noah.

Matt asked Ira to cover the front so he could follow Liz and Emily to the car. As he moved closer to Liz, she recoiled. "Leave me alone! Don't bother coming home! Sleep on the couch in the office tonight," she said sharply.

As Liz settled into the car, Emily texted Drew. "Matt hurt Liz. Need your help. Meet @ Liz's!"

"Damn! Be right there."

Emily suspected Drew's career choice as an EMT would come in handy tonight as she saw him pull into the driveway at Liz and Matt's. She went out to the porch so they could talk without disturbing Liz. Emily hugged Drew hard.

Emily found the words tumbling out of her mouth. "I'm glad you're here. Liz is settled on the couch. We have to talk fast. I'm worried that Matt might show up during the break between sets."

"What happened? Tell me what my brother-in-law did now," insisted Drew.

"Drew, I need you to listen so we can figure this out together." Emily was confident that Liz could look critically at her marriage if they approached her in the right way.

"I think the honeymoon is over," Emily continued. "Matt let his true colors show. He shoved Liz against the wall hard enough to hurt her. I saw it happen and so did Ira."

Drew was frantic. "I'm going over to the Cafe. Then, I'll call the police and get him charged with assault."

The last thing that Emily wanted was for Drew to create a scene at the Cafe, disrupt the show and have it get back to Liz.

"Hey!" Emily grabbed his arm. "Don't be rash. That'll just alienate your sister. What you need to do is be present, right here and right now." Drew looked surprised that Emily lapsed into her fast-talking New Yorker style, with a heavy Brooklyn accent.

"You're right, Em. I'll check Liz to see if she needs medical care. She may have to go to the hospital."

"Now, that's the Drew I know and love. Go in and tell Liz you're here for her. I hope she doesn't feel like we're ganging up on her."

"Something was always missing for me with Matt. Now it's finally all coming out. Just a matter of time."

"I'm not surprised either. Matt's been out of control lately. Most of us at work tiptoe around him these days, avoiding him as much as possible."

As she opened the door, Emily called out, "Drew's here to see if you're okay."

"No, I'm not okay. What are you doing here, Drew?" Liz snapped.

"Emily texted that you were hurt, so here I am."

"Drew, I don't need you to rescue me."

He saw the ice pack on her wrist. "You've been injured. Let me look at it."

"Okay, Dr. Drew. Take a quick look. I've taken some ibuprofen and will go to the doctor in the morning if the pain doesn't let up."

Drew carefully examined Liz's wrist. "It may be broken. By the amount of swelling and the way you're holding your arm, it should be x-rayed. We'll drive you to the hospital, just to be safe."

"I don't know what Emily has told you, but I tripped and fell against the wall. I could have taken care of this myself. I'll go to the hospital if you don't say a word or come into the exam room. Got it?"

"Okay. Whatever you say." Drew nodded. "Let's roll."

Liz grabbed her bag and walked toward the door. As she reached for the door handle, she flinched. "Damn, that hurts."

Drew slipped Liz's bag off her shoulder and gently guided her out the door to Emily's car. He helped her in and then hopped in behind the passenger seat as Emily started off.

"Thank you both for being here. I'm sorry I'm being so impossible. I feel so stupid for being such a klutz."

They were both silent for a minute. "You're not a klutz," Emily said.

"You're not acting impossible," Drew said, stifling his anger as he envisioned Matt attacking his sister.

Liz chose the Emerald Emergency Room, the closest of the two local hospitals.

"Alright. Whatever you say. At least you're willing to get your wrist checked out," Drew piped in.

When Emily pulled up to the entrance, Liz slowly got out of the car with Drew's help. "You seem shaky, Lizzie. Take it slow," Drew warned.

Liz walked up to the only available intake desk in a row of eight stations. She quietly explained the injury and was given a clipboard with forms to complete. She handed it to Emily since it was too painful for her to use her right hand. Emily quietly read each question and recorded Liz's responses.

Within thirty minutes, the intake worker reviewed her forms, noting that Liz was four months pregnant. She said, "Your pregnancy moves you up in the queue. Would you like to lie down while you wait?"

"Yes, I'd like that." Liz turned to Emily, sounding terrified and whispered, "I'm praying the fall didn't hurt the baby." The nurse grabbed her bag and Liz followed her slowly down the hall.

Emily took a moment alone and walked outside. She found a bench and decided to call Becca. Emily was crying intermittently as she frantically described the incident at the Cafe.

"I get how upset you are. You've been close to Liz for a long time, Drew too, right?"

"It's so complicated because of my relationship with Drew and Liz."

"Tell me more about it," Becca said in a calming voice.

Emily told her how much Drew and Liz meant to her. Since she started working at the Cafe five years ago, the three of them had become like family. She knew the complexities of their relationship. Drew was a strong business partner to Liz and was something of a second father to her. The six-year age difference and life circumstances had dramatically changed their roles in the family. Drew essentially raised Liz in her teenage years.

Becca winced when she learned Liz's mother, Sally, was diagnosed with breast cancer when she was 11. After completing surgery, chemotherapy and radiation, she seemed to be on the other side of it. Drew was at UW Seattle when the cancer recurred a year later. When it metastasized to her bones, no further treatment was possible. Drew flew home every weekend to help his father, Jonah, care for her. Just nine months after Sally's death, their Dad died suddenly of a heart attack at 54. Liz was only 15 and Drew 22 when they lost both parents.

When their father's sister and her husband offered to raise Liz in Corvallis, she was vehemently against it. She confided to Drew that the move would be another loss she couldn't handle. Drew convinced them to let Liz finish high school, living in their childhood home. He would leave school in Seattle and move back to Eugene immediately.

In addition, their father's best friend, Jim Leonardi, offered to help. He lived a couple of blocks away and planned to make dinner for them several times a week. He would stop by most mornings to check-in and was always there in case of emergency. "Uncle Jim" had been a constant in their lives. He was attentive and kind, parenting both of them as much as they would allow. It was a patchwork family. But it somehow worked.

Drew had planned to go back to college in Seattle after Liz graduated. In the meantime, he enrolled at Lane Community College in Eugene and became an Emergency Medical Technician (EMT). He needed a good job to support them. He was quickly drawn into the adrenalin rush of doing emergency work and never returned to Seattle. He had accidentally found the right career for himself.

"Now, I understand so much more about why you are so connected to those two," said Becca.

"I gotta go. I need to check in with Drew." When Emily got off the phone, she walked back inside.

Across the waiting area, she noticed Drew hugging a small, stocky woman in light blue scrubs. She figured he'd run into an old friend.

"Long time, Anna," Drew said as he lifted her off the floor and embraced her long and hard. She couldn't help but smile.

"How's it going?" Like Emily, Anna was small, only a

little over 5'2", but her presence was big. She had a booming voice and a striking look. Her short, curly red hair dominated her face, giving her a pixie quality. Yet, Drew knew when she gave orders to staff, they moved quickly into action.

"Oh, not too bad. I switched jobs. I stopped working the graveyard shift to get some decent hours, so I could be with my daughter. That's why I never see you anymore. She is a bit of a crazed middle schooler so I have to keep a close eye on her. What are you doing here? You're not in uniform. Things okay, my friend?" Anna's eyes furrowed with a look of concern.

Drew noticed from the ID badge, hanging around Anna's neck, that she had been promoted to Nurse Manager. When Drew didn't answer her question, Anna pointed toward a room down the hall where they could talk privately. "Let's chat for a moment before I'm off to debrief the next shift."

Drew walked back with Anna as far as the staff door. With their backs to Liz, Drew lowered his voice. " I don't know if you ever met my sister, Liz. Seems she had an 'accident' with her husband at the Cafe." They exchanged looks as Matt emphasized "accident."

"Got it. She'll be seen fairly soon. When Liz is done being assessed, she'll get triaged. Looks like about three people are ahead of her."

Half an hour later, the nurse called Liz's name. Liz touched Emily's arm and said, "Thanks, Emily. I can take it from here. Go buy my brother a cup of coffee and get the story on that nurse he was so cozy with earlier. I'll be out soon."

Emily and Drew went to the coffee kiosk down the hall.

As they sat down, Emily asked with a teasing smirk, "Drew, I can't go anywhere without some random woman giving you a hug. Another old lover?"

Drew leaned in to talk quietly to Emily. "Give me a break. You remember Anna Goldsmith. She ran the graveyard shift here when we first started hanging out together. You met her the night your friends had a bike accident and we drove them here. You even complimented Anna on her take-charge approach and got your friends treated quickly. You said her style made her look like she was six feet tall."

"That's right! She was a powerhouse," recalled Emily. Just then, a doctor approached their table.

"I'm Dr. Maloney. Are you Drew Lodde?" Drew nodded.

"Your sister's wrist is broken. A nurse is sizing her wrist brace. We took some additional tests since she's pregnant. She should be out in a little while and her nurse will give you details. Any quick questions?"

Drew looked at the doctor. "No. It seems pretty straightforward. Thanks." The doctor turned around and headed back toward the sliding glass doors. From Drew's experience as an EMT, he immediately understood Liz's wrist was low priority considering the number of other patients waiting with more serious medical issues. He would get details about the break, pain medication, recovery time and impact on the pregnancy from the nurse.

Drew looked at Emily and said, "I really want to take Liz back to my house. Could you convince her she'd be safer with me?"

"I'll try, Drew, but Liz needs to choose. If we force her before she's ready, it will alienate her and drive her back to Matt."

CHAPTER 7

Liz was fast asleep. The pain killers had kicked in. Drew felt like he could leave her alone safely. He left a note: "If you need anything, call me." He closed the door to the guest room quietly so as not to disturb her.

When Drew got into his car, he called Ira.

"Is Matt still at the Cafe?" Drew asked when Ira picked up.

"No. He just left with Kofi and the band. They went over to Hector's Burrito to get a late-night snack. Apparently, our food is too healthy for them."

"Well, I'm headed over to Hector's. Want to come? I may need you to stop me from giving Matt a taste of the physical pain that my sister is feeling. You've heard by now what happened?" Drew was probing to find out what Ira knew or witnessed.

"Yeah, I actually saw it. I was putting a meal out on the counter for a server to deliver and watched it happen."

"So, both you and Emily were witnesses?"

"Yeah, but Matt's got a good cover story. Rushed, crowded, turned the wrong way and Liz tripped on the stool and fell against the wall. Total bullshit. Such a liar. Sophie thinks he's a con man. We both tried to convince Liz not to marry him so fast."

"Okay, then. We're on the same page. We need to scare the hell out of Matt, so he won't even think of messing with Lizzie again. I need you for backup. Also, you're the only one I know with a black belt," Drew said.

"Yeah. I'm nearly done here. I'll meet you for a hot burrito in a few minutes. Do me a favor though, and don't go in without me. I think we should wait until Kofi and the guys leave before we get in Matt's face. See you soon."

Putting his phone into his pocket, Drew took a deep breath to try to calm himself. He started the engine, drove down High Street and turned left on 16th. He saw Matt on the outdoor deck with the band, laughing and talking. Four patio heaters around the deck made it warm enough to sit outside even at this late hour.

Drew was beside himself with anger. How could Matt be having a good old time? He's acting like the big shot businessman, gloating over two sold-out shows with Kofi Harper. In the meantime, his wife is drugged out in bed, fighting the pain of a broken limb. Damn him!

Adrenaline rushing, Drew decided not to wait for Ira and climbed out of his car. Just as he swung his door open, Ira turned the corner. Lucky for Matt, Drew thought to himself when Ira pulled up next to him.

"Breathe," demanded Ira, as he locked his car and gave him a bear hug. "We'll deal with this fiasco. Let me start the conversation."

Ira and Drew walked toward the table of seven and

greeted the band warmly. Ira said, "You guys were outstanding tonight. I liked the way you did 'Don't Ever Leave.' I always thought it was the best song you ever wrote."

Kofi smiled humbly. "You've always been a sucker for my depressing love songs, Ira, even before they started to get traction."

Drew noticed the guilt on his brother-in-law's face as they sat down. Matt looked away and stared at the three empty beer bottles sitting in front of him. Drew's expression and Ira's stern gaze jolted Matt out of his alcoholic high.

"Hey, guys. We were just wrapping it up. Kofi and the band are heading to Portland tonight, so they need to get going."

"Sorry we didn't have time with you guys," Ira said to the band. "Actually, Matt, we wanted to talk with you about some Cafe business."

Matt looked annoyed. Drew suspected Matt figured they had come to blame him for Liz's fall. He was probably feeling safer in a public place rather than being alone with them.

The band got up to leave, pay the check and say goodbye. Drew and Ira moved into two chairs directly across from Matt under the umbrella. A family with two teenage sons, seated nearby, were engrossed in conversations and didn't notice the three of them.

"Just a second. I'm going to call Liz and see how she's doing." Matt grabbed his cell phone and pushed back his chair.

"Don't bother," Drew said, "I think you've done enough for one day. She's fast asleep at my house, on drugs to kill the pain you caused. Quit acting like you give a damn. Or are you having a bout of remorse for breaking her wrist?"

"What are you talking about? I didn't break Liz's wrist," Matt shouted.

"That's not what the ER doctor said!" Drew shouted back.

"Whatever happened, it wasn't my fault," Matt snapped.

Ira looked at both of them and intervened. "Okay, guys. Let's take it easy here. One at a time. Matt, you start."

"There are no sides to what happened tonight," interrupted Drew angrily. "In fact, Matt, I'm guessing that you had the same type of 'accident' with your first wife, Anne. No wonder she left you so soon after you got married." Liz had shared the little she knew about Anne with her brother.

"Where are you getting this bullshit from?" challenged Matt.

"Well, do you know what happened to Anne or where she is?"

"My first marriage is none of your business. Anne's depression is what made her leave. That's all I'll say."

"Yeah, right. Knowing how you treat my sister, I can believe your first wife was depressed." Drew was getting louder. He noticed the customers on the deck staring at him.

"You're no shrink!" retorted Matt.

Trying to calm himself down, Drew said in a quieter voice, "It's convenient for you that Anne isn't around to tell her story."

"Don't you dare blame me for Anne's leaving!" Matt

pounded the table with his fist. A beer mug fell to the patio floor and smashed to pieces.

"Now look at what you've done," Drew said with contempt.

"I never hurt or threatened Anne, or Liz for that matter! Her injury was an accident. Ask her if you don't believe me!"

"I don't need to ask her. I already know what you're like," Drew scoffed.

"You know, Drew, it really doesn't matter what you think. I only care if Liz believes me."

"Cut it out, both of you!" Ira had raised his voice, only slightly, startling Drew and Matt. Ira was known as centered, always calm, never rattled.

"You're right, Ira," Drew said, looking away. Drew was still furious. But he clenched his fists, struggling with the impulse to smash Matt's face.

"Maybe it's time to let Liz decide what she wants. And that's not your business," Matt seethed.

"You really don't understand family, do you, Matt? I'll be here for my sister no matter what happens. I'll do whatever I can to get her away from you!"

"She's my wife. She'll listen to me," Matt said smugly.

"You're being an asshole. I'm going to convince Liz to get you out of our business. You're done reaping the benefits of years of our family's hard work," Drew threatened.

"Keep it down," Ira cautioned Drew.

"I can't get through to this idiot," Drew shouted, rising to his feet.

The family with teenage sons got up quickly and went inside. After complaining to Hector, they hurried out of the restaurant.

Matt was about to reply as Hector rushed to the table, hissing, "All of you, out of here now or I'll call the police!"

They stood up quickly, responding to Hector's command. His disgust squelched their anger and brought them back to reality.

"Sorry, Hector. We screwed up. We'll leave right away. Just a little heated family dispute," Drew offered.

"You're lucky we go way back. I run a family restaurant here. It's my livelihood, just like yours. You know better than to act like this."

"I can't apologize enough. I'll make it up to you," promised Drew.

"Take your family business to your own place! Just get out!"

As Matt got into his car, he imagined this incident would be all over town. He hoped the Chamber of Commerce wouldn't hear about it. It could easily ruin his reputation. He would convince Liz to side with him and see her injury as an accident. Liz was tired of Drew's interference and would come back home once she heard about the scene at Hector's. Maybe it's good that this confrontation happened.

Before he drove off, Matt looked around to see if Drew and Ira were actually gone. He would call Liz in the morning when Drew was at work. He'd get her back. He knew he would.

CHAPTER 8

Becca woke suddenly from a deep sleep when she heard a voice from the top of the stairs calling out: "Becca, are you awake? Time for our debrief." She quickly jumped out of bed, threw on her robe and pulled open the door. It was 8:30 and Lily, the shelter's night supervisor, was at the top of the basement stairs, grinning down at her. Lily's hair was an even brighter color of orange than it had been the week before. Her hair color was a moving target.

"I hope you got a good night's sleep. I had a hectic 12-hour shift," Lily said as she came down the stairs and plopped down on the couch. As Becca put the kettle on, she realized how much she envied Lily's 25-year-old agility. Becca had been athletic in high school and her height and speed landed her a center position on the Ohio University's women's basketball team.

The former basketball star glanced around the cramped living room. It was filled with a well-used couch and two hand-me-down overstuffed chairs, community donations to furnish the shelter. The rental market was tight, so Becca had been staying in the shelter's basement apartment for the last few months until she found a place. Lily told her that the shelter was now a full house. "Today, you'll have to turn women and children away or refer them to a shelter in another city. I know it's an option we all hate."

"Are you suggesting I'm in for another rough shift?"

"Yeah. The last couple have been wild. I had three late-night crisis calls and sent back up staff out on one assessment. Pat met a woman with three kids at my favorite 24-hour restaurant. After assessing the situation, she brought the family in. I did a brief intake at 4:00 am and got them settled in for the night."

"I promised never a dull moment when you took this job. Fortunately, we both feed off the adrenaline that comes with this work," Becca teased.

"The household's been hectic all week, but Molly and her children seem to be settling in. The residents are already connecting with her and Jason is a sweetheart. They're both terrified Danny will get out of jail. Fortunately, Molly will meet with her advocate today to develop a plan," added Lily. "We should move her out of here as quickly as we can!"

"Is there anything else I should know?

"Yes. Four families here. Two are working on finding housing. We may need to give them an extension. Then there's Melissa, the one with the new baby. She's been on the phone a lot with her mother-in-law and is toying with giving her husband one more chance. During the group last night, one woman talked about how much less isolated she feels now. They love telling their stories to people who get it. They feel stronger and less alone. Great when that happens."

"By the way, Molly told me Danny has a good friend who's a cop with the Eugene police. Since he probably knows our location, we should be ready to move her to the Corvallis shelter or to the motel at a moment's notice. I'll call both to check availability when I go upstairs," Becca said.

"Did you talk to the officer you met at the hospital with Molly?" Lily asked.

Becca got up to take the whistling kettle off the stove and made a pot of Earl Grey tea. "Yes. I called Susan last night and she's keeping tabs on Danny. She has my cell phone so can reach me quickly if she hears about an early release from the custody referee's office."

As she poured a cup of tea for Lily, she asked, "Milk and sugar, right? Or would you rather just have lemon?"

"God, it's like a fancy tea house down here. A bit of lemon would be nice," Lily said with a fake English accent. Becca valued her job because Jill's Place saved women's lives. Plus, she was part of an exceptional team of women who were smart and used their humor to balance out the seriousness of their work.

"What happened when you went to get Molly?" Lily asked in a more serious tone.

"It was really risky. Don't ever do what we did," Becca responded with a heavy sigh.

"I heard you went out to her house in the middle of nowhere by yourself."

"I did, but not alone. Emily was with me. Molly's husband could have come back at any time. She told us he always has a rifle in his truck."

Lily stared at Becca shaking her head.

"We had no choice."

"I'd never take that risk," Lily said.

"I guess that's where we're different. I did get approval from Katrina, our fearless leader. She agreed we were out of options."

As Lily finished her tea, she said, "I still disagree. I'm sure Katrina weighed out the risks. I know she trusts your judgment. She's told me more than once how glad she is that you landed here."

"Thanks for passing that along," Becca smiled. As Lily bounded up the stairs, Becca cleaned up the cups. Then, she joined the residents upstairs in the kitchen and checked in with the two women who would make dinner. They didn't have quite enough rice so Becca went to the pantry and hauled out a 20-pound bag. The residents laughed at the size.

"Are you planning on feeding an army tonight?" Molly asked.

Becca laughed, "I want to keep all of you well-fed so you have the physical stamina and inner strength to keep moving forward."

"This is the place where that can happen," Molly replied, as she got up and looked around at the kitchen, dining room, and living room. There was enough space for five families of various sizes to be together comfortably. All the children were in the living room and playroom so the mothers could keep an eye on them while chatting with each other.

Becca went into the office to check in with the Corvallis shelter. That shelter was full, as were all the shelters in towns up and down the Willamette Valley. She then realized it would be better to get Molly and the kids out of state where a connection with the local police would be less likely. She called the shelter in Vancouver, Washington and explained the situation. She was in luck. Two families had checked out. They would hold a space if Molly could get up there by tomorrow on a bus or train.

Since Jill's Place had a standing reservation at a local motel when the shelter was full, Becca called to alert them she might need a space tonight. After she rejoined the families around the dining room table, Becca first fed Jenny and then held another baby so their mothers could have a moment to relax while eating.

Becca looked over at Jason and asked, "How's it going?"

"Good," he replied. "But where's Emily? She said she would come over to play checkers with me."

"Well, if she said it, she'll do it," Becca reassured him. "If she doesn't come in a little while, I'll give her a call. Remind me if I get busy, okay?"

"Yeah, I will."

Jason asked Mark, the boy across the table from him, if he knew Emily.

"Yeah, she's awesome," Mark replied, stuffing some scrambled eggs into his mouth.

Becca's cell phone vibrated in her pocket. The caller ID said "Susan Brody." This won't be good, she thought as she answered.

"Hi, Susan. This is Becca. What's up?"

"I'm afraid I have some news that you need to share with Molly. Six men were just released from jail because we needed the cells after a drug bust and Danny was one of them."

"I better get Molly out of here fast! Thanks for the heads up," Becca said.

She motioned to Molly to come into her office. "Susan Brody called to tell you that Danny just got out. Grab your purse and the kids and we'll head to the motel we use for emergencies. One of the volunteers will get the rest of your stuff and bring it over."

For a split second Molly looked like she would fall apart. She took a deep breath, looked at Becca with fear in her eyes, but managed to calmly reply, "Okay, let's get moving." As Molly was putting on her kids' jackets, Emily walked in.

"I'm glad you're here, Em. Let's talk for a minute." Becca pointed to the office so they could talk confidentially. "Will you take Molly and the kids to the motel?" Becca asked. "Danny just got out of jail. I need to stay here to deal with anything that could come up. I'll call for staff back-up."

Emily went into the kitchen and picked up Jenny from the high chair. Molly took Jason's hand, turned back to the women sitting around the table, and said, "Got to go! I hope I'll see all of you again sometime under happier circumstances."

The women all stood up and gave her hugs with words of encouragement.

"Now where are we going?" Jason asked in a resigned tone.

"We're going to be fine," Molly responded. "We're going to stay somewhere else to be extra safe."

Jason looked at Emily and asked, "Still want to play checkers?"

"Sure. When I come back here to get your stuff, I'll

grab the board. We can have a marathon tournament."

Suddenly, they heard a loud pounding on the front door. The women stopped talking and hushed their kids. No one ever used the front door. As Becca went toward the door, Emily whispered to the residents to get their kids and go upstairs quietly. Becca motioned for Emily to follow the families.

When she looked through the peephole in the door, Becca saw a Eugene police officer standing on the porch. She opened the door with the chain on.

"Can I help you?" she asked.

"EPD, Officer Phil Anderson. Open the door. I'm looking for a woman who kidnapped two kids and is reported to be here," the officer announced brusquely. He was taller than Becca, but not by much.

"Can I see your identification?" Becca asked, trying to sound bored rather than terrified.

"I don't have time for that. We're talking about kidnapping here. Let me in," he shouted, pushing against the door. The chain held, but Becca knew he could break it if he decided to.

"Let me get my supervisor. Wait just a moment," Becca said and closed and double-bolted the door. The pounding began again as Becca punched 911 into her cell phone.

"I'm at 2250 Pierce Avenue. There's someone claiming to be a police officer banging on my front door. He says he's here to investigate a kidnapping. I don't know what he's talking about. Says his name is Anderson, Phil Anderson. Can you check and see if this is real?" Becca said loudly enough for the officer to hear. He stopped pounding.

"Did you ask for his ID?" the dispatcher asked.

"He won't show me his ID. That's why I suspect he's not a real officer."

"One moment please. I'll check that location. Please stay on the line."

As the phone went silent, the police officer called out, "Hey, we don't have to go through all this. Just open the door. I'm sure we can straighten this out." Becca didn't respond.

His voice became more urgent. "I'm just trying to help out a friend. Just open the door so I can see that his wife and kids aren't here and I'll be on my way."

Still no response.

Then the dispatcher came back on the phone. "I don't show any officers sent to that address. No Phil Anderson on shift today. I'll send a squad car over to investigate."

This is what Becca was dreading. If a squad car came and there was a scene in front of the house, it would threaten the confidentiality of the shelter. She took a chance by opening the door slightly and spoke in a loud voice: "You need to leave right now or a squad car is coming to sort this out!"

The cop muttered something she couldn't make out except for the word "bitch" at the end. He quickly ran down the porch stairs. Seconds later, she could hear his tires screeching down the street.

"I think it's okay. He just drove off," Becca said.

"I understand," the dispatcher responded. Becca could tell from her tone she recognized the address of the shelter and understood the problem of sending a squad car.

"Thanks."

"No problem. We're always here, so call back if there's any further problem."

As soon as she hung up, Becca grabbed her cell phone and called Katrina. "A cop friend of Danny's banged on the door trying to find Molly. I managed to get him to leave, but the women are pretty freaked out and I need to get Molly out of here," she blurted out when Katrina answered.

"Are you sure Danny wasn't with him?" Katrina asked.

"Not 100% sure. But by the way the cop acted, I'm pretty sure he was alone."

"I'll be right over. Get Molly ready to leave. If the cop comes back or Danny shows up, call the police even if it means exposing our location."

Becca took a deep breath, looked out the front and back windows, and checked that all the outside doors and windows were locked. Then she ran upstairs.

Emily had separated the families into two groups in two of the bedrooms so the women could help each other and keep the kids calm. Becca saw immediately that it was working. The atmosphere was amazingly quiet.

"He's gone. You can all come downstairs now. It's safe." The women cheered and hugged Becca, thanking her for her bravery. Emily looked over at Becca and gave her a thumbs up as the women left the room. They paused for a moment, looking at each other intently.

As they came downstairs, Katrina rushed in through the backdoor. Her 14 years of work in Portland and Eugene shelters had taught her that situations like these can go sideways fast.

"What's your plan?" she asked Becca.

"First, I want to drive behind Emily over to the motel to make sure they're not followed. Then I'll talk to Molly about her options. I have the Vancouver shelter holding a room for tomorrow."

Katrina nodded. "Great. You should call Susan Brody and tell her we moved Molly and the kids out of town to get that rumor started. Then, Danny's friend on the force will stop looking for her here. Next, we can arrange transportation for Molly to go to Vancouver, assuming that's what she wants."

As they were talking, Molly walked up. "I heard what you said. I'm ready to go wherever you want to take me. I don't want to put the other residents in any more danger."

"Let's go," Emily said, noticing that Jason was carrying a bag and the checkers game.

She looked back at Katrina and Becca. "I'll stay with Molly and the kids as long as they need me and get them to the bus tomorrow."

Becca went out the back door first, to make sure no one was there. Emily opened her car and Jason climbed in next to his sister as Molly was strapping her into the car seat. When Jenny started whimpering, Jason made funny faces to distract her. She started to giggle.

Once everyone was settled, Becca pulled out to the alley. She looked both ways for Danny or the police car, then gestured for Emily to pull ahead of her. She drove at enough distance to spot anyone following them.

After checking in at the motel and getting Jenny down for a nap, the postponed checkers tournament began between Jason and Emily. Becca walked outside with Molly to talk privately.

"You're calling the shots, Molly. So, what do you want to do now?" Becca asked.

"I'm ready for a major change," Molly said, with a confidence that surprised Becca. "I see how I got into this mess and I want out. I have to stop Danny! I won't let him hurt us anymore!"

"OK. then. How about the shelter in Vancouver? If you have other places you'd rather go, just tell me," Becca said.

"Vancouver could work. One of my best friends from high school lives there. She tried to contact me a while back, but Danny grabbed the phone from me and hung up on her. He kept cutting me off from people who cared. When I call her now and explain, I think she'll understand. Do you think Danny will try to find me?"

"I don't know him. What do you think he'll do, Molly?"

"In the past when I've left he's come after me. Since I've been at Jill's Place, the women here have taught me a lot. Some men won't quit and hunt you down non-stop. Others just move onto the next woman they can push around."

"I've seen that too. It can go either way," Becca said with a sympathetic nod. "The staff at the Vancouver shelter will show you ways to stay safe once you leave the shelter."

"Vancouver sounds like my best bet."

"Good. I'll make bus reservations online for tomorrow and alert the shelter that you're coming," Becca said. "Now I need to get back to Jill's Place."

When they went back into the motel room, Molly looked at Jason and Emily playing checkers. She thought about how different her life would be if Emily and Becca hadn't come to her house in Cottage Grove. Danny could have come back dead drunk and killed her. Maybe the kids, too. She never would have escaped him alone.

As Becca started out the door, Molly turned to hug her. "You and Emily saved my life."

"We're glad it's all working out. Good luck! You'll get to the other side of this, Molly."

Emily turned back to Jason. "After we finish our checkers marathon, I've got to go. I promise to come back tomorrow. I'll wait at the bus station with you in the morning."

Molly interrupted. "I'm going to take a quick shower while you're finishing the game. Then it's fine for you to leave. Danny would never think of looking here, an old motel tucked away off Highway 99."

Fifteen minutes later, Jason was struggling to keep his eyes open. The past chaotic 24 hours had done him in. Emily tucked Jason into the bed next to his sister. She said goodbye to Molly and headed to the shelter before going to work at the Cafe.

As she pulled up behind the shelter and let herself in the back gate, Becca came out to the porch. "Glad it's you. Every small noise makes me jumpy," she said. "All good at the motel?"

"Yeah. Molly is ready to make the next move. She'll figure out a way to reclaim her family's farmhouse from Danny, but that will be down the road. Now she needs to get her kids to a safe place," Emily said, climbing up the creaky, wooden steps to stand next to Becca.

"It takes time," Becca agreed with a sigh. "I think this family might make it. Got a feeling."

"We can only hope."

"Hey, how would you like to get away from all this craziness for a while? Tomorrow night, we could go and hang out at Sam Bond's Garage. Great bar food and Babes with Axes is playing. They play music like the Indigo Girls."

"Sounds like fun. I love their bluesy and rock songs. They're good songwriters too. I've been a groupie ever since I first saw them at Oregon Country Fair a few years ago. Let's do it!"

"Great," Becca said. "I'll pick you up at 6:30."

Emily gave Becca a lingering hug before starting toward the gate. She turned and waved as she opened it to leave. Becca stood there for a moment. A wave of unexpected elation washed over her. Things are finally going my way, she thought.

CHAPTER 9

The morning after the disaster at Hector's Burritos, Drew cracked open the door to the guest room to check on Liz. The painkillers were working and she was still fast asleep. Because he'd been called in for an extra shift that morning, he didn't get a chance to tell Liz what happened. So, he left a note saying he had a confrontation with Matt and wanted to talk to her about it when he got home.

Unfortunately, Hector called Liz first and described what had happened. Since Liz and Hector were friends, they would often commiserate about work challenges and treat each other like royalty at one another's establishments. They had opened their businesses the same year a mile apart. When Hector called, he told Liz that he was concerned about her. He described the fight between Matt and Drew. The server had overheard Drew accuse Matt of breaking Liz's wrist. She assured Hector that it was just a clumsy accident at work and she would be fine. The conversation unnerved her. After she hung up, she turned off the ringer on her phone.

While waiting for Drew, Liz sat at the kitchen table, sipping tea. She looked out the window at the hummingbirds swooping into the feeder five feet away. At least three of them were flitting back and forth making the feeder sway wildly as they grudgingly shared it. She had lost that kind of endless energy. Watching them made Liz realize how listless and alone she had become.

Her earlier attempt to take a shower by covering the velcro splint with a plastic bag had failed. When she tried to take a sponge bath, it was awkward washing herself with her left hand. If only it weren't her right wrist that was injured, things would be easier. As she bathed, she recalled the chain of events leading to her injury.

Trying to keep the customers happy when the band was so late had been challenging for the first forty-five minutes or so. Turning on the charm, going from table to table, chatting with customers and making personal connections were important parts of being a club owner. Liz had watched Matt out of the corner of her eye and could see he was getting more and more agitated. She went over to calm him down and the next thing she knew she had crashed against the wall behind the counter. The blurred memories of their argument replayed in Liz's mind. Her growing annoyance with Matt. His face turned red with rage. Her fall. Could he have pushed her intentionally? Would he do such a thing?

As she went to get another cup of tea, she wondered, who is Matt? Liz had always prided herself on being cautious in relationships. Probably why she hadn't married earlier in life. She sometimes wondered what it would have been like if she had stayed with the men in her past who had been safe and easy to manage. She couldn't imagine herself getting serious with any of them at the time. Now she questioned if she had been wrong.

But with Matt, there was an excitement she hadn't felt before. He had layers she wanted to uncover. He was complex and passionate which was what she loved about him. Better not to overreact. They loved the outdoors, the same music, and similar politics. Most of all they wanted to create a family together and share that equally. She couldn't just walk away from the marriage without giving Matt a chance.

Liz picked up the phone and dialed Matt's cell. After four rings, it went to voicemail. She hesitated leaving a message and quickly hung up before the beep. After the chaos at the Cafe and what she heard about the confrontation at Hector's, she knew they couldn't work it out by texting or a phone call. She wondered if Matt was sleeping late or had his ringer off.

Just as she settled back to read the newspaper, there was a knock at the door. It was the secret one they used for each other. Two knocks. Pause, then three more. Liz hesitated for a moment before answering. She opened the door slowly. "I just tried to call you, but then put down the phone because I wasn't ready yet," she lied.

"And here I am. We're so connected. You think it and I show up," Matt said, with his infectious grin. Liz couldn't help but smile slightly, but still wouldn't give into his light banter. He ducked past her into the house. He had ridden his bike over and took off his metallic blue rain jacket, placing it on a hook by the door.

As he looked around, Liz could tell he was making sure Drew wasn't there. When he noticed her wrist in a splint, he looked horrified. "How did your fall get that serious? You're in a splint."

"I'm having a hard time remembering the sequence of events. I'm blocking it or something. Did you mean to break my wrist? Did you do this to me to teach me a lesson or something? Emily and Ira think you meant to hurt me. Drew thinks I should be afraid of you."

"Are you kidding me? Why would you ask me that? You fell because you were exhausted. You lost your balance!"

"Then why didn't you call after the show? And why did Hector call me this morning to ask me about my broken wrist?"

"Hector wasn't there when you fell. I wonder where he picked up that rumor?" Matt said, looking annoyed.

"His staff overheard Drew accuse you of breaking my wrist."

"You remember how chaotic it was before the show? Everyone came in at once. The band and customers crowded the reception area. Suddenly there you were up against the wall and falling to the floor. I've replayed your fall in my mind over and over all night."

"So have I," Liz said, shaking her head. "I remember you getting tenser as the band got later and later. I tried to calm you down. Apparently, a bad move."

"I love you, Liz," Matt said. He tried to lead her over to the couch. Liz instinctively pulled away. Simultaneous feelings of fear and relief confused her.

She looked intently at Matt. "It's too hard to admit you would do this to me. I do remember you panicked and were bossing me around."

"I know. I know. I'm acting kind of crazy lately. The

idea of being a father has really thrown me off. I have to admit it. I'm overwhelmed just thinking about it. What if something goes wrong or we lose the baby? What if I lose you?" Matt's fearful tone didn't sound like him.

Seeing Matt so vulnerable, she took his hand. Something in her softened. He seemed so genuine. "You can't control everything, Matt."

"I know. My life is more together than it's been in years. I don't want to mess it all up."

"Matt, you hurt me. Badly. Look at me. My wrist is broken. This is a big deal. You blew up under pressure. You caused this. I'm not only physically hurt. I'm terrified to think you could do it again."

"Quit blaming me!"

"Who else should I blame? Because of what you did, I'm in constant pain. I can't do the basics, like driving or using my computer. I won't get a cast until the swelling goes down, maybe in a week. I'll be out of commission for six weeks. This is serious."

"You think I deliberately hurt you? No way! Let me tell you how I see it."

"Go ahead. I'm all ears."

"You were between the front desk and the kitchen. Customers were heading to the restroom. I was trying to move you out of their way. You tripped over the stool and fell back against the wall and landed on the floor. Your balance has been off from the weight you've gained being pregnant."

"Are you kidding me? Blaming the fall on my pregnancy? I put my hand on your arm to calm you down. You pushed me away so roughly, the next thing I knew I was up against the wall. You shoved me that hard. I fell to the floor with shooting pains in my right wrist and cuts on my hand from the glass breaking." She stared angrily at Matt. He looked back in total shock, speechless.

"Why do you think the emergency room nurse gave me a domestic violence assessment? She actually referred to you as a possible batterer, suspecting you caused my fall and broken wrist. She even gave me a brochure about Jill's Place."

Matt had tears in his eyes. "I'm so sorry, Liz. We were both at our worst and it simply got out of hand. I didn't mean to hurt you. I love you. Please forgive me!"

At that moment, Liz wanted to believe him. Had she misread what happened? Matt noticed her guard drop and reached out to hold her left hand. Liz was so relieved Matt understood his part in what had happened, believing that together they could get through this. They just needed to keep talking and lessen the pressure at work.

"Maybe we could schedule the staff better so we're not so stressed out all the time?" Matt suggested.

She looked at him. "Okay. It would reduce the stress at the Cafe. I'm willing to give it a try. The bigger problem for you is Drew and Emily. They both think you meant to hurt me."

"I honestly didn't mean for you to fall. I'll do whatever I can to get them to trust me again. I know it'll take time, but I can do it. Drew has such a hard time letting go of you. We just need to show him I'm taking good care of you."

Liz pulled her hand away in astonishment. This conversation was a roller coaster. She couldn't help but glare at him.

"What is it now? I can't say anything without setting you off!"

"You still don't get it, do you? You make it sound like I can't take care of myself so you're taking over for Drew."

"That's not what I meant!"

"You act like a father handing over his daughter to her husband at their wedding. You may as well throw 'love, honor, and obey' into this conversation. I don't want that kind of relationship with you!"

"Calm down, Liz. That's not what I meant at all."

Liz looked at him, feeling confused in a way she never had before. How was this supposed to work? She wanted to believe Matt. While she loved him, he continued to frighten her.

"I don't know what to believe. Part of me feels like I could just walk away and simply admit that it's just too hard. I can't do this."

"Don't leave me. We love each other so much. Don't give up."

"It may be a bit late to say this, but we've got to slow things down. I need time to think about what I want. I'd like this to work out, but it has to be as equals."

"I want that too," he responded, leaning forward and touching her knee. "Come home with me. We can figure this out together."

"No, Matt. I'm not ready to do that. I'm going to stay here at least another night. After spending hours at the hospital, I'm exhausted. I plan to take the rest of the week off. You and Emily will have to make things work at the Cafe."

Liz could tell he wanted to argue her out of staying another night, but he held back.

"Okay, I get it. I'll back off."

"Good. That's what I need from you."

"Oh, Liz, just one more thing and I'll go. I almost forgot to tell you my father called this morning. He wants to visit next month on his way to San Francisco for a law conference. I hope that's alright."

Liz stared at him in disbelief. "We're struggling right now. Is this the best time for him to visit?"

"You're probably right. Considering all of this, I can tell him not to come. Make up some excuse," Matt said, though not very convincingly.

Liz saw his disappointment. "I guess we could try to make it work. I'm relieved it's next month and not any sooner. More stress is not what we need right now. Would he stay with us?"

"No. At a hotel. I'll call the Valley River Inn. Upscale enough for him. Maybe we'll go fly fishing while he's here. We could take him to the Metolius River."

"I don't know if I'll be up for the river right now, but you two should definitely go."

"He'll be disappointed not to fish and hike with you. I've told him how outdoorsy you are."

"Well, he'll just have to be disappointed," Liz said with a slightly annoyed tone. There he goes again, she thought. It always has to be Matt's way. We're going down the same path.

"You're right. I'm sure Dad will understand with the pregnancy," Matt said hesitantly.

"Of course he will, Matt. I'm exhausted. You need to go," Liz said.

"Wait, Liz. How about this? Something that could work for all of us. Let's all go to the coast for a couple of nights."

Liz paused for a moment. "That's not a bad idea. As

long as it's my favorite hotel, The Purple Haze."

"Would you be up for reserving two rooms?"

"I can do that."

"I'll get out of here. Why don't you get some rest? When you come home, I'll make you a special dinner." She watched him stand up and bend over to kiss her. She only lifted her cheek for a peck and fell back onto the couch. Matt simply shrugged and quietly walked out.

She lay on the couch replaying their conversation. Would a quick leap into marriage and sudden fatherhood make him act this way? It seemed too simple an explanation.

As Liz fell into a restless sleep, she had a strong feeling of uncertainty about what lay ahead.

CHAPTER 10

During the next month, the tension lessened. Matt was acting like he had when they first met. Romantic. Little gifts. He'd leave love notes about how he'd miss her when he went off to work.

Going out to pick up his father, Matt and Liz drove to the Eugene airport. Liz was anxious about seeing her father-in-law. She felt like a small child on her way to meet someone she was expected to impress. Because of losing her parents so young, she wasn't sure how adult children related to their parents. She started to remember scenes from her childhood, driving along Highway 99 with her parents when they traveled together to Portland and beyond. They always preferred driving through small towns and farmlands rather than speeding north on I-5. Over the years, there were inevitable transitions in the rural and urban landscapes. The old motels in west Eugene had been turned into homeless shelters and housing programs. The Gilbert Shopping Center had been replaced by a street food scene, "Barger Drive Food Cart Pod." A half-dozen food trucks featured a variety of foods, including Mexican, Thai, Jamaican, Hawaiian, and, of course, vegan cuisine. What would her parents think of these changes?

"You're unusually quiet today," Matt interrupted her reminiscing. "Is the idea of seeing my father scary? It always is for me!"

Liz laughed. "You know me too well. Sure. I'm nervous about spending time with Quinn. I barely talked to him at the wedding. Mostly I remember how odd it was he left early to get back to Wisconsin. Hard to imagine what emergency could be so important that he'd leave his son's wedding."

"Work is always a priority for him. Why would our wedding be any different?"

"Not so for my Mom and Dad. They always said that family came first and acted like it. I hope that we'll be those kinds of parents."

Matt redirected the conversation. "I'm glad we decided to take him to the coast first. This way we'll all have a little room to breathe. You can get to know each other slowly. Anyway, he's only here three nights. How bad can it be?"

"You tell me. How bad can it be?" Liz replied in a more serious tone.

Matt hesitated. "You just never know with Dad. What's in your favor is that he's a politician first and foremost. Always looking for approval whether it's at the polls or any woman he meets, including you."

"That's reassuring," Liz responded sarcastically. "We had talked about taking him to the Shady Grove for dinner before we head to the coast. He'd get a close look at our lives. I know you weren't big on the idea, but I want him to see how successful our business is. He'll be impressed."

Again, Matt hesitated. "It's not exactly his scene. He'd prefer French farm to table cuisine or upscale Italian fare where the menu calls for a translator."

"We both know it's not about the food at the Cafe. I just don't get it. Are you embarrassed by our business? Sounds like you don't want to show it to him at all," Liz challenged.

Matt glanced over at her and then looked away. "Let's not decide now. We'll just see how the weekend goes. Maybe by spending time with us, Dad will get why living out here is better for me than becoming a lawyer. He'll see that it's a healthier lifestyle. If that's the way it goes, we could stop at the Cafe before taking him to the airport."

Liz was disappointed. She looked out the window, wondering what it would be like if her parents were alive now. She was certain they would have been so proud of the Cafe. But, would they like Matt? Quinn? She wasn't so sure.

Matt's easy-going manner and attentiveness over the past month was a promising and welcome respite. In spite of the change, Liz scoped out the Jill's Place website at Sophie's suggestion. She learned that after an explosive incident the partner is often highly apologetic. They act romantically and promise things will be better. It's called the "honeymoon phase."

"What are you thinking now? You're so quiet again," Matt said, interrupting her thoughts.

"I keep thinking about my parents. So different from how you describe Quinn."

Matt turned off Highway 99 toward the airport. "You

had a healthy family. Me? Not so much. Listen, we're almost there. Let's not overthink this. Just be prepared for my charming and unpredictable dad!"

"We rarely talk so openly about your past. Maybe Quinn's visit can help me understand you better. I want to figure out his true impact on your family."

"I wouldn't bet on it!" Matt replied. "Saying any more is too loaded. One thing I know for sure, my father's presence rarely brings people closer together."

Matt pulled into the parking lot of Eugene's small airport with its two baggage claim areas and four gates. After pacing for fifteen minutes in the lobby, he saw his father coming down the escalator. Quinn smiled and waved as he spotted them. Liz relaxed a bit, imagining that he wouldn't be as harsh as Matt made him out to be.

Judge Quinten Mathew Foley was about 5'11" with gray hair and a stylish, short-stubble beard that turned white at the sideburns. His hair was short but curly and framed his face along his high forehead. When he took off his University of Wisconsin Badgers cap, Liz noticed a bald spot on the crown of his head. He looked younger than his 55 years. The only resemblance between Matt and his dad were the blue eyes and bushy eyebrows, which on his father, seemed too long and sprang in all directions.

"Welcome to Oregon, Dad," Matt said, giving his father a quick, sideways hug.

"It's good to be here and to see the mother of my grandchild," Quinn said, stepping forward and giving Liz a long bear hug. "How are mother and baby doing?"

"It's all going well."

"Matt told me you were past the morning sickness. Is that right?"

"Yeah. The second trimester is easier. I'm actually sleeping much better and my energy is picking up. There's a reason they call it the most comfortable period of the pregnancy. I'm still ready for it to be over though," Liz said, laughing as she patted her stomach.

"I don't think I've ever met a pregnant woman who didn't feel that way," he responded, confidently putting his arm around her shoulders, guiding her toward the luggage area. "You are glowing!"

Liz looked back as Matt rolled his eyes, looking like a rejected little boy. She quickly turned and grabbed his hand, so they were walking three abreast.

Meanwhile, Quinn was telling an amusing story about catching his flight in San Francisco and how the airport felt larger than the whole city when you had to catch a flight to the hinterlands. "I got enough exercise for a week," he laughed.

"It's funny, Quinn, out here we think of Wisconsin as being the hinterlands."

Judge Foley's laugh was so raucous that several people turned around and looked at him. "I like your feistiness. We'll have a great time getting to know each other. I've been looking forward to this visit all month."

Quinn stepped forward when the luggage carrier started moving and bags began appearing.

"Watch out," Matt whispered, giving her arm a squeeze. "He can turn on you in a minute."

"He's just trying to figure me out. I'm okay."

Looking dubious, Matt pulled away and announced, "I'll go get the car and meet you out front."

Quinn shrugged and looked at Liz. "What's up with him?"

"I don't know. Why don't you ask him?" Liz said, looking him in the eye.

"It was a rough adolescence. I don't think we've gotten past it. Matt often gets angry at me for no reason."

"It might be worth finding out why he's still so angry with you."

"You're probably right. Matt is lucky to have someone like you in his life. You're more suited to him."

"More than his first wife?"

Quinn hesitated as he turned to look for his luggage. "Let's put it this way. Matt married well the second time around."

Looking at her father-in-law, Liz realized Matt was right. His dad was a piece of work. How rude of him to compare her to Matt's ex-wife.

By the time Quinn's suitcase came off the carousel, Matt had retrieved the car and was sitting at the curb out front. He got out and loaded the suitcase into the trunk while his father opened the front door for Liz. He waited to close it until she was comfortable and buckled in.

Then he climbed into the backseat behind Matt.

"Dad, we made plans to take you to the coast to our favorite place, The Purple Haze. It's an 18-room rock and roll music-themed hotel," Matt said, looking at his father in the rearview mirror.

When Quinn nodded, Matt continued nervously, "Every room is decorated in the style of a musician, reflecting their life and songs. I thought about reserving either the Jimi Hendrix or Janis Joplin room for you. In the end, I decided on the Grateful Dead because I remembered how much you loved Jerry Garcia. Didn't you follow him around the country when you were in college and consider yourself a Deadhead?"

Quinn laughed and said, "That was a lifetime ago."

"Anyway, all the rooms have an ocean view and most have fireplaces or hot tubs. Liz chose the Jefferson Airplane room for us. Her all time favorite song is 'Somebody to Love.' Remember that it was the first song we danced to at our wedding? Liz just loves Gracie Slick. I was leaning towards the Rolling Stones room, but Liz made the reservations. She's big on strong women songwriters."

Liz noticed Matt talking too fast. To help relieve his nervousness, she chimed in, "There's a third-floor ocean-front library, with sheet music, old records, cassettes and CDs. You can even find DVDs of musical movies like the Beatles' *Yellow Submarine*. Also, memoirs and old rock and roll magazines. Kind of like a shortened version of the Rock and Roll Hall of Fame, but you get to sleep over. They offer family-style seating for breakfast and dinner. The place attracts music lovers from all over the country."

Quinn couldn't help but laugh. "Sounds like a clever concept. Whatever you want to do is fine by me. I'm in your hands for three days. My only request is to take you to a good restaurant with fresh salmon and the great Oregon wines I've heard about."

"Because you're only here for the weekend, Matt thought that we should go directly to the hotel. It happens to have one of the best restaurants on the Coast with exceptionally good wines from local vineyards," Liz said, looking over the seat at him. "Or we could drive into Eugene first and show you the Shady Grove so you can see our business in action. Your choice."

Quinn smiled at Liz. "Maybe we can save the Shady Grove for the end of the weekend before heading to the airport." Matt rolled his eyes at Liz.

For the rest of the three-hour drive to Cannon Beach, Quinn regaled them with tales of court cases and political life in Wisconsin. He also mentioned there had been talk of him running for Governor, but the possibility was still in exploratory stages.

They stopped once and got out at Strawberry Hill to visit their favorite tide pools. The tide was out so they could walk onto the rocks and see a variety of anemones, starfish, crabs, and other creatures. The sea lions were lolling on the rocks a short distance out in the water. Quinn was fascinated and asked question after question. Liz was glad that the sea life of the Oregon coast was one of her hobbies. With few exceptions, she could answer his questions. Matt had to drag them away, so they could get to the Purple Haze in time to check in before dinner.

They arrived at the hotel and found out that dinner would be served in a half-hour. They headed to their rooms to drop off their bags and agreed to meet in the dining room at seven.

When they entered the restaurant, they could see the surf pounding along the rocky beach through panoramic windows. Quinn spotted a table with three people. One, in particular, caught his eye. "Let's sit at that table," he suggested, striding across the room.

He smiled at the attractive woman in her 50s with dark brown curly hair that hugged her face. She was laughing hard as she listened intently to a young woman across the table. Quinn assumed that the man, in his late twenties, was the young woman's sibling. They almost looked like twins.

He excused his interruption and asked, "Do you mind

if we join you?"

"Please do. I'm Bridgette," said the older woman as she offered the chair next to her. "I've been getting to know our dinner partners, Rachel Adler-Roth, and her brother, Josh."

Liz watched as Quinn sat down and checked out Bridgette's body. He then turned to look at Rachel, taking in her large brown eyes, and hair coiled in an African head wrap knotted like a turban on the top of her head. He looked disapprovingly at Josh's locs that were wound tight. Liz was embarrassed by Quinn scrutinizing the group without saying a word.

She decided to get the conversation going and learned that both were Portland-based. Josh was a video game designer for a fast-growing company and Rachel was a part-time manager at a microbrewery whose beers could be found on tap at restaurants across the Northwest.

Next, Liz turned to Bridgette and asked where she was from. Bridgette owned a financial investment company in San Francisco where she had lived all her life. She was on a solo vacation, taking her time driving along the Coast Highway to visit her daughter and baby granddaughter in Seattle. Since she was an old rock and roller, she had to stop at The Purple Haze Hotel. One of her clients had raved about it.

Once the Foleys had ordered drinks from Lupe, their server, Bridgette learned about Quinn's run for governor of Wisconsin. It drew her interest since she was active in the Bay Area Democratic Party and had been a delegate during national elections.

"We seem to have a lot in common," Quinn said.

"Yes, except our work," Bridgette replied. "Tell me

about the most exciting court cases in your career. I love legal shows." From her expression, Matt could tell she was charmed by him and admired his ability to tell what could have been dull court stories in a riveting way.

After a few minutes of storytelling, Quinn said, "Hey. I'm about to join you as a grandparent. Should I get Matt and Liz to move to Wisconsin?"

"Good luck with that," Bridgette said with a laugh.

"You're probably right. I'll have to come to them. Maybe we can plan to meet once a year when I visit?"

"Let's see how the dinner goes before we schedule our annual rendezvous," she teased.

In the meantime, Liz and Matt described their cafe to Rachel and Josh. They liked connecting with musicians, customers and staff, and offering good food and music. Since Rachel and Josh had worked in restaurants, the four of them could compare their experiences as workers and managers.

Overhearing Quinn's conversation with Bridgette about his rise from lawyer to judge, Rachel caught Quinn's glance and said, "I once considered law school but decided to work for a while before making the commitment."

"Seems like working at a beer hall restaurant is a waste of your good mind. You could do more with your life, don't you think? I've read that trendy microbreweries have a high failure rate."

Rachel replied emphatically, "Really? Ours doubled its profits in the past year. It's not like the Miller Brewing Company in Milwaukee, swallowed up by a huge corporation like Coors."

"Yes, things have changed since the old days, Judge Foley. Got to keep current," Josh added before Rachel could finish putting Quinn completely in his place.

Rachel smiled at her brother and turned to ask Bridgette about what she liked best about San Francisco. She talked about what it was like growing up there in the '70s and how much it had changed.

After the first course had been served, Lupe politely broke into the table chatter to say it was time for a group game. She explained the rules for *Two Truths and a Lie*. "This game is a way for our guests to get to know each other. Each person tells two things that are true about themselves and one that's not. The other guests have ten minutes to ask questions. They'll work together to try to determine the lie."

Quinn laughed, "Let's give it a try. Could be fun."

"We've done this game before and it's really a great way to connect with strangers," Liz added.

"Okay, I'm willing to start," Bridgette offered after the five minutes they were given to come up with their two truths and a lie.

As Liz studied her father-in-law, she wondered what his two truths and a lie could possibly be. She could only imagine how easy it would be for him to come up with the lie.

Bridgette began, "I have driven a car 140 miles per hour on the Utah Salt Flats. I have been to Antarctica twice. I won the state lottery in California."

Liz jumped in. "What's the most memorable thing about Antarctica?"

"The obvious answer would be the cold, but that's not what I remember. It's the stillness when the wind dies down for short periods."

"That sounds to me like the response of someone

who's been there. Or else, Bridgette, you're an impressive liar," chided Liz.

Once everyone stopped laughing, Matt asked the next question about the Salt Flats which was answered just as smoothly. They went around the table once, ending with Quinn. "All I can say is that I hope you never end up in my courtroom. The jury would never be able to figure out what was true."

After much discussion and more questions, the group decided that Bridgette's lie was racing on the Salt Flats.

"Wrong," she said. "My lie was Antarctica. Never been there!"

"That's too funny, Bridgette. I don't think of an investment adviser as a race car driver! You've ruined my stereotype," Rachel teased.

The game continued while they ate savory Peruvian roasted chicken. Each person revealed intriguing facts about their lives. When it was Matt's turn, Quinn said, "I better opt out of this one. I don't think there's much I don't know about my son."

"Oh, you'd be surprised, Dad," Matt replied. "Think about the things you did that your parents never suspected."

Deep knowing grins appeared around the table, followed by a few snickers. Quinn looked at Matt and smiled broadly, proud of his son's clever remark. It was a look that Matt rarely saw.

Matt began his two truths and a lie. "I joined a practice session with Barcelona's soccer team while traveling in Spain. I met Ray Charles at a concert in Milwaukee. I spent six days walking and camping on the Great Wall of China. It's so wide there's room to camp."

"Wow," Rachel said. "You've got some unusual experiences there. I wonder which one is a big fat lie! How sore were you after playing soccer in Barcelona?"

"I couldn't move for two days, but it was worth it."

"Who did you know to get a backstage guest pass to meet Ray Charles?" Josh asked. Matt exchanged a look with his father, who seemed amused. "My father knew Ray Charles' attorney."

They all looked at Quinn who smiled and shrugged. "I belong to the Madison Democratic Lawyers Association. We do each other favors now and then, especially when we've graduated from the same law school." The group seemed nearly convinced the Ray Charles story was true.

Yet, Liz knew it was a lie and she was fascinated to see Matt and his father lie together so convincingly. Well, at least they were connecting about something. In the end, the group agreed that practicing with the soccer team in Spain would be impossible. Once they discovered how wrong they were, the group laughed and teased Quinn about what a great attorney he must have been defending guilty criminals. They all believed the Ray Charles story.

"Criminal law involves great acting. Any good attorney could go on the stage and make millions, but most prefer to make the country a functioning democracy," Quinn said, directing his comment at Matt.

Liz noticed how humiliated Matt looked. She wondered if his father would ever get over the fact that he had dropped out of law school.

By the time the group had finished the main course, each had a turn at the game. While waiting for dessert and coffee, Liz polled the group on everyone's most memorable meal. Quinn's was at Claudia Bergmann's German restaurant in Milwaukee. Her Wiener schnitzel was the best he'd ever had, including when he was in Germany.

Rachel asked how he could eat veal when he knew how they were raised. Quinn's look of disdain made Liz embarrassed for him.

"I noticed you didn't hesitate to eat the poor, tortured chicken tonight," he said. "Do you think they have a great life cooped up and force-fed until they are ready to be butchered? I thought the cliché on politically correct food was Portland-based, not Cannon Beach."

Rachel looked directly at Quinn with an offended expression. "I have met people like you before and am happy to set you straight. The Purple Haze uses free-range chickens, as they describe on the menu, buying from local farmers. I'm not a vegetarian, but I do care about how the food I eat comes to my table. I always read the small print. You might want to try that next time. So easy to miss," offered Rachel smugly.

A strange smile formed on Quinn's face and he nodded. "Got me," he admitted.

The moment passed, but a coolness settled over the table. Rachel noticed her brother looking at her approvingly as she quickly switched topics. She told the group how she and Josh had tossed the idea around of opening a liege waffle food truck. They described the year they had lived in Belgium, the home of the perfect waffle, while their college professor mother had a year-long sabbatical.

"I went to a law conference in Belgium just last year, and those Belgian waffles are to die for. Pearl sugar is what does it!" Quinn added as he poured the table another glass of wine. Liz passed. Lupe appeared to serve the baklava brownie pie with pecans, honey and chocolate drizzle that melted in their mouths. Other diners returned to the game as they ate dessert, but their table inhaled the sweet treat the minute it was served.

Bridgette moved her empty dessert plate to the side and asked if anyone would like to go up to the library and play Scrabble. "I'm a bit of a Scrabble addict. It's an old family tradition. We even play online with each other." Josh and Rachel said they would love to join her.

As they were leaving, Rachel raved over the dessert. "I make it a rule to have chocolate every day as part of a healthy diet," she laughed.

"You must have spent most of college studying nutrition," Liz teased. "Let's get together tomorrow. We have a lot in common, chocolate and restaurant work!"

"Yeah, good idea," Rachel said, hurrying off to catch up with Josh and Bridgette.

Liz yawned and used her exhaustion as an excuse to go back to their room. As the three got up from the table, Quinn nabbed the guest check from Matt's hand. "Let me get this. I know you must be living on a shoestring owning a small business."

"We're actually doing great, Quinn," Liz responded. Looking at Matt, she regretted that she had intervened. Matt shook his head at her and walked silently away towards the stairs to their room.

When Quinn and Liz got to the landing, he mentioned wanting to stop at the gift shop to get some chocolate for later. So, Liz caught up with Matt and they headed to their room. They had been looking forward to some time alone. Their room had a picture of the lead singer, Gracie Slick, holding a white rabbit to highlight her hit psychedelic song of the same name. A funky old electric guitar hung above the bed with more photos of the whole band. Strobe lights, an antique lamp with a fringe shade, Day-Glo posters and a huge picture of Jefferson Airplane at Woodstock covered the east wall.

✖

After buying the chocolates, Quinn went to his room but had trouble reading since the energy-saving bulbs weren't bright enough for him. He had been trying to review some early drafts of documents developed by his lawyer and campaign manager, Lyle Oliver. Lyle needed his comments in two days in order to schedule meetings. Quinn would have to gain support from numerous special interest groups to be nominated for Governor.

Quinn put his iPad aside on the oak nightstand. He was having trouble focusing as his mind wandered back to the evening. He may have been a bit pushy with Rachel but he believed it was her way of flirting. He'd seen that type of come on before.

He had overheard Liz and Rachel talking about Janis Joplin's tragic life and her best album, *Pearl*. They agreed she was a feminist heroine and some of her music pointed out how often women were used by men. He hoped that his daughter-in-law and Rachel weren't die-hard feminists. He had dealt with too many of those in his professional life, law school, the courtroom and his personal life. His ex-wife, Joanne began taking Women and Gender Studies classes, dabbling to see if she might want to change careers. Her return to school created havoc and contributed to the end of their marriage. Tough times, he recalled resentfully.

One night, after 15 years of marriage, Quinn had come home to their two-story, red brick house overlooking both Lake Mendota and the Capitol. He had been out with colleagues at the Plaza Tavern after work. He discovered the locks had been changed and found two large suitcases and a wardrobe hanger sitting near the front door.

Joanne always had a strange sense of humor and had duct-taped a sealed letter in a business-sized envelope to one of the suitcases. The hanger held three suits and light blue and lavender shirts with matching Jerry Garcia ties. He was mystified as he took a seat on the top step of the porch and read the note: "Quinn, I need a serious break from you. You need help. I won't be your punching bag anymore. Once you've had treatment for your anger, I might consider meeting with you in a public place to talk. Stay away from me or I'll get a restraining order."

He was shocked. A few months later, Joanne filed for divorce and moved to Chicago with Matt. Surprisingly, his artist wife began law school at Loyola and now managed a nationally known women's legal advocacy center.

To escape these memories, he went over to the window and looked out at the crashing waves. Then he decided to check out the library. He grabbed the "Blissful Chocolates" he had purchased earlier hoping to offer them as an atonement gift to Rachel. As he headed out the door, he recalled she was in the Janis Joplin room just down the hall. The group had shared their room's unique musical themes over dinner. A mural of a Mercedes covered the door with the song title, "Oh Lord, Won't You Buy Me a Mercedes Benz."

Quinn decided to turn this depressing night into one of passion and pleasure. He knocked softly on Rachel's

119

door. No answer. He knocked louder. Rachel came to the door, looking startled, wearing jean leggings, a light teal, thin strapped tank top, and purple Nike sneakers. Quinn's face had a pleased look as his eyes moved across her body, from top to bottom.

"Rachel, I'm so glad you're still up."

She quickly interrupted. "It's a little late for a visit, Quinn. Can it wait until morning? I'm pretty tired. Good night." Not waiting for a reply, she began to shut the door. Quinn's foot jammed it.

"Wait! It will just take a second. I want to give you these chocolates to apologize for being rude at dinner," he said as he tried to hand her the gift. He maintained his foot's position. As she hesitated, he pushed his body through the entryway and shut the door.

"Take your chocolates and get the hell out!" Rachel shouted.

He grabbed her by both shoulders, pulled her roughly to him and kissed her hard on the lips.

When she put her hands on his chest and tried to shove him away, he clutched her wrist and pulled her toward him. Reaching under her shirt, he grabbed her breasts and kissed her roughly up and down her neck. As she fought to get released from his grip, Quinn tore her shirt.

"You're disgusting! Let go of me," she shouted, pushing him away. Quinn spun her around and put his arm tightly across her neck. He whispered in her ear: "You want this!"

"Stop it! You're choking me. I can't breathe," she gasped.

He'd been here before with other women, including his own wife. They loved the struggle but eventually gave into the passion.

Thinking quickly, Rachel stopped fighting to change tactics and get this monster out of her room. Once he relaxed his grip and stepped back, she motioned for him to go into the bedroom. She looked at him seductively and said, "Hold on. We got off to a rough start. Let's take this slower. I need to get something from the bathroom first."

Now we're talking, he thought to himself. He sat down on the bed and began to unbutton his shirt. Rachel grabbed her purse where she kept her cell phone and rushed into the bathroom, locking the door. She quickly texted Josh: "Help. Come over now. Quinn's here!" He texted back: "On my way."

At that moment, Quinn called out from the bedroom, "What's taking you so long?"

"Out in a minute. It will be worth the wait!" When Rachel heard Josh pounding on the door, she raced out of the bathroom to let him in.

Quinn saw Josh and asked, "What are you doing here?"

"Protecting my sister. Get out!" shouted Josh.

"Rachel wants me here!"

"I know my sister. She'd never let a pig like you into her room! Get out before I call the police."

"Hold on a second. This is just a misunderstanding. The police would have no interest in this." He grabbed his shirt and pushed past both of them on his way out the door.

Rachel walked over to the bed and burst into tears. "I don't know what would have happened if you hadn't come so fast!" Josh put his arm around her.

Once she stopped crying, he asked, "What should we do now? Call the police?"

"No. Calling them won't help. Especially when we got

him out of here before he raped me. Do you think we have enough physical evidence to go after him? He's a powerful guy who gets what he wants."

"You have bruises on your neck. Your torn shirt is on the floor. He tried to rape you, Rachel! We can't let him get away with this," Josh burst out.

"Whatever I do, I want to make sure he never does this to another woman."

"Should we call Mom and Dad? They'll know what to do." He had often turned to his parents for advice over the years.

"No. I want to deal with this on my own. Or at least with your help, Josh. We've always been there for each other."

"Of course, I'll help you. Maybe Matt could get his dad to leave the hotel. Or should I report Quinn to the management? Once he's gone, we can talk about how to make him pay for this."

"Those are possibilities. Let's find Matt first."

Josh rushed out toward the end of the hall to Matt and Liz's room. As he passed Quinn's door, he saw it was wide open. He stuck his head in. The room was empty. His luggage was gone.

CHAPTER 11

Josh returned to Rachel's room and declared, "Quinn is out of here. His room is empty!"

"Unbelievable!"

"Let's find that bastard!"

"I'm going to make Matt tell me where he's gone," Rachel said.

"I'm game," Josh responded, following Rachel to Matt's room.

When Matt answered the door in his pajamas, he looked surprised. Rachel demanded, "Where the hell is your father?"

"Keep it down," Matt said, holding his finger to his lips. As he closed the door to their bedroom, Rachel and Josh went into the sitting room.

Matt shrugged. "Not sure. Probably in his room or in the library looking for a legal mystery." Meanwhile, his gut reaction was a familiar one when it came to his father. Suddenly, he could barely breathe.

"No, he's not!" Rachel said emphatically, looking him straight in the eye. "He left the hotel after assaulting me!" She was so angry her body was shaking. Still, she observed his shocked reaction. She had no way of knowing that Matt's worst suspicion had been confirmed.

After an awkward silence, Matt's cell phone chimed with a text. He glanced at the caller's name and said, "It's someone connected to my father. He'll be able to tell me where he is. I'll come up to your room once I find out what's going on."

"Even after leaving the scene, Quinn's calling the shots," Josh said, exchanging a look of exasperation with Rachel.

"I'm so sorry this happened. Try having him as your father."

"I'm sure it's hell," Rachel said, noticing the hurt in his eyes. "I can give you an hour before I talk to my lawyer."

Before Matt texted back, he went out to the parking lot and saw that his car was gone. Quinn was the last to use it when he went into town earlier to get flowers for Liz. Matt told Liz how startled he was by his father's thoughtfulness. Quinn had also left a tender note about Liz's future motherhood.

Not only had Quinn fled the scene of the crime, but had stranded them. Matt was left to clean up his mess, and with no transportation home. With a business to run, a pregnant wife and a marriage growing shakier by the minute, Matt was frantic and overwhelmed.

His cell phone chimed again. He grabbed it out of his back pocket and read a text from Lyle Oliver. "Working on agreement and payment. Stall her til I have something."

Once again, Lyle is my father's fixer, Matt thought.

Acting on instinct, Matt texted back: "You have until 1:00 am. Need it fast!" His gut told him Rachel could act quickly.

It made Matt feel conflicted since he was negotiating for his father, but still felt compassion for Rachel. He wanted to get the best deal for her when he was supposed to be his father's advocate. He knew something about Rachel's circumstances because of Liz's conversation with her after dinner. She had wandered to the library, found Rachel in the fiction section and asked about the *Scrabble* game. Rachel had confessed it was just an excuse to get away from Quinn as she'd had enough of him for the night.

After a half-hour of drinking tea and talking about their lives, including their college experiences, Liz returned to their room. She described the enormity of Rachel's undergraduate student debt. Her Psychology Ph.D. program at Lewis & Clark was only partially funded through scholarships and grants. She was considering dropping out of grad school to manage the microbrewery full time.

Matt gave this information to Lyle to craft an offer that Rachel would find hard to refuse. He got the go-ahead to offer Rachel $90,000 with a negotiating cap of $125,000. Lyle would send Matt the non-disclosure agreement once he texted him the final amount.

Matt made it to Rachel's room with five minutes to spare. He sat in the straight-backed chair across from Rachel and Josh. "I know this doesn't make up for what happened, but my dad's lawyer wants to try to make things right," offered Matt.

"Nothing can make this right," Josh said.

"Of course not. But here's the deal. I was told to offer

you $90,000, but the real cap is $125,000. I tell you this because I don't want to play games and I want my father to pay for what he did."

Rachel sat with a stone face. "I want to consult with my friend who is a criminal lawyer."

"No, the deal is that you can't talk to lawyers or anyone! I have a non-disclosure agreement for you to sign."

"Then I'll consult with Josh alone. Wait here." Rachel and Josh went into the bedroom. Should she call the police or take Quinn's offer? Rachel was torn. They were both shocked by the size of the offer.

"Dirty money, huh, Josh?" Her face was drained.

"Sure feels like it. That sleaze gets away with assaulting you. You know he'll do it again. If he becomes the next governor of Wisconsin, he'll have even more cover."

"True. Think of all the women who have taken on influential, abusive men, just like the judge." Rachel knew they had taken a big risk.

"They had everything to lose." Josh could play both sides of a decision Rachel had to make.

"Women have gotten raked over the coals for exposing them. All it takes is for one woman to come forward for more to do the same," Rachel added.

"On the other hand," reasoned Josh, "Litigation will probably involve a long, expensive legal battle. We could talk about this all day, but you have to make a decision right now."

"I don't have that kind of money. If I took the offer, I could pay off my college loans and finish grad school out of debt. I could move forward, practicing my profession as a child psychologist."

"Sounds like you've made your decision."

"I think I have. Let's tell Matt." They joined Matt in the sitting room.

"I've decided to accept the offer with one stipulation. I want an additional $15,000 to donate to the Sexual Assault Support Center at Portland State University. I'll make the donation anonymously, but I want your father to know that he's paying for what he did."

"Okay. I'll convince Dad's lawyer to come up with the extra money."

Matt relayed Rachel's counter offer to Lyle. Once it was approved by Quinn, Matt received the agreement for Rachel's signature. Quinn wanted it over fast, so the funds were transferred by noon that day.

After Matt left, Rachel turned to her brother. "I wish I felt better about this." It was easy to read the disappointment in her eyes.

"Let's find another way to make Quinn pay for what he did to you."

CHAPTER 12

When Matt made it back to their room, he looked at the clock. It was 6:00 a.m. Knowing Liz's sleep challenges while pregnant, he hesitated waking her to tell why his father had left suddenly. He sat at the edge of the bed and gently woke her from a deep sleep.

"What's going on? What time is it?" Liz asked in a startled voice, sitting up abruptly. "It's still dark outside."

"You're not going to believe this. After going to Rachel's room last night, Dad came on too strong. She managed to get away from him for a few moments to text Josh for help. She has accused him of assault."

"Are you kidding me?" Liz asked incredulously, pulling the covers over her shoulders protectively.

"No. Trust me. It's no joke. Dad is gone. So is our car. I got a text from Lyle Oliver. He was the fast-talking, pretentious man you found so annoying at our wedding. Anyway, he offered a $140,000 cash settlement with a non-disclosure agreement to prevent Rachel from going public. It's amazing how Dad and Lyle were able to respond so quickly. Almost like they'd done it before."

"Not so amazing," Liz said with disgust. "Want to know how I really feel?"

"You're pissed off. It's obvious. But I did the best I could."

"Not good enough. I'm so angry at Quinn, I can't imagine him being a grandfather to our daughter."

"Hold up for a second." Matt started to speak.

But Liz interrupted him, "You warned me to be careful around him, but you didn't tell me he rapes women."

"He didn't actually rape her. He just came on too strong."

"Your father attacked Rachel. He does more than come on too strong. Last night, we watched him being rude and judgmental to Rachel. The next minute he was flirting with her. She felt it."

"He's impossible. He may have assaulted Rachel, but it wasn't rape. According to her, Dad did hurt her. She was definitely shaken and he intimidated her. But right now we have other things to deal with. Dad took our car. Let's figure out how we're going to get home."

"That's really what's most important to you?" Liz challenged. "You know what's sad? I'm not at all surprised about the attack. What shocks me is how you tell the story."

"I'm just repeating what Rachel told me."

"Damn it, Matt. You should be angrier at Quinn and his goon for paying Rachel thousands of dollars to silence her. Whose side are you on, Quinn's or Rachel's?"

"Of course I'm on Rachel's side. How could you even ask?"

"I think it's sheer luck that Rachel got away before he raped her. Isn't he known as a champion for civil rights? Doesn't seem to translate to women's rights. Frankly, your father makes me sick. And right now, so do you!"

"Hold on. I've been up all night dealing with this. Could you cut me a little slack and hear me out?"

"Go ahead but I can't imagine what you could say to make it sound any better."

"I agree. What my father did was questionable, but don't blame me. He thinks all women are attracted to him. I saw it growing up." Matt collapsed on the bed in exhaustion. At that moment, Liz felt a wave of compassion for Matt.

"You need to get some sleep and I need some time alone to digest this. I'm going to the library for a while before breakfast. I'll wake you when I get back." Liz threw on her clothes and decided to go to Rachel's room instead of the library. She was unsure if she should disturb her, but wanted to offer support. She knocked lightly on the door. Josh pulled it open with a look of anger.

"Oh, it's you," he said with relief. "Rachel, it's Liz."

Rachel appeared from the bathroom, grimacing. "I'm guessing you've heard everything from Matt."

"I'm so sorry!" Liz cried out, throwing her arms around Rachel. "I really don't know my father-in-law very well, but I didn't know he was capable of this!"

Rachel stepped back, looking relieved. "I'm not surprised that you get it. But, you never know these days who will get what I went through and who won't."

"I get it. You stood up to him and fought back. It must have been terrifying."

"Thankfully, Josh came when I needed him."

"Rachel, you fought him off and texted me for help," Josh said.

"I hate that Matt is so involved in this," confessed Liz. "He's beginning to remind me of his father."

"Where is Matt?" asked Rachel.

"I left him in our room after chewing him out. He referred to Quinn's attack as coming on too strong. He refused to come right out and call it what it was."

"Funny, it seemed like Matt believed me. He was sincere and was trying to help," Rachel insisted.

Josh sighed. "I'm afraid you were dealing with the devil, Rachel, and Matt was simply his messenger!"

"Well, the devil had me sign a non-disclosure agreement. So, I can't tell anyone about the assault."

"Matt told me about the pay-off. A financial settlement is the least Quinn could do, but prison is where men like him belong. And then, to top it off, he took our car and left us stranded."

"Liz, come with us when we leave later today. We can take the long way and drop you off in Eugene on our way back to Portland," Josh said.

"It will give us time to decide the next steps in dealing with Quinn," Rachel said.

They talked for a while longer, giving Rachel a chance to vent. She cried as she described the attack to Liz. A loud knock on the door startled them. Josh got up and slowly opened it.

"I thought I'd find you here. I've rented a car. Are you ready to go?" Matt asked.

Liz got up quickly and stepped into the hall to join Matt, closing the door behind her.

"No," Liz replied. "I'm going to stay here and help

Rachel get through this." She stared past him.

"How about me? I've been through a lot dealing with all of it."

"I don't see it quite that way. We can talk more about it when I get home."

"If that's what you want. But, keep in mind that I'm the one who fought for Rachel. I made Dad pay." Liz saw the disgust on Matt's face as he abruptly turned his back on her and stormed off.

Liz went back into the room and collapsed into the chair. Rachel grabbed her hand, pleading, "I couldn't help but hear you two quarreling in the hallway. Don't let Quinn poison your relationship. He ruins just about every-thing he touches, doesn't he?"

"Considering how Matt fought for Rachel to get the best deal, he appears to be a better man than his father any day," Josh said.

Liz looked from one to the other and then suddenly stood up saying, "Matt and I have a lot of unfinished business. This just adds another layer to it."

Later, as they were checking out, Liz looked sadly around the lobby thinking she would never feel the same way about this hotel that she had loved for years.

They decided to drive down the coast to Florence rather than cut over to the freeway. It would give them a chance to calm their nerves. They stopped to walk along the beach and watch the waves pounding against Haystack Rock, 235 feet tall. They were captivated by the puffins who flew around their nests on the rock. The repetitious sounds of crashing waves had a consoling effect.

As they headed out of Florence and up the Siuslaw River, they started to form a plan. Liz insisted that despite the tension between her and Matt, the priority was to go after Quinn. She offered to consult an attorney to determine if Matt had nullified the non-disclosure agreement by telling her about it. Liz knew a good contract lawyer from college.

As they were driving past Veneta, Liz's phone rang. Seeing it was Emily, she answered.

"Liz, I don't know what to say. When Matt came in this morning, he was super angry and fired me," Emily blurted out. "Are you still at the coast?"

"No, I'm on my way home. You've been caught in the middle of a drama that you won't believe. I'll fill you in when I see you. Don't worry about your job. I'll take care of it."

"Will you be home soon?"

"Probably a half-hour or so. I'll give you a call."

"Good. Talk to you later."

After she hung up, Liz said, "Matt's on a rampage. I need to help Emily, our restaurant manager. Let's finish up. I'll take notes on my iPad."

"Where should we drop you off when we get to Eugene?" asked Josh. "I assume you don't want to go home."

"I texted my best friend, Sophie, while we were packing. I'm going to stay there. I'll keep a low profile. Matt will think I'm still at the coast."

Fortunately, Liz had a key to Sophie's since she was out when they arrived. Josh and Rachel helped take her luggage up to the bedroom.

"Before we talk at the end of the week, Rachel, why don't you find a detective agency to look into Quinn's history?" asked Liz.

"Will do," Rachel said.

"We're in this together," Josh declared as they both hugged Liz goodbye.

Before Liz called Emily, she wondered if she was on the right track. Was she putting herself and her baby at risk? Matt had been violent once and could be again. Would their plan result in Quinn facing consequences for what he did or would Liz be the one to pay?

CHAPTER 13

The next morning, Liz told Sophie that Matt had called four times and texted twice during the night. She had a voicemail from Natalie who, with her husband Marcus, had been close friends of Matt's for quite a while. The two couples went hiking together and hung out at each other's homes. Since Liz liked Natalie and considered her a friend separate from the couples' relationship, she decided to call back.

"Hi, Natalie. You called. What's up?"

"Thanks for getting back to me. I have a hard question for you."

"Go for it."

"I'm up to speed on your hideous weekend at the coast."

"I figured as much. I know Matt confides in you."

"Well, he's pretty stressed out that you're taking another break from him. He's obsessing about it. I have to butt in. I can't help myself."

Liz frowned. "Honestly, Natalie, I feel like I have no privacy these days. Between Matt and Quinn, my life has been on display at the Cafe and at the hotel. It's embarrassing."

"Well, I happen to have a suggestion. I can personally create some privacy for you two to talk things out."

"You're a born mediator, Natalie. I'm not sure I'm ready for that yet."

"Hear me out. Just come over to our house. Marcus and I will disappear. We have a project going in the garage, making stained glass windows. You and Matt could talk about the Quinn Horror Show. We'll be nearby if you need us. Are you willing?"

Liz hesitated. "I just don't know. My life is beginning to feel like a drama with too many scenes. Scene 5: Matt and Liz Try Second Reconciliation at Friends' House."

"Is that such a bad thing?"

"Constantly forgiving Matt and getting back together is getting old. The only reason I'll even consider this is because the baby is due soon."

"How about tomorrow at one o'clock?"

"I'll come if you tell Matt no more calls or texts until then."

"I can do that. I think you two can get past all this. I'm on both your sides."

"I'm not so convinced we can, but I'll come by tomorrow."

Before leaving the house the next day, Liz considered canceling. Realizing she wasn't ready to be a single mom and trying to imagine going through childbirth without him, she forced herself to go. Maybe Matt was worth another try.

Just as she was about to ring the doorbell, Matt opened the door and said, "Liz, I'm so glad you're here. Let's go sit in the living room. I made your favorite orange spice tea."

Liz walked slowly over to the couch with an expressionless face. As she sat down, Matt poured them both some tea. "I'll start if that's okay."

"Go ahead," Liz said curtly, looking away.

"I'm so sorry you had to be a part of the disaster with my father. How can I make it up to you?" He moved closer to Liz on the couch, being careful not to touch her injured wrist. When he reached for her other hand and kissed it gently, Liz pulled back as though she had brushed against fire. Matt recoiled.

"I don't know what to say, Matt. I'm disappointed you'd help your dad cover up such a heinous act." Liz noticed Matt's expression had changed. What was it? Anger at her or disgust at his father? Maybe both.

"I can't completely blame you for your reaction. I don't know how to convince you that I had no choice. I've never lived up to Dad's expectations. When I'm with him, my mind is muddled, trying to decide if I want to do what he wants or what I want."

"It's pretty obvious which path you chose at the coast."

"I never want you to see that shaky, insecure side of me again. I thought I left that behind when I moved here from Wisconsin. I should have told Dad not to visit."

"No. I want to get to know your family. It's part of our problem. You've kept your childhood a secret from me until now."

"It's not about secrets. You got to see Dad in action and how disrespectfully he treats me and the people around him. I'm ashamed of him."

"I wish I had known more about him. He reveals his ugliness more each time I see him."

"It's too painful to talk about my childhood, Liz. My old therapist encouraged me not to re-traumatize myself by telling my story over and over. I can't seem to win. Talk about it or repress it? No matter what I do, it's wrong."

"But I'm your wife. You needed to tell me the truth about your father. Has he always been like this?" Liz asked, turning to face him on the couch. Matt moved slightly away so he wasn't touching her.

"Dad has always believed he was irresistible to women. When I was a little boy, I would hide in the hallway by the living room when my parents had parties and watch. I saw how Dad spoke to women. Later, I understood he was flirting, pretending he was glued to their every word. Everything he did was a setup to get what he wanted from them later."

"On the prowl in front of your mom? How awful for her."

"He hurt Mom in so many different ways. After the guests left, Mom was humiliated and accused him of hitting on every woman there. He'd get defensive and explode. I was upstairs in bed by then. I'd hear a commotion making me think he shoved or kicked her. Maybe even worse. I'd put the pillow over my head to block it out."

"So, you weren't surprised when she left him?"

"Not really. While Mom always reassured me everything was fine, I wondered if it was just an act so I wouldn't worry. Did you believe whatever your parents told you even though the opposite was right in your face?"

"Yeah. I get that. My dad always acted like everything was fine during the first few months after Mom died.

Then, I would hear him sobbing in their bedroom at night. It made me crazy, but I thought I had to go along with the pretense."

"You do understand." Matt breathed a sigh of relief. "My mom will probably tell you more when she visits, but it's obvious you want to know everything. Let's see. Where should I start?"

"Start with what you think I need to know."

"Okay. I was a junior in high school when Mom walked out. My entire life pretty much crumbled when we moved to Chicago. I left my school, my friends and my life in Madison. It was hard, but it was still better than living with my father. I'll never forgive him for hurting us so much and leaving Mom with only one option. She had to get out, take me with her and leave my childhood home. The only thing that saved me was my Aunt Eleanor, Mom's sister. She had two teenage sons and I went to high school with them. My cousin, Kit, was a life saver. He was a junior and his brother was a senior. They asked me to play guitar in their band. It was a great way for me to make friends." Matt was looking at the floor

When he looked up, Liz gave him a bewildered look. "Slow down! You've been such a mystery to me. Why have you waited so long to tell me all this?"

"Honestly Liz, there's a lot I've kept from you."

Liz was quiet as she looked sadly out the window at the steady rainfall. It always had a calming effect on her. When she looked back at Matt, she saw his anguished expression.

"Say something to me," he begged. "Sometimes you give up on me and just shut down. I see it more and more these days. I can't take it."

"It's because we have these clashes so often. It's exhausting."

Liz wondered if she could forgive him and come home. In truth, he was the one who often shut down emotionally, not her. She was tired of coaxing him to be more open. How long would he keep his cool if she continued to criticize his behavior at the hotel? She looked at her wrist and remembered the night at the Cafe. Arguing with Matt seemed more and more dangerous these days.

After a few minutes, Liz began slowly, "Our life together is on shaky ground. Between the push at the Cafe and you covering up Quinn's sexual assault, I don't think the good parts outweigh the bad." She saw that he was trying to hide his anger. She suspected it was "the push at the Cafe" remark.

"Again, your fall was an accident. I would never do anything to hurt you or our baby. I want to make a family with you. I know it will bring us closer."

"You're just telling me words you think I want to hear."

"No, I'm not. I know everything isn't perfect right now. But our baby will change things for the better."

"Probably for a while," she said. "Having kids is exciting but also discombobulating. The baby will be our whole life."

He paused, looking thoughtfully at her. "Sure, it'll be a big adjustment."

"Maybe taking parenting classes. I heard of a program for new parents that could help us."

"No way!" Matt responded without hesitation. "I'm not sitting around spilling my guts with a bunch of people who think they don't know what they're doing."

"We wouldn't go there for counseling. It would educate us about how to care for our baby and understand how children develop. We'd meet other new parents who are trying to figure it out, too. Think about your dad. Did he have a clue about how to be a good father?"

Matt took a deep breath. She could tell he was trying not to blow up at her.

"Do me a favor and don't compare me to my father! If it's so important to you, I'll think about joining this group. Even without it, we can still be good parents. We're naturals! We can do this, Liz. I know we can."

How likely was that? Liz doubted that Matt would magically become the opposite of his father. She wondered what he would have to do to not carry on the abusive parenting he learned growing up.

"Let's get back to why I came here. We need to work through what happened with your dad at the hotel. What was your take on dinner that night?"

"Do you mean what did I think of how Dad acted? The Two Truths and a Lie game went surprisingly well," Matt said, taking a sip of tea and touching her hand lightly.

"I saw it differently. I thought your Dad made snide remarks to you during dinner, especially the digs about being a lawyer. Why did you look so wounded?"

Matt stood up and walked over to the window. He turned around, looking furious and hurt. "It's always like that, so passive. It's about his disappointment with me for dropping out of law school. I'm surprised you caught it."

"What I caught was your reaction."

Matt looked at her in a way that she'd never seen before. He seemed vulnerable. Sad and scared. When he sat down by her, Liz leaned over and took his hand. They sat silently for a moment.

"Dad could be mean and heartless. My earliest memories of him were teasing me in front of other people for mispronouncing words when I was two or three years old. You know, toddler language with cute, goofy words. He would laugh at me, so they would laugh. I'm sure some thought it was funny and others thought it cruel. I can't remember anyone ever challenging him. It's why I was so shocked when Rachel called him out on his rudeness. The little kid in me expected him to verbally annihilate her. To demean her. To get the entire table laughing at her expense. I was surprised he didn't slap her."

Liz felt his pain. It was hard not to. "Your dad got where he is today because he can control his anger when he has to. His public image is what's most important to him. That's what you told me. If he had humiliated Rachel, he would have been ostracized by everyone. Would that have included you?"

"To be safe, I never criticize Dad. He's a complicated man."

"Explain."

"Don't forget he has a humane side too. He's done so much good for people who are in desperate situations. He's not as simple as you paint him." Matt moved his hand away from hers. "It's hard to read a man that you hardly know, Liz. Some prominent people believe Dad has a good chance of becoming the next governor of Wisconsin. They wouldn't back a tyrant, would they?"

"Sure they would! We've had candidates before who were tyrants or had monstrous pasts. Do you think he can keep this assault a secret in today's environment? It's impossible to keep anything out of the press and social media these days. I wonder who else was paid off for their silence?"

"Everyone has secrets. No one is perfect. What secrets do you have?" he asked, standing up and looking down at her.

What a ridiculous question, Liz thought. She couldn't stop herself from jumping up from the couch and staring at him with disbelief. "So, which is your dad? A cruel, violent man who tried to rape Rachel or the Honorable Quinn Foley? Do you want your child to spend time around him?"

Matt was escalating, but he quickly composed himself enough to ask, "Here we go again! Before the weekend at the coast, everything was fine between us. If I promise to keep him out of our lives, can we drop this?"

"I don't know. What happened at the coast shook me up. Give me some more time to think about how we should deal with your dad in the future," Liz said, trying to lower the tension. She was glad she had learned the many ways women postponed violent incidents from the Jill's Place website. She had immediately erased her browsing history in case Matt used her iPad.

When Matt was interrupted by a phone call from the Cafe, Liz was relieved. After he hung up, he said gently, "I'm so glad we talked and are clearing things up. You know, Liz, I miss you at work and feel lost without you."

"We still have more work to do before I can come back."

"I do have to leave in a few minutes to go back to the Cafe."

"Right. You need to get ready for the Beatles vs. Rolling Stones tribute bands competition." Liz loved that it was always a sold-out show with the audience singing along and knowing all the words by heart.

"I wish you would come. It's one of your favorite shows."

As they began walking to their cars, Liz promised to come if she had the energy. Matt kissed her lightly on the mouth while gently rubbing his hand up and down her back. For a brief moment, Liz liked how good it felt to have Matt soothing her. There it was again, the honeymoon stage. Liz could tell he thought the conversation had patched things up. She quickly looked away so he wouldn't see the fear in her eyes. She shuddered to think what the future held.

CHAPTER 14

After two more visits with Matt where he acted open and reasonable, Liz agreed to move home. She told Sophie she still felt tentative about going back but would give it one more chance.

A week later, Matt took a bike ride to clear his head. He called the Cafe and asked one of the staff to help the band set up so he could grab an hour to himself.

He rode along the Riverfront Bike Path, glancing at his bike speedometer, hovering around 10 miles per hour. Bicycling often alleviated his stress, especially when there was tension at home or at work. Today was different. He couldn't stop thinking about his chaotic relationship with Liz.

After Liz pushed to rehire Emily, Matt's annoyance festered. When he finally relented, he begrudgingly admitted to overreacting by firing Emily. Now, whenever he worked with Emily, he felt watched and judged by her. Emily had won that battle and it was humiliating.

Even though he and Liz weren't openly fighting, Matt noticed the tension between them increasing again. Their relationship was beginning to look like his parent's, anger followed by an explosion and then periods of calm. The sexual assault accusation seemed to be growing in stature in Liz's mind. She saw his father as pure evil. Liz still didn't know everything about Matt's childhood. On the one hand, he was raised by an abusive father and wife batterer. Yet, the same man was seen as charismatic by so many. He couldn't convey his conflicting feelings to Liz. Should he tell her about the man he despised or the man he idolized? Could he tell her about the pain he and his mother experienced? If he did, would she give up on him?

As Matt rode over the De Fazio Bike Bridge, he looked down on the wide and roiling Willamette River. Taking a deep breath, he was finally able to relax a little.

Matt remembered watching his father in court. He worked in a well-respected civil practice that also litigated pro bono criminal cases. The most memorable one stayed with Matt to this day and had once inspired him to pursue a law career.

He was only in sixth grade when his father took on the Willie Wyatt case. Quinn was in such a positive mood while working on it. He talked about it at dinner for months, using Matt and his mom as sounding boards.

Ultimately, Willie Wyatt won a huge financial settlement, over $1.2 million, for having been severely beaten during a racially motivated incident.

The case was even more political because Mayor Sorenson's 18-year-old son was the major perpetrator of the crime, along with a friend. Both boys were in the top 5% of their high school class. The mayor's son, Hunter

WALK OUT THE DOOR

Sorenson, was slated to go to Princeton in the fall and his friend, Carter, to Yale.

Quinn described to Matt how this was reminiscent of 1960s civil rights cases where vigilantism against black men was ignored. To this day, black men were frequently falsely accused of sexually assaulting white women. White community members became judges, jury and executioners.

The story went that Willie Wyatt was proud of his two-year-old catering business. He was the president of the Madison Black Entrepreneurs Association and had just landed one of his biggest accounts through the University of Wisconsin's Development Department. Things were clicking. He was catering a party at a wealthy UW donor's estate overlooking Lake Mendota. His company, Wyatt's at Your Table, had just finished serving a holiday gathering for 200 guests. The hundred-year-old mansion had a winding staircase to two upper floors. The catering staff served appetizers, a sit-down dinner and bar service. The dinner had been a great success with guests raving over the baked halibut with orange avocado salsa and couldn't stop talking about the chocolate caramel turtle cheesecake.

"Do you do cheesecake home deliveries?" asked the president of the University.

"If the entire football team is there, I'm happy to deliver. Go Badgers!" Willie teased.

As he finished coordinating the kitchen breakdown, Willie breathed a sigh of relief. Since this one went so smoothly, he thought more University events this size may come his way. Andre Gold and Katie Wilson, and a dozen others staffed the event.

"We just have two more carts of food to haul out,"

Andre called out to Willie as he and Katie began loading the van. They headed back into the house one last time. While arranging the boxes in the back, Willie heard a scream from the front porch. He saw Claudia Morris, a drunk and teetering guest, take a bad fall by slipping on black ice at the bottom of the stairs. Willie jumped off the back of the van and ran to her rescue. Feeling humiliated by her fall and Willie's offer to help, Claudia shouted belligerently, "Get away from me!"

Her words were slurred and barely understandable. Fortunately, Andre and Katie had come back outside. They were maneuvering a large cart through the doorway and heard the commotion. Andre rushed over to help. Willie was patiently asking if Claudia could move her legs. When she did, Willie explained she was too drunk to drive and offered to call a cab or get a friend to drive her home. She might even need an ambulance.

As Claudia slowly began to calm down, two teenage boys appeared from out of nowhere. The leader, Hunter Sorenson, grabbed Willie and began punching him in the face, shouting, "You black bastard. Get your dirty hands off her or I'll kill you!"

Claudia, having come out of her stupor, yelled, "Stop it. I fell. He was helping me. Get your hands off him."

Hunter ignored her and yelled at his friend, Carter Franklin, "Let's give him what he deserves."

Andre tried to stop the brawl but was knocked unconscious when Carter punched him in the face and then threw him against the car fender. Katie, shocked by the rapidly escalating violence, ran into the house to call for help.

Hunter then grabbed Willie and shoved him against a

tree, increasing his grip around Willie's neck, nearly strangling him while bashing his body repeatedly. He continued his racist slurs. Carter egged him on.

Another friend, Leon Campbell, a 6'2", 245-pound high school football player, came around the corner of the house. He had lagged behind when he ran into an old friend. He was horrified to see his friends behaving like animals. Without a moment's pause, Leon physically pried Hunter off Willie and threw him to the ground. "The crack cocaine has made you crazy, man! Back off!"

Next, Leon found Andre lying unconscious in the driveway. He turned to Carter and yelled, "What in the hell have you done, Carter?"

Like a child caught in the act, Carter fumbled over his words. "But, but...we were just trying to help that poor woman from getting raped by that black guy."

"Just shut up, Carter. You two have done enough," retorted Leon.

When Leon saw Abe and Aviva Altman, the party hosts, standing on the second-floor porch, he shouted, "Call an ambulance!"

Abe ran down the steps to assess the situation and Aviva went into the house to call 911. She quickly learned that Katie had already phoned and an ambulance was on the way. They could hear a siren in the distance.

The repeated punches to Willie's stomach and chest resulted in two broken ribs on his left side and a spleen laceration requiring surgery. Carter's throwing Andre against the car caused not only a concussion but also an orbital fracture, breaking Andre's cheekbone near his eyeball. It required surgical repair of his left eye socket. Willie was out of work for three weeks. Andre was out of commission for well over a month. Carter was treated for a boxer's hand fracture from punching Andre in the face. Willie and Andre also experienced emotional trauma, so the size of the settlement in the lawsuit was significantly increased.

Since Willie could only afford a legal aid attorney and the crime was racially motivated, the local NAACP chapter offered to find stronger legal representation. The NAACP president approached Marks and Silverstein on Willie's behalf. While the firm had impressive civil rights advocacy experience, the partners considered the case reluctantly. They preferred to keep local government and media entities as allies. Because the main perpetrator of the crime was Mayor Sorenson's son, the case became highly political.

Since Carter's family owned the Madison Chronicle, little came out about the incident. Nothing at all related to race. Because the boys were minors, they weren't named in the article. The NAACP met repeatedly with the newspaper's editorial board, accusing them of treating the crime as a simple assault in spite of numerous witnesses. When Marks and Silverstein saw the civil rights aspect of the case, they decided representing Willie and Andre was the ethical thing to do. The partners suggested Quinn take the case. It seemed likely that the Franklins and the Sorensons would want to quickly settle out of court.

The Franklin family and Mayor Sorensen both offered a sizable settlement to Willie Wyatt. Hunter Sorenson had a history of getting away with criminal violence. He had been in trouble as early as middle school where he was suspected of arson after being suspended for punching a teacher. Hunter managed to avoid detention and the state juvenile facility due to his mother's political connections as a city councilor at the time. In the end, the arson charge was dropped to menacing behavior. Since it was his first offense, Hunter was diverted to a residential drug treatment program for six months. His drug problems continued throughout high school.

Willie refused to accept the out-of-court settlement because he wanted the public to bear witness to the brutal hate crime he and Andre had survived. So, the case went to court. When the verdict was read at the end of the trial, Willie had tears streaming down his cheeks. He hugged Matt's father. Willie's wife and three children formed a circle around Quinn, arm in arm.

"You've changed my life forever. I don't know how to thank you," said a highly emotional Willie Wyatt.

"The win is thanks enough for me," Quinn said as he warmly embraced Willie in return.

The NAACP and UW Black Union protesters moved from the hall into the courtroom to celebrate the win. At the time, the award of $1.2 million was unprecedented. Quinn was clearly the hero of the day.

As Matt and his father left the courtroom, reporters from Madison, Milwaukee and Chicago bombarded Quinn with endless questions. He later learned that the *New York Times* had also covered the story. Quinn was high on victory when a poignant photo of young Matt looking up at him with deep admiration was published by numerous newspapers. The photo was credited to the *Milwaukee News*, not the Franklin family's *Madison Chronicle*. No surprise there, Quinn had joked with his family as they reviewed the unforgettable climax of the trial.

Afterward, Matt and his parents joined the Wyatt

family at a local barbecue spot in Madison, owned by Willie's brother, Henry. Matt would never forget watching complete strangers shaking his father's hand, hugging him and showering him with accolades for his successful battle against racism. Even Matt's mom seemed happy and was smiling. Fortunately, she had no bruises on her face that day. Quinn hadn't lost his temper with her since the Wyatt case began. All was well.

In lieu of a second trial with Gold vs. Franklin, focusing on Carter's role in the attack, the Franklin family paid a hefty out-of-court settlement to keep their son from entering the system. They wanted to avoid publicity that might harm the newspaper's reputation. Quinn disapproved of his firm's position to do an out-of-court settlement. As a result, another lawyer at the firm was assigned to handle the case.

Because Andre's wife was only weeks away from delivering their first baby, he accepted the settlement. Months later it became clear to Quinn that his firm's partners resented his vocal stand on the Franklin family settlement. He would never make partner there. Nonetheless, his prominence based on the Wyatt case catapulted his career. He was offered positions at a number of prestigious firms. Quinn realized that bigger opportunities were in store and confided to Joanne that political office could now be a possibility.

X

The Wyatt Trial was his father at his best. But not all of Matt's memories of his dad were as positive. As young as three years old, Matt could recall overhearing the night-time fights when his father returned home from work. Matt was in his room, after his mom had finished reading his three nightly stories. He loved the routine of always being tucked in for the night so affectionately. He felt so safe in his mother's warmth in contrast to his father's unpredictability.

Matt could also recall the yelling and crying when he was in elementary school. At first, his mom would scream back when his father taunted her. She was often angry when Quinn came home late from work. He had no time for dinner with his family or a chance to play with his young son before bed. Joanne accused Quinn of lying about working late when he came home drunk and teetering. She wondered if he was out with that new lawyer at his firm, Alicia Anderson, who often called him at home.

Matt painfully watched his mom absorb constant shouting and threats. She seemed to take it in stride. This made no sense to Matt. And things got worse. They became so severe that his mother would curl up on the couch and go deep into a world he couldn't reach. Increasingly there were bruises or cuts. He'd offer to get her ice or bandages and she wouldn't answer. He had no idea what to do. It scared him. He sat down next to her, watching and waiting until she eventually came back to life.

Later, in middle school, Matt overheard his mother talking to Aunt Eleanor. She confided that Quinn was beginning to direct some of his anger towards Matt since he had become more outspoken at home and challenged his father's violence. Quinn's belittling and profanities became more and more frequent.

By the time Matt was 14, he felt his father's physical wrath directly. Shoves, punches, slaps and kicks replaced name-calling and put-downs. Quinn disapproved of nearly everything Matt did. He hated how he dressed, his choice of friends, and his grades. While he told Matt that he was proud when he made the debate team, he was bitingly critical of Matt's performance the few times he attended his debates. Matt lived in constant dread of a certain look from his Dad, a sudden rise from the dinner table or simply the sound of his father's car coming up the driveway.

Matt couldn't predict what might trigger his father's physical or emotional abuse. It was crazy-making. Part way through high school, it all came to a head. Matt and his mom began to openly discuss the terrifying life they shared.

Early one evening when Joanne got home from work, she found Matt studying at the kitchen table, munching on chips and salsa with melted Wisconsin cheddar cheese, his favorite snack. "Hi, honey. Have a good day at school?"

"All good." Matt's brief synopsis of his day at school was normal.

"How was dinner at the Hewitts' last night? You got home after I'd fallen asleep. Your dad got in even later than you."

Matt began to describe, in intimate detail, his dinner at the Hewitt's. Matt's best friend, Sam Hewitt was on the debate team with him and the two had been close since middle school. Matt ate meals and stayed overnight at his house whenever he could. Sam's parents were loving to each other in front of everyone. Along with sisters, Jamie and Nicole, they carried on animated conversations about politics, work, school and life. All topics were open for discussion and disagreement. At times, they all talked at once and that was okay, too. Dinners were filled with stories, sarcasm and laughter.

"Mom, the best part of hanging out at Sam's house is how they all care about each other. They even care about me! They're never afraid of saying the wrong thing. When I'm there, I'm part of a family. I bought a card for Mr. Hewitt for Father's Day, but I was too embarrassed to give it to him."

"You're breaking my heart."

"The Hewitts celebrate when good things happen to their kids and don't blame them when things go wrong. No yelling. No name-calling. No beatings."

"I can see why they've become a second family to you. I like them. Sam's parents are always warm to me when I see them at school events."

"Let me finish, Mom. I've got an important point here."

"OK. Go ahead."

"I can't take it anymore."

Joanne's eyes filled with tears. "I'm not surprised, Matt. You've been spending more and more time there. I don't blame you. It's easier for me if you're not here when your dad is home. He gets so furious when you challenge him. When I try to defend you, he makes me pay for it later."

"Don't defend me, Mom. I can take care of myself."

"I'll never forget when you spent the night in detention for protecting me from your father. When you grabbed a kitchen knife and pointed it at your dad, I was terrified. You threatened to stab him if he didn't stop choking me."

"I thought Dad was going to kill you. I had no choice. Now, I have one. I want to go live with the Hewitts."

"Wait, Matt. Hear me out! Something snapped inside

me that night. Since then, I've been working day and night to get things together so we can leave."

"Really? You'd leave Dad? I had no idea you were even thinking about it," Matt exclaimed.

"I've met a few times with an attorney at Domestic Violence Intervention Services. I'll get a restraining order to get Quinn out of the house. Then, I'll file for divorce and sole custody with limited visitation. I've been warned the most dangerous time in a violent relationship is when you leave."

"How can we be safe?"

"I thought about that. We'll go to Chicago and stay with Aunt Eleanor and Uncle Chris once the restraining order is served. When your dad accepts that he legally can't come near me, we'll return, pack up our things and then make the permanent move to Chicago. We won't be his punching bags anymore."

"Mom, I'm glad this is finally happening, but I can't believe he'll let us go without a fight. If anyone can stop us from leaving, it's him," Matt said in a voice that sounded considerably older than his 16 years.

"The law is on our side, Matt. If he violates a restraining order, it will be all over the papers which he would hate. You'll finish your school year here and we'll move to Chicago in the summer." Joanne suddenly stopped, noticing that Matt looked bewildered. "Matt, what are you thinking?"

"It sucks to leave my friends and my life here. But you're right. We've got to do this."

Joanne walked over and hugged him. "I'm so sorry it's taken me so long. I didn't want to break up our family, but your dad has given me no choice. By leaving, we'll lose a lot. Our friends. This house. My job. You won't get to graduate from high school with all your friends."

"We can't wait two more years until I graduate."

"Promise you'll keep this to yourself. I did tell the Hewitts what I'm up to since I know they can be trusted. They'll help us in any way they can."

This conversation was a turning point in Matt's life.

Now, years later, as he was riding his bike along the Willamette River, he could remember it in vivid detail. All this time, he had compartmentalized the horrible memories of his childhood. Recent tension with Liz had pried open the tightly sealed box.

CHAPTER 15

Joanne was at work when she got a phone call from Ade Coleman, a private investigator, about an incident at the Oregon coast last weekend. She hated to take personal calls at work because it was too distracting and she despised talking on the phone in general. When Joanne didn't recognize a phone number, she'd let it go to voicemail. She saw the call came from an Oregon area code. The only people she knew in Oregon were her son and various family members of her ex-husband. Listening to the message during lunch, Joanne couldn't stifle a deep sigh when the investigator mentioned Judge Quinn Foley. This inevitably meant that something big and problematic was about to enter her life. Historically, this proved true 100% of the time.

Joanne felt anxious, almost sick, as she returned the call. She choked over her words as she identified herself to Ade. They spoke briefly and all Joanne could muster was to arrange a call back after eight o'clock that night. She wondered what she could contribute to an inquiry about Quinn. They'd been divorced for over a decade.

By the time Joanne got home, she had gotten over the shock of Ade's call. Her condo in Chicago's Lakeview neighborhood was her safe haven. She kicked off her shoes as she walked in the door, and quickly got out of her work clothes. She slipped on her speckled black and white cotton leggings and her favorite gauzy purple tunic. After pouring herself a glass of rosé, she sat on the couch to look through the day's mail. She had fifteen minutes of peace before the phone rang. Joanne picked up her cell and answered, "Hello, this is Joanne."

"Hi. This is Ade Coleman, from the Go Girls Agency. Is now still a good time to talk?"

"It's fine. Thanks for sending me a PDF of your private investigator license with your photo and resume. It turns out we used your firm once in a domestic violence case originating in Portland and you did a great job."

"I'm so glad to hear that. Please call me Ade. Since everyone asks, it's spelled A-d-e, but pronounced Ah-day, Nigerian in origin."

"Thanks. You're right. I would have asked. It's a powerful name. Call me Joanne. How can I help you?"

"I'm working on a case involving your ex-husband, Quinn Foley. It involves sexual assault, intimidation, and threats towards a hotel guest. I used the Madison, Wisconsin Court records to research Judge Foley's criminal background and found a restraining order you filed against him. Mind if I read that statement to you before I ask you some more questions?" Ade spoke with an urgent but compassionate tone.

Joanne hesitated for a moment. She knew this line of

questioning, a typical domestic violence drill she often used in interviewing clients. It had taken two years of therapy in Madison before she could leave Quinn. During that time, she began to consider changing careers from working artist to lawyer, eventually specializing in women's rights. Her therapist warned she might suffer from Post-Traumatic Stress Disorder by pursuing a career that dealt with issues from her own past. Having overcome this barrier, she still wondered if she could handle listening to the restraining order statement from so long ago. Deep breath, Joanne Zimmer, she coached herself. That monster can't hurt you anymore!

"Okay, Ade. I'm ready. Go ahead."

Ade began: "Your statement says: 'My husband and I have been married for fifteen years. In a recent incident, I was pushed against the wall and punched in the face, directly on my right cheek. The force of the punch caused me to fall to the floor, knocking over a table and lamp. Quinn Foley kicked me in the side three times after I had fallen, causing additional bruising (see attached photos). He told me if I ever talked about leaving him again, he would kill me. I fear for my safety and for that of my son.

"'One month ago, our son Matt spent a night at the Dane County Juvenile Detention Center when he threatened his father with a knife to stop him from strangling me. Matt had witnessed his father strike me in a separate incident two nights before, resulting in a bloody lip and black and blue eye. Because I had proof that Matt had met with a school counselor related to his father's violence, the juvenile judge released him after only one night. He believed Matt was defending me from life-threatening violence.'"

"Yes, that sounds accurate," replied Joanne.

"Were there other reasons beyond the domestic violence that caused you to file for divorce, not that those aren't enough?"

"I need to ask you a few things before we go on."

"Sure."

The questions spilling out of Joanne's mouth were from her personal experiences as well as from years of legal work.

"Who hired you to investigate Quinn?"

Ade hesitated before crafting a response, "I'm unable to disclose the identity of my client. However, your daughter-in-law told me to use her name so you'd know this inquiry is legitimate."

The news took Joanne by surprise. What could Liz have to do with this? She knew Matt would find Liz's involvement infuriating. "That's interesting. What will your client do with the results of your investigation? What's your client after?"

"Without going into detail, I can say that our investigation has political and legal ramifications for Judge Foley."

"I see where this is going. I've heard a rumor Quinn is running for Governor. This type of scandal could hurt him," commented Joanne. "How is Liz involved? Did Quinn assault her? I wouldn't put it past him."

"No, Liz wasn't hurt and didn't witness the actual sexual assault. However, Matt was involved in the resolution of the incident and gave Liz the victim's version of what happened. Since she journaled that conversation, Liz was able to supply me with a second-hand report which could be used as evidence, if I need it."

"What?" asked Joanne incredulously. "My son helped his father dodge a sexual assault charge? I'm not comfortable answering any more questions until I've talked with him and Liz. Luckily, I plan to visit them next week. I can get back to you after that."

"Would you mind calling them about this matter before your visit?"

"No, I need to check in with them face to face before I become more involved in your investigation."

"Of course. This affects your whole family. Call me as soon as you're ready to talk. You could be a key informant to this investigation."

"I'll decide what my role will be. I have to think carefully about how immersed I'm willing to get into Quinn's world. Honestly, I thought those days were over." Joanne hung up.

A second glass of rosé was in her hand by the time Joanne scrolled down her contact list to select her sister, Eleanor. "Hey, El Belle. It's me."

"Hi, Jo. It's not like you to call me on a work night. What's up?"

"Freaking out a bit. It's a Quinn thing."

"Yuck! What's he done now? It's been a while since you've talked to him. Matt's wedding, right?"

"That's right. We never talk unless we absolutely have to. He didn't call me. An investigator called me about him."

"Are you crying? Your voice sounds shaky or something."

"I'm shook up. It's easy to go to that dark place. I was crying for a few minutes after talking to the investigator. I wish Quinn still didn't have that effect on me after all this time."

"It's the damn PTSD again. You're the expert. We both know it happens to women who've been through hell like you. You always say it to your clients, so it must be true."

"Flashbacks to the past. Pops right up. So does the pain."

"Sorry, Jo. What did Quinn do now?" Joanne shared the details of Ade's call.

"Jo, you shouldn't have let her read the restraining order to you. It must have been torture to relive it."

"Too late now, El. Was I right to wait until I talk to Matt and Liz in person? I got the feeling that the investigator thought I was being neurotic."

"Follow your instincts. Yes, you need to hear Matt and Liz's renditions of what happened. Still, it must be tempting to just jump in to help nail Quinn. Maybe his luck has finally run out."

"I have to be careful how I handle this. I don't want to hurt Matt. He's been torn between Quinn and me for years. I just want to help him to stay out of Quinn's craziness."

"Yes, he's your priority. Go talk it out with him when you get to Eugene. Make Matt tell you what really happened at the coast."

"It won't be easy."

"Feel free to call me from Eugene. I'll help you think it through. You know how this stuff shakes out all too well. It's a balance. Don't let Quinn strain your relationship with Matt. But don't let Matt rescue his dad either. You've got a lot to grapple with."

"All true. Thanks for your advice, El. It helps. The restraining order brings up another tear-jerker memory. Guess what it is."

"I bet I can. It was during your first year in Chicago. You and I were blubbering fools at a bar mitzvah where the kids' band played. Matt sang a song he wrote."

"That's it."

Matt had been in the band for six months when they got the gig. Joanne and her sister attended because the parents were old friends of Eleanor's. While Joanne knew Matt had a good voice, she'd never heard him sing a solo and had no idea he even wrote songs. Towards the end of the first set, Matt walked up to the center microphone. He introduced his song "Good Enough." He said it wasn't a party song but hoped it meant something because today's Jewish ritual focuses so much on family. He dedicated it to those in the room who understood the experience of never feeling safe or good enough. The chorus was:

No respect or love
take off your boxing gloves,
nothing is good enough
never proud of me

After Matt finished, the applause was overwhelming. Even the band clapped. Matt's verses described the desperate search for approval and being denied over and over.

"It sounded like it was written by an adult, not a teenager," said Eleanor. "It took our breath away. Matt suggested the audience help friends who have this experience. It would be a good deed, or a 'mitzvah,' like the bar mitzvah boy mentioned in his speech."

"And Matt still struggles with wanting approval from Quinn. Some things never change."

"I know you'll get through to him."

"I'll try. I'm sure I'll be calling you from Oregon." She paused. "I do have to crash now. I have an early staff meeting in the morning. Give my love to Chris. And again. thanks."

"Night, Jo. Love you."

"Sweet dreams, Jelly Bean." The sisters both quietly laughed as they hung up.

CHAPTER 16

A week later, Liz opened the door and found Joanne dripping from head to toe.

"Hey, Joanne. Get in here. Welcome to the land of rain," Liz said as they kissed each other's cheeks. "When Matt told me you were coming, I was so excited. Let's get you dry and settled in."

As Liz reached for Joanne's suitcase, Joanne smiled and picked it up. "This is a time when I'm the one who should do the heavy lifting."

"You're right," Liz stepped back with a grin and patted her stomach. "You know where your room is, so why don't you get changed and meet me in the kitchen. I'll make you an espresso."

"I'd love some coffee. Flying is a burnout these days."

When Joanne came downstairs, Liz handed her the hot espresso with her left hand. Joanne immediately noticed the cast. "How's your wrist healing? Matt called to tell me you had slipped and fallen during a busy show."

"Yep. Just a clumsy fall and I ended up with a broken wrist. In the employer biz, we call it a work-related injury. Should be healed in another few weeks."

"I'm so sorry. It must be hard to be pregnant and do that kind of work. Funny though, I thought you were managing the operation these days and only helping out in the kitchen or waiting on tables when you're short-staffed," Joanne replied, giving her a doubtful look.

"You got it right. I back up staff when I need to, especially on hectic nights. A sold-out show with a personal friend of mine performing. I had to be there."

"Of course."

"This isn't new to me. I've had job injuries before with kitchen burns and cuts, but this is the first time I've broken anything. With the pregnancy, my reaction time must be off. I just couldn't stop the fall."

"What does your doctor say? Will it have any impact on your pregnancy?"

"Emily took me to the emergency room. They asked me lots of questions and ran tests. They decided that the baby was fine, but my wrist was broken."

"That's a relief." Something was off. Joanne wondered if she was getting the whole story, but quickly changed the topic. "Before I forget, I got a strange call last week from Ade Coleman about Quinn."

"I know. I told her to call you but never thought she'd do it this fast. Sorry I didn't let you know beforehand. The woman he assaulted hired Ade and I'm trying to help."

"She's gathering evidence against Quinn. I need to understand what happened at the coast before I'm willing to help."

"Long story. Let's talk about this later. I need to get

some work done. I usually work from home in the afternoons. Why don't you go over to the Cafe to see Matt?"

"Sounds good."

"Once Matt finishes the sound check with BeauSoleil, you two can head back here. Why don't you text Matt that you're on your way?"

"Will do. Anything you need while I'm there?"

"Yes. You need to be my delivery woman. Why don't you bring home three Cajun dinners? I'd like shrimp gumbo and Matt will probably want chicken jambalaya. You can decide what smells good once you get there. Don't forget bread pudding with praline sauce for dessert."

"I love BeauSoleil and Louisiana Cajun tunes make me want to dance!"

"You'll be in heaven, then. Matt will want you to meet the band and listen to their sound check."

As Joanne was getting up to leave, she asked, "One more thing. Does Matt know about Ade?"

"No. He has no idea. I'd like to keep it that way. He'd get upset if he knew about the investigation. He has such mixed feelings about Quinn."

"Too many secrets in this family," replied Joanne. "Don't you think that Matt has a right to know if the incident goes public?"

"At some point. Not just yet."

"How would Matt react if he knew that his wife and mother are talking to a private investigator about his father? He's your husband, Liz. Wouldn't it be better for him to be prepared if he gets a call from the press?"

"I'm hesitating for good reason. Matt and I are having some serious problems." When Liz noticed the alarm on Joanne's face, she quickly added, "I want to work things out. Telling him about my involvement with Ade's investigation would make things worse."

"Understood. I'll go over now to get some alone time with Matt. I won't say a thing."

When Joanne arrived at the Cafe, she found Matt in his office. He jumped up, running to give her a hug. When she pulled away, she noticed a sadness in his eyes. It confirmed her gut feeling from the moment Ade Coleman phoned her. Quinn had disrupted Matt and Liz's life in some big way.

Since it was mid-afternoon, Matt offered his mom a glass of pinot noir from Provence's Côte du Rhône valley. They had traveled there together for Matt's high school graduation with Aunt Eleanor, Cousin Kit and Matt's childhood friend, Sam Hewitt. They toured through France and Italy for two weeks. Then the three boys went off to Paris and Barcelona on their own. Joanne and Eleanor knew that they got the sanitized version of their travels. They didn't believe for a minute that it was all about museums and cathedrals. Eventually, they learned that the three hitchhiked with some people they met at a youth hostel in Barcelona. They hung out at clubs, went to a music festival, slept on beaches and ate large quantities of street food. Later, Joanne and Matt jokingly referred to the trip as their "Quinn European Recovery Tour."

Matt led Joanne over to his favorite table. "This is where I met Liz two years ago. We literally fell in love over a cup of coffee and a cinnamon streusel muffin. We couldn't stop talking or staring at each other. It was love at first sight."

When Emily came over to their table, they exchanged a warm hug. "It's great to see you again, Joanne. Liz has been excited about your visit. Something about grilling you for parenting wisdom."

"My wisdom is ancient. I hope I can still pull it up. I'll do my best."

"You raised me, Mom. You'll be fine," Matt said with a grin. "Em, Mom's starving. I know just what she likes."

Minutes later, Emily reappeared with a small redwood cutting board displaying three imported cheeses, red grapes and sliced organic apples to go with their pinot noir. A basket of warm baguette made it the perfect light lunch.

After Matt and Joanne finished their meal and began to drink their cappuccinos, they shared a slice of Bailey's Irish Cream cheesecake and were poised for a long talk. Matt had mentioned their stay at the Purple Haze hotel in an email. Now he wanted to describe the weekend in detail. Joanne kept in mind her promise to Liz to not discuss the investigation.

"Liz wants us to bring home dinner. You still need to do the sound check, right?" asked Joanne.

"I sure do. The band wants an early one so they can hike Skinner Butte before sunset. I told them it's the best view of the Willamette Valley. Once we get a second cup of coffee to wash down this cheesecake, I have 15 minutes to give you the short version of the hotel fiasco."

After Emily refilled their cups, Matt described the sequence of events leading to Quinn's attack on Rachel. The dinner, the Two Truths and a Lie game, the verbal sparring between Quinn and Rachel and his late-night visit to her room where the assault took place.

"You know that nothing your father does ever surprises me. My biggest worry is how you got drawn into protecting him. Nothing good comes out of aiding and abetting Quinn Foley. I have fifteen years of trauma to show for it."

Matt heard intense anger and contempt in her voice.

"Mom, you don't think I know all that? But I'm still his son. You got out, but he will always be my father, whether I like it or not."

"I know, honey," Joanne said, looking contrite. "And here you are in another impossible situation with your father. It sure is hard to refuse him. Bet he convinced himself that Rachel's disagreeing with him was a come on. How many times do women have to say no to him before he gets it?"

"I know. I watched it when I was growing up. When Rachel told Liz about Dad attacking her, she explained how her self-defense training helped her get away. He hadn't done enough to be charged with a felony." Matt paused.

"Did Rachel call the police?"

"No, Mom. Things went another way. Dad's fixer involved me."

"The great Lyle Oliver! What a sleaze."

"He's effective, though. Saves Dad every time!"

"Matt, you know that Quinn assaulted Rachel. And I know it's not the first time. He harassed a young colleague early in his career. There were others and he managed to get away with it each time. He had his lawyer pay off the victims in exchange for non-disclosure agreements. When I accused Lyle of being his fixer, your father was furious with me for calling him out."

"You're sure going to hate what happened next. Dad fled the scene with our car, leaving us stranded at the coast. He texted he was flying home for a work emergency.

Next thing I knew, Lyle contacted me to negotiate Rachel's pay-off. At first, I refused to be part of Dad's deal to hush her up. Lyle's no fool. He reminded me of the stalking order Anne filed against me. She attached copies of texts and cell phone records, with an affidavit from her school principal claiming I was menacing. Dad got the judge, an old friend, to deny the order. I owe him for that. When I refused to act as the negotiator, Lyle threatened to tell Liz about the stalking order."

"Couldn't you just explain how desperate you were at the time? Liz would understand. Don't let Lyle intimidate you."

"All I know is Dad must have been in a panic. He has a lot to lose if Rachel goes public. In his run for governor, a sexual assault accusation would be a political bombshell. It would ruin his chance for the Democratic Party endorsement."

"Why would you help the father who tormented you and made your life hell for years? Who was violent to you! Toward me! Where does it end?"

"I get to decide what to do when Dad asks for help. I don't need your approval."

"That's harsh, Matt. Stop it! You owe your father nothing. Now, I'm beginning to understand why Liz is so angry."

"She's furious because she thinks I'm being sympathetic to Dad. She has no idea how Dad saved my ass!"

"It's surprising how little Liz knows about your father, the batterer. She has no idea what your Dad did to our family, does she?"

"I'm afraid it would overwhelm her. Since the coast trip, we can barely be in the same room without getting into a fight. She even stayed with Sophie for a while after she got back from the coast. Sometimes if I look at her the wrong way, she storms out of the room. You've got to help get Liz to see it my way."

"I need for you to answer me honestly. How did Liz break her wrist?"

"What does that have to do with what we're talking about?"

"You tell me."

"I already told you what happened on the phone. Liz fell at work. It was crowded at the front counter with the band coming in. When I tried to move her out of the way, she tripped, lost her balance and fell against the wall."

"Really, Matt?"

"What does that mean?"

"You're scaring me. Remember what your therapist said about your anger being a problem for you. She helped you find ways to express your feelings and not resort to violence after the knife incident. Does that ring a bell?"

"Of course, it does. But, I'm not Dad. I would never hurt Liz or the baby. I know Anne told you I scared her sometimes. I'd raise my voice when I got mad, but I never threatened her or hurt her. To this day, I don't know why she left or where she went. It kills me to even think about it. So, I just told Liz that Anne left because we were both too immature to make the marriage work."

Joanne was silent. It was a lot to digest. She loved her son so much, but his defensiveness and excuses were typical of abusive men. Matt was beginning to remind her of cases that came across her desk. And of Quinn in the early days.

"Matt, let's put this on hold for now. I should have

waited until we had more time. Sorry."

"It's okay, Mom. I know you worry about me."

"Go do your sound check. I'll order our take-out. But promise me you'll tell Liz the whole truth about our family before I leave?"

Matt had a confused look of relief and trepidation. "Uh... okay."

"You have to let Liz in, Matt. You've got to. It will help."

"Okay, Okay. I'll do it."

As Matt walked away from their table, Joanne closed her eyes for a moment. A painful memory came up. She was six months pregnant when Quinn came to the art gallery and demanded she stop working. When she refused to quit, he shoved her against the wall and stormed out. Once Joanne steadied herself, she got some ice for the hip that took most of the impact. She felt terrified, being alone in the gallery. She immediately phoned her obstetrician for an urgent appointment where she was assured that she and the baby were fine. When Matt was born healthy, she breathed a sigh of relief.

She hadn't thought of the incident in years. After the flashback, she was beginning to realize her granddaughter's safe arrival into the world came before anything else.

CHAPTER 17

It was after seven o'clock when Joanne and Matt returned with dinner. After they stashed the Cajun food in the kitchen and Matt went upstairs to take a shower, Joanne walked into Liz's office to let her know they were back. Liz was cozily stretched out on her window seat with a purple polar fleece blanket wrapped around her. When she saw Joanne, she put aside Lauren Kessler's *Stubborn Twig*.

"Hi, we're home. What are you reading?" asked Joanne.

Liz showed her the cover. "It's a story of the Japanese internment camps. It's one of those books that breaks your heart and gives you hope at the same time. I'm struck by how resilient humans can be, even when being treated cruelly and unjustly."

"So true. Don't I know it from the work I do every day. Hey, I'm coveting that window seat of yours. I'm going to have to get one built for my condo."

"Matt calls it my 'perch'. A long time ago I told him

how I love staring out at my domain, like the caretaker of a small park. It's where I feel grounded. I can think clearly here. I think Matt's bike riding is like that for him."

"I hate to be such a city woman, but Lincoln Park near my condo does the same thing for me."

"You're so lucky to be on Lake Michigan. It's your Pacific Ocean."

"I was checking out the baby's room. Major progress there. I love the exotic background in The Elephants Mural. Matt told me that Leah, your old college friend, painted it. The mural at the Cafe too."

"Leah's quite the artist. When we were in school together, she was doing things on large canvases. It was all about bigger-than-life women, focusing on women of color. Now, she's branched out to entire walls. When the City of Eugene does mural tours, the Cafe is the first stop. Because, as Leah would say, she's kinda famous."

"Her work is so intense. She's not afraid to use bold colors. Her life-size figures look like they're on the move. They almost dance off the wall."

"You sound like an art critic. You can see why I wanted Leah's art in our home, too."

"I miss painting. Someday when I'm not so crazed with my law practice, I'll go back to it."

"My work of art is the backyard. Drew and I used some of our inheritance to start the Cafe with Sophie. The rest of mine was the down payment for my country house in the city. See my half-acre out back. I built the half-dozen raised beds and filled them with organic vegetables and fruit. I love the persimmon tree right smack in the center of the yard. I put a bench in memory of my parents in that shady spot. I asked a Saturday Market woodworker to handcraft an oak bench and he engraved my parents' names on it, Peter and Sally. Matt and I like to sit out there with a glass of wine after work and go over the day together."

"What a beautiful gesture, Liz. I want to sit out there with the two of you some time."

Matt walked into the room and smiled at both of them. "I see you're holding court from your perch, Liz."

"I'm so happy that your Mom is here. She's the best."

"Can't argue with that. I'm starving," Matt said, heading for the kitchen to carry out the food.

Once they were seated, Matt poured a glass of wine for himself and his mother who said, "When we talked this afternoon, Matt agreed to fill you in about how he grew up. It's a hard story to tell."

"I'm ready to hear it. I know talking about your past rattles you."

After a long hesitation, Matt began, "I was afraid you'd give up on me if I told you how awful Dad was to us. I honestly think we can get back on track if we cut him out of our lives. He's pretty much the cause of all our problems."

Liz looked at Joanne and sighed.

"What does that mean?" Matt asked, looking from one to the other.

"You can't blame everything on your Dad. You have a role in our problems," Liz responded.

Joanne jumped in. "Matt, you're right that Quinn is at the root of the arguments you've had lately. But, it's the way he treated you when you were growing up that is spilling over into your life now."

"Okay, Mom. Let's just tell Liz what happened and not dance around it."

"Matt, why don't you start with what you remember?"

"I'll tell it my way, but I don't want to go into all the gory details," Turning to Liz, he began, "Dad was violent toward Mom when she wouldn't see things exactly the way he did. I saw or heard what happened between them when I was little."

"Matt saw the results of the violence more than the violence itself. I tried to keep Quinn calm when Matt was home, but I never knew what would set him off. When Matt got older and could reason more, he asked about the black eyes, my bruised legs and broken bones. I had feeble excuses."

"I knew more than you thought. Remember the time I called the police when I was in sixth grade, Mom? I thought Dad was going to kill you. When I saw the police pull up and heard the doorbell ring, I hid at the top of the stairs. Dad told them that everything was okay. You just smiled and didn't say a word. They apologized for bothering him. I went to the window and heard the police talking. 'Just another family fight. I recognized the husband from court. He's a hotshot lawyer. Not our job to do marriage counseling.' Dad finished what he started after the police drove away. I never called for help again."

"I always thought it was a neighbor who called. I had no idea it was you." Joanne looked shocked.

"I just made it worse. I sure wasn't about to tell Dad it was me," Matt said, turning back to Liz. "By the time I was thirteen, he was furious when he couldn't control me. He retaliated when I tried to defend Mom during arguments. He belittled me constantly. I became his new punching bag. He began to slap, kick and punch me. One time, as I was running out the sliding glass door to get away from him, I turned around and yelled 'Go to hell!'"

Matt stopped abruptly to take a deep breath and continued. "He picked up a heavy paperweight off his desk and threw it at me. He missed. It shattered the door into fragments, cutting my face. He screamed 'Don't come back' as he saw the blood running down my neck."

Joanne didn't say a word. She watched Liz's expressions and waited for her reaction. She could see a mix of disbelief and empathy.

"That's when I started hanging out at my friend Sam's house as much as I could," Matt said.

"I get it. You had to get away from your Dad," Liz said, looking back at him compassionately. "You figured out a way to protect yourself."

"Matt was searching for a healthy family and found one," admitted Joanne.

"That's one way to look at it," Matt responded.

"By being with Sam's family, you took back control of your life," Liz observed. "These days, you seem on edge all the time. You act like you have to control everything."

"See what you're doing, Matt? It affects people you care about," Joanne pointed out.

Matt jumped up and blurted out, "That's not fair. Maybe if you had left sooner, I wouldn't have learned how to be a man like Dad."

"But you are a better man than he is," Joanne said.

Liz nodded. "I agree with Joanne. I saw at the hotel how your father treats people. You're unlike him in so many ways. Yet, maybe some of him rubbed off on you." Liz looked up at him towering over her, hoping he would sit down again.

Matt did sit down, though still looking agitated. Liz

continued, "We learn the basics from our childhood. Losing my parents at an early age made me scared to get too attached to anyone. It wasn't until we met that I figured that out."

"So, what's changed? I'm the same person you fell in love with."

"But are you? You act differently now. This helps me understand why."

"How do we stop it?"

"Here's one example of something you could change. It was your idea that I work remotely after the first trimester. It made no sense to me. I never wanted to stay home and be isolated, but you insisted."

"Then why did you go along with it?"

"I shouldn't have. You know the Cafe is where my people are. I love being around our staff, the musicians and customers. I have way too much time on my hands now."

"I just wanted to take care of you during your pregnancy."

"You've got to stop telling me what to do. No more demanding that I go home early or work less."

"I'll try to stop. In exchange, you need to stop comparing me to Dad."

Joanne interrupted. "You don't have to relive your entire past in one conversation. You've both made some headway." She looked from one to the other. "Why don't we call it a night?"

Matt looked at his wife hopefully as he cleared the plates. "We can fix this, Liz."

Liz looked away and wondered, can we?

CHAPTER 18

After Matt left for the Cafe the next morning, Joanne poured her first cup of coffee and bit into one of Liz's warm Irish scones, slathered with butter and cherry jam. "Whoa, Liz. I may have to stay another week if this is the treatment I get in the morning."

"I love this recipe too. Whenever I make it, I think of my Dad. He was the baker in our family. He taught me how to make these when I was six years old. I made a dozen this morning. Help yourself to more!"

"Okay. You've forced me to have another. Every time you talk about your parents, I feel like I get to know you better. I'm picking up little pieces of your family history."

"Thanks for saying that. What's best in me comes from those two."

"They raised a strong daughter and not too shabby a baker. These scones will give me the energy I need to take you shopping for baby clothes, toys and books. Plus parenting tips over lunch. Does that plan still work for you?"

"Let's do it!"

Two hours later after shopping for onesies, cloth diapers, sun hats, overalls, an oversized panda bear, and some children's books, Joanne and Liz settled into a booth for lunch at the Old Time Bakery. "In the bookstore, you asked me about what my other relationships were like before Matt. Tough topic while skimming baby books. I'll fill you in now."

"Not to mention the hyper twin toddlers who were crawling around your legs in the bookstore." They both laughed before Joanne continued, "You left off with finding guys who were stable and predictable."

"I think I meant safe and boring. Safe was the key word. I was going for no surprises. Matt was the opposite from the day we met. He was a puzzle I couldn't quite figure out, more complicated than I was used to. A couple of years later, he's still a puzzle to me. But not in a good way."

Seeing Liz's forlorn look, Joanne searched for a way to give her hope about her son.

"He's worth it, Liz. He's got some evolving to do. My theory has always been that men don't grow into themselves until their mid-thirties. Matt is a perfect example. He bottles his feelings up inside. He's got to work on that. Deep down, he's a good, compassionate man."

"When I met Matt, I still missed Sophie, my best friend and business partner. Two years before, she had gone into the Peace Corps with her new husband, Pete. I was finally getting used to running the Cafe alone, using Drew's help when I needed it."

"Sounds really challenging."

"I wasn't sure I had the confidence to do it solo. We

dissolved our business partnership and Drew and I bought out her share."

"Big change!"

"You're not kidding. My support system was shattered, just like when I lost my parents. I felt so alone after working closely with Sophie every single day. She had known my parents and extended family for years. She is still family. Do you know who saved the day, both when my parents died and when Sophie left?"

"Tell me."

"My big brother. Drew changed his whole life to raise me. He left his pre-med program during his senior year at UW Seattle to move back to Eugene to raise me. And then after Sophie left, he got more involved in the business again."

"Your brother stepped up. You were lucky."

"We were all each other had. I trust him more than anyone," Liz said, tearing up.

"How could you not?"

"Now, I'm about to become a mother. I'm at a loss here. I don't fully trust my husband. This isn't where I imagined I'd be at this point in my life." By now, Liz had begun to cry. "Just talking to you makes me miss my mom so much." Joanne moved over to Liz's side of the booth and held her until she stopped crying.

After the food came and Liz bit into her sandwich, she changed the subject by asking Joanne how she met Quinn.

"Are you ready for the whole courtship story?"

"I'm all ears," Liz said, content to listen for a while.

"Quinn and I fell in love in the summer of 1974 in Washington, D.C. I was a junior at Berkeley. I got a summer internship at the Art of Social Change Museum.

My department chair had gotten her Fine Arts degree with Laurel Fineman, the museum director. That connection plus my social protest portfolio landed me the internship."

"What was in your portfolio?"

"I made anti-war protest posters. One had hundreds of National Guardsmen standing at attention in front of my dorm, holding M-1 rifles. My 'Make Love Not War' poster captured a circle of women dancing mid-air and was picked up by the Chicago Tribune and the L.A. Times. My personal favorite was a Jerry Garcia poster with The Grateful Dead playing in People's Park."

Liz listened intently, holding up her chin with her knuckles. "Impressive. No wonder you got the internship."

"Thanks. I couldn't believe it at first. Laurel's mentoring was like an initiation. I stepped into a broader world of art. She took me to exhibit openings and introduced me to the new wave of 1970s political artists. I drank in every new experience. People playing music on Dupont Circle, the rallies, Watergate. Wild times."

"Thanks for the history lesson, Joanne." They both laughed.

"I hung out at a cafe-bookstore on Connecticut Avenue in Northwest D.C. called More Than Words. They had the best books, magazines and newspapers from all over the world. Good coffee, triple-layer deli sandwiches and desserts made it my personal hangout to sketch after work and on weekends."

"That must be where you met Quinn." Liz grinned with anticipation.

"You guessed it. I couldn't help but notice a blondish-brown, curly-haired guy sitting by the window. He had round wire-rim glasses and was lost in a book. There was something about how the light fell on his hair and his serious expression. I sketched him for an hour. I was fearless in those days. I walked up to his table and laid my sketch pad down in front of him. He closed his book, *Zen and the Art of Motorcycle Maintenance: An Inquiry into Values.* When I saw the cover, I had a feeling we were of the same tribe. Quinn said that I obviously have an eye for fascinating and attractive subjects."

Liz began cracking up.

"I teased Quinn back, asking if he thought it was him. Then explained it was actually the guy at the table behind us."

"Too funny! And so, the romance begins," Liz said.

"Quinn was flattered by my sketch and we talked for hours. He was so different from the pseudo-radical guys at Berkeley. He appreciated how I looked at things in an off-beat way, not at all like his law school friends."

Joanne went on to describe that once the summer ended, they reluctantly went back to their separate lives. Quinn went to UW Law School and Joanne to UC Berkeley Art School, 2,000 long miles apart. They exchanged countless letters, talked long-distance with little money. No cell phones then. No emails. They spent school breaks and summer together. Finally, Joanne transferred to UW-Madison and finished her art degree there. She had to be with him. They married soon after her graduation.

"What a sweet story," said Liz.

"I found work at a local gallery and volunteered to teach an art class at the Juvenile Detention Center. Life was busy. We'd fly to Oregon and spend time in Cottage Grove for Thanksgiving and summer vacations with Quinn's parents, Ben and Vivie. I loved those two. So did Quinn."

"So far so good. I'm waiting for the bomb to drop."

"I don't want to admit it, but things didn't go sideways until I got pregnant with Matt. We weren't planning to have a baby so soon. Quinn was working for Legal Aid and I was an assistant gallery manager. We both worked long hours, but we were doing exactly what we wanted. It was kind of sudden when Quinn started to change."

"In what way?"

"He wanted my attention constantly. He kept asking me to reassure him that nothing would change between us once the baby came."

"Sounds like he wasn't quite ready to be a father."

"No kidding! First I thought Quinn was afraid the baby would slow down his career. He had big plans. Later, I realized the baby wasn't the threat. The real problem was Quinn had an addiction to control. When I was six months pregnant, he gave me a new insight into who he was. One day he stopped by the Celeste Gallery to take me to lunch. He always seemed jealous of my good friend, David Powell, the gallery owner. It was annoying."

"I can guess what's next. Did Quinn's jealousy become a problem at work?"

"To say the least. When Quinn walked in that day, David said hello and asked how he was doing. Quinn turned his back on David and insisted I leave immediately. I was so irritated with him, but I said nothing to avoid a fight."

Liz interrupted. "I know all about avoiding conflict."

"I did what I could to keep things peaceful. I acted like nothing happened. So, we headed to Aviva's Deli and Bakery, the best challah in town. On the way over, Quinn warned me to watch out for David. He was sure my boss had a 'thing' for me."

"Did he?"

"David was a mentor and close friend. There was nothing between us then. I told Quinn he had to stop obsessing about him."

"Good. You stood up to him."

"I did, but I paid for it. As we walked into the restaurant, our conversation got more heated and Quinn raised his voice. He grabbed my arm. He was so rough, I cried out. The customer behind us asked if I needed help. When I didn't say 'no,' Quinn went ballistic and the manager asked us to leave."

"How humiliating!"

"Absolutely. I was livid with Quinn for acting like a bully. I was sick and tired of it."

"I know what you mean," sympathized Liz.

"Things changed for a while after Matt was born. Quinn seemed almost content. I hoped his strange behavior was over."

"What a relief!"

"As you already know, it didn't last. We had a honeymoon stage as new parents, madly in love with our baby boy. When Matt was about six months old, Quinn began to come home later and later. I suspected he was having affairs. Next, he began to track my every move."

"How?"

"Initially, he called constantly from work and asked where I was and where I'd been. It was suffocating."

"Sounds unbearable. Why did you stay?"

"I was a new mom. I didn't have any income except Quinn's. My fear was he'd screw me in a divorce if I left."

"Tough times. The romantic courtship turned into a

marriage from hell."

Joanne took a deep breath. "Now I'm the one who needs a break. My therapist advised me to share my trauma to help me heal. Over time it's supposed to lessen the pain. I'm surprised it's still difficult for me to talk about it."

"I can see why."

"Let me drop you off at home. I'll go over to Amazon Park and walk this off. I need to remind myself I was the best mother I could be under the circumstances."

"Wait. One more thing. Thanks for telling me the truth about Quinn. Now I finally know more about him – and Matt. I wish you had left Quinn sooner."

"So do I, Liz. So do I."

CHAPTER 19

After they got home from lunch and put the gifts in the baby's room, Joanne drove Liz's car to Amazon Park. The large, urban park was 100 acres bordered by streets lined with maple and alder trees, and a creek running through it. Numerous walking, running and bicycling trails weaved in and around the park. Flat and tree-lined. A walker's dream.

As Joanne pulled into the parking lot near the dog park, she realized the irony of choosing this spot to clear her mind. Some of her fondest memories during her marriage to Quinn were at this very park. When they came to Oregon to visit Quinn's parents, they would leave Matt with them for the day and go to Eugene. Walking the dogs and visiting Maude Kerns Art Gallery were perfect ways to spend a day together. Quinn would pack a tasty picnic lunch with Joanne's favorite foods. They often devoured chicken apple salad sandwiches with gruyere cheese. He topped it off with a prize-winning apple cake from a

Bayfield, Wisconsin recipe.

Then they would go to the dog park with Gus, a rescued German Shepherd, and Sammy, an English Sheepdog. Gus had an unpredictable temper requiring a high soprano voice to settle him down. Joanne felt more comfortable around Sammy who was mellow, playful and faithfully obedient. They would run the dogs in the park while chit-chatting with other dog people. Comparing their pets' personalities and behaviors was sort of like talking about kids. It always amused Joanne, a cat person, how paternal Quinn was with his two gigantic dogs. When Gus got belligerent with other dogs, their owners complained angrily to Quinn. He was Gus' greatest defender, explaining that he had been abused by previous owners. As a rescue dog, he was still in training to tone down the aggressiveness. Some dog owners were more receptive than others. Joanne was still astonished that Gus' training period extended to ten years and Quinn never acknowledged it.

As Joanne passed the Amazon Dog Park, she thought about how Quinn was not unlike Gus. They were both unpredictable and sometimes violent. As she strolled past the Amazon Pool, she heard screams and laughter from the children splashing in the kiddie pool and racing down the water slide into the larger pool. She finished the loop trail around the park before heading home.

One thing was bothering Joanne about her earlier conversation with Liz. She hadn't been completely truthful about her connection to David Powell, the gallery owner. At one point, their collegial relationship became more than a close friendship.

As Quinn became more distracted by work, he often

came home late. He would be irritable and impatient with Joanne to the point of shouting. Joanne gradually confided fears about her deteriorating marriage to David. They'd go out for long lunches and leave the gallery assistant in charge. Sharing their life stories gave David a chance to talk about his painful divorce three years earlier.

Joanne dreaded the long weekends when she wasn't with David. He started to call her under the guise of work questions, but she knew it was more than that. She looked forward to hearing his voice. When Quinn shoved her at the gallery, Joanne felt guilty, guessing Quinn had figured out she had fallen in love with David.

After Matt was born, Joanne stopped all contact with David. She let him know that instead of a leave of absence, she wasn't coming back. David failed to convince her to postpone the decision. Joanne was clear she wanted a family and intended to make it work with Quinn.

Years later, Joanne's Chicago therapist described Joanne and David's changing relationship as an "emotional affair." While not sexual, it was intimate. Joanne had been getting her emotional needs met by someone outside her marriage. While Quinn might have been jealous and suspected something was going on between the two, it didn't justify his violence. Her therapist pointed out, "Even though battered women may be imperfect, nothing they do warrants abuse."

When Joanne came into the house, Liz was at her computer, reviewing the Cafe's bi-monthly music schedule. She looked up. "How was the walk?"

"It helped."

"While you were gone, I thought a lot about how hard life was for you and Matt."

"I wish I had figured it out sooner and left. As terrifying as my life was, disrupting it was even scarier."

"I get that," Liz said, looking down at her wrist.

"I had so much to plan. Law school and the move to Chicago were big changes. I had to make sure I could get sole custody and decent child support."

"How did Matt deal with it?" Liz asked.

"During the two years before I left Quinn, Matt was never home. As he told you last night, he spent most of his time at Sam's house. Sam's parents were everything Quinn and I weren't. I knew I was losing him."

"When did you tell Matt you planned to leave?"

"The spring he turned fifteen. I wanted to leave in July so he had two months to get settled before he started school. I asked him to keep the move to himself. We had the most honest talk we'd had in a long time, mostly about his fears."

"Was he relieved or angry?"

"Both." Joanne sighed and continued. "I hired a lawyer specializing in domestic violence. She told me to collect photos of my injuries, the breaks and bruises. I found photos of Matt with a black and blue eye after a particularly brutal attack. She also requested the assault documentation from the hospital, session notes from Matt's school counselor and detention records. She made a strong case for why I should get custody, child support and alimony. I began to hide money in a separate account for the move."

"I'm so impressed you knew exactly what to do," Liz said.

"I couldn't have done it without the help of the local domestic violence program. I talked to them numerous times before I got my plan figured out."

Liz's cell phone rang and she checked the caller. "I'm sorry but it's Sophie and we really need to talk. Do you mind?"

"Not at all. I'll go upstairs and deal with work emails. Let me know when you're done."

After Joanne left, Liz returned Sophie's call, sobbing so hard Sophie could barely understand her.

"Talk slower, Liz. What's going on?"

Liz took a few deep breaths and started again. "Sophie, do I really know Matt at all? I've been such a fool! Joanne said Matt was beaten and she was physically and emotionally abused by Quinn for years. Matt was even in therapy to work on his anger towards his father."

"That's a shocker! Still, it must feel better to know more about Matt. I wish I knew how to make it better."

"All I need is for you to listen for a while."

About an hour later, Joanne heard a soft knock on her door. "Come on in."

"Sorry it took so long. Talking to Sophie helped. I don't know what I'd do without her!"

"It's good to have a friend who is always there for you. My sister, Eleanor, is that person for me."

"You're not going to like this but Sophie felt uneasy about Matt from the beginning."

"That's funny. People usually like Matt right away. There's a certain warmth about him. You felt it when you met."

"Well, Sophie was just not feeling it. She tried to support our relationship. But, when she returned from the Peace Corps, she wondered why we got married so quickly. It was a sore point between us. Still, we've stayed close friends in spite of it."

"Sometimes our closest friends don't always see what we do."

"But I actually think Sophie was onto something I missed!"

"You know what's hard, Liz? If I say the slightest good thing about Matt, you dismiss it."

"Well, how about you don't paint Matt as if nothing is ever his fault?"

"I don't feel like I've done that."

"When I checked out the Jill's Place website, it said keeping secrets about the violence is a big mistake. It isolates women who are battered. Also, batterers frequently abuse their children. You two are a case in point. You were battered and Matt experienced child abuse."

"That's right. I know from my legal work and my own experience that the violence only gets worse over time."

"Hot issue for us, Joanne. Brings up a lot of feelings that we've both bottled up. Is Matt different or is he following in his father's footsteps?"

"Matt's a kinder and better man than Quinn could ever be. It's hard for me to be impartial, but I believe Matt can change."

"You're more optimistic than I am, Joanne."

"Maybe all Sophie sees in Matt is the part Quinn damaged. My own mother used to ask me over and over why I stayed in my marriage. I couldn't admit to her I still loved him and kept hoping he would change."

"That's the hard part, isn't it?"

"I'll tell you something else. My parents noticed early on that Quinn was isolating me. He felt threatened when they visited or called and hated when I spent time with them in San Francisco. Feeling their disapproval, Quinn talked negatively about them and discouraged me from visiting. As he grew more insistent over time, it was harder for me to say 'no' to him. While I didn't see it clearly at the time, my mother did."

"His strategy worked."

"You're right. It did. I'd do almost anything to postpone his threats and violent outbursts. It infuriated my mother that I rarely saw her. She accused me of being an obedient wife, something she would never have predicted. One day she asked me what happened to her feminist daughter. That hurt!"

"I'm surprised they didn't drag you and Matt out of there."

"I think Mom and Dad would have if they'd known Quinn was physically hurting us." Joanne paused. She was flooded with regret for ignoring the repeated warnings from people she loved.

"When you left Quinn, did they help you?"

"They did. They were proud of me for going to law school, even more so as a single parent. They understood by choosing law school, I had exchanged the work I loved for financial stability. Art became a hobby instead of my life's work. It was a huge sacrifice and I promised myself that one day I would be an artist again."

Joanne shared how her parents and sister jumped from their seats and hooted when she crossed the stage to receive her law degree. "It was totally embarrassing, but I loved it. My parents helped me financially for the first few years. Five years after practicing law, I began to repay them."

"You were so lucky they stood by you."

"You're right. Their love and support made all the difference."

"Was it an ugly divorce?"

"Surprisingly not. Once Quinn got past the shock and anger about our leaving, he didn't put up much of a battle. My divorce lawyer knew Quinn was pursuing a judgeship at the time and wouldn't want bad publicity surrounding his appointment."

Joanne suddenly stopped talking. She looked away from Liz and sat silently for a few minutes. Liz walked over to her, gently putting her hand on her mother-in-law's shoulder.

"Hey, where'd you go? You got quiet all of a sudden."

"I can visualize walking out the door of my upscale lakeside home, leaving my community. I left a comfortable, upper-middle-class life. Status and privilege vanished. I yanked Matt out of a small, prestigious Quaker high school and enrolled him in an overcrowded Chicago public school. I turned our lives upside down and felt immense guilt about it."

Liz looked at her sympathetically. "If it helps, I think you were incredibly brave and did the right thing."

"I wish I had been brave much sooner," Joanne said remorsefully. "Ultimately, Matt ended up doing well. His cousin, Kit, paved the way by adding him to his band, *State Street Driveby*. Matt replaced their lead guitarist who had just moved to California. The other band members welcomed Matt into the fold, not only as a musician, but as their manager. Matt began booking gigs and helped them become a money-making band. They played at parties, school events across Chicago and at the Great Lakes Music Festival. He even got them a gig at the UW-Madison

Autumn Music Festival."

"Impressive that Matt had so much initiative. He lucked out by having a lot of support. High school is hard under the best of circumstances."

"Our lives fell into place about six months after we made the move. Sam Hewitt came to visit when he could and Matt saw him when he visited Quinn. In the beginning of his senior year, Matt refused to follow the visitation schedule that was in our custody agreement. At first, Quinn pretended to care and was angry but, in truth, he was on the prowl and sleeping around. Matt was in the way of all that."

"Matt seemed to bounce back after your move and divorce. He wasn't as resilient after his own divorce from Anne. When we moved in together, Matt kept pushing to get married. I thought it was too soon because we were still getting to know each other. Now I wonder if he ever really got over his first marriage."

"That was my question, too. It's something you'll have to ask Matt. All I know is his first marriage was over in a flash. I didn't see it coming. It bothered me, but whenever I brought Anne up, he would shut me down. Off-limits."

"You know Sophie warned me that I was his rebound relationship. I ignored her."

"What did Sophie say about your broken wrist?"

"She didn't think it was an accident at all," answered Liz as she stood up. "I just don't want to talk about it now."

"I'm sorry. I'll back off."

Liz sat down to collect herself and realized she had to face the truth. The broken wrist was no accident. She added in a quieter voice, "Good."

"I'm not always sure what to say. You want the truth

about my past, but you're hesitant to be honest with me. I keep asking about your wrist because I'm worried that Matt is acting like his father. I can't sit by and watch your lives unravel if I can help."

Liz got up slowly, holding her pregnant belly and breathing deeply. "I need a break. I'm going to lie down for a while."

"Are you alright?" Joanne asked, looking worried.

"I was just feeling the baby kick. My obstetrician warned me to be careful about my blood pressure shooting up. I get angry and then scared when I talk about my life."

"You can be angry at me and be honest, too. I warn you, I'll do the same. I won't walk away, no matter what you say."

Joanne sensed Liz's remorse. The two of them had been walking on landmines. Liz's reaction was identical to hers when she would get angry with friends or family who suspected violence. They saw through the flimsy excuses for bruises, bumps and no-shows.

Was there time for her son to change? Matt needed help immediately. Joanne promised herself that she would find a way.

CHAPTER 20

After a day of shopping and constant conversation with Liz, Joanne decided to catch up with her son. When she arrived at the Shady Grove, she parked in the back since the band was unloading their sound equipment through the front door. Instead of going inside, Joanne darted over to the deck and ordered a glass of rosé. It gave her time to call Emily. She sat four tables away from the other customers, creating a modicum of privacy for herself.

Joanne took a sip of wine as she called Emily, who picked up after a couple of rings. "Hey Emily, it's Joanne How are you doing?"

"Hi, Joanne. I'm good. I'm glad you called," Emily said warmly.

"I wondered if you had a few minutes to talk. I've spent the day with Liz and have some questions."

"Sure. I bet she told you about Matt's erratic behavior over the past few weeks. Maybe you've witnessed some of it since you arrived."

"No, it's about Liz's wrist. She seems uncomfortable telling me what happened. I don't believe it was accidental. I know you were there that night. What really happened?"

"Joanne, are you sure you want the answer? It doesn't bode well for Matt."

"Of course, Emily, I want the truth. Hold on a second. I'm out on the Shady Grove deck and three people just got seated at the table next to me. I need to move into the office for more privacy."

Once Joanne closed the office door, Emily began: "I was waiting on a table near the front of the Cafe with a clear view of the check-in area. Matt was frantic because the band was so late. Liz knew that the audience could manage a later showtime. She explained from the stage why the band was running late. After offering free drinks and future updates, everyone applauded. We have understanding audiences!"

"That's the advantage of being in a smaller city like Eugene where people know each other."

"So true. Later, as I took the dinner order to the kitchen, I heard Matt and Liz arguing in loud whispers. Liz was assuring him that the show would go off fine. When I saw the band pulling up, I decided to go up front and give them a hand."

When Emily hesitated for several seconds. Joanne said, "Go ahead, Emily. I want to know what happened."

"Okay," Emily said with a deep sigh. "I had barely gotten three steps toward the front door when I saw Matt grasping Liz's shoulders and shoving her against the wall. She didn't trip. She didn't slip. I watched her hit the wall and shriek with pain, collapsing to the floor. As I raced over, Matt turned and saw what he'd done. When he offered to help, Liz told him to get away. I got her up and out to the car. The whole incident happened in minutes. Ira saw it too, from the kitchen."

"Are you sure? Maybe Matt was only trying to help Liz."

"Sorry, Joanne. I won't lie to you or second guess myself. His story was Liz tripped over the high stool by the front counter when she turned to direct the traffic coming in the front door. It's a common scene for the front to be a bit chaotic before a show. Still, this was not like the usual mayhem. His hands were on her shoulders before she fell. And, then she ended up in the emergency room with a broken wrist!" Emily's voice was so loud that Joanne adjusted the volume on her cell.

Joanne knew Emily was a close friend of Liz's, so wasn't surprised by her angry tone. "That's even worse than I thought. No accident. I wonder what I can do now to turn this around. Matt is going to lose everything if he keeps this up."

"If I can help in any way, let me know. If you're thinking of a batterer intervention group, you know as well as I do they often aren't effective. Definitely a big 'no' to couples counseling. It puts the woman in more danger. Maybe you can get his friends to convince Matt to attend a group, although it could be like pulling teeth."

"Emily, which friends could convince him to get help?"

"Let me think. Oh, I know! Marcus and Natalie Bernstein could do it! They're the bass player and fiddler in Matt's Shady Grove String Band. If anyone could, they're the ones to get Matt to see he could lose Liz and their baby."

"Right. I met them when they played music at Matt and

Liz's wedding. What's their story?"

"Natalie's a social worker and a big supporter of the shelter's Dating Violence Workshops in the schools. She's been to my classroom presentations more than once. She told me about a couple of her students that she suspected were in violent relationships. One ended up calling me. She joined our support group and broke up with her boyfriend a couple of months later. In fact, Natalie and Marcus are coming to tonight's show."

"I'll try to stop by their table tonight." Joanne felt a small sense of relief. The situation was awful, but at least there were possibilities.

"Good luck with all this. I'm so glad you're here to help Liz and Matt. They need it."

"One more thing. Can you email me which batterer intervention groups you'd recommend? We both know religious ones wouldn't work for Matt."

"I'll send the agency names with contact info of staff I know personally," offered Emily. "If anyone can turn this around, it's you."

"At first I was going to encourage them to keep working on their relationship while Matt got help. But Liz's broken wrist, combined with her pregnancy, makes me worry."

"It should! When I went to the hospital with Liz for her wrist, the nurse gave her the domestic violence talk. She warned about the high rate of miscarriage or premature birth connected to battering. But, that's not news to either of us."

"If Liz decides to live separately for a while, it may be just the incentive Matt needs to save his marriage. When I left Quinn, he offered to do anything to get us back. But I realized he wasn't sincere. It was way too late for him."

"You have high expectations Matt will change. And I hope he will."

"I'm no fool. He'll need lots of support. I'd even take a leave of absence from work if that would help. We'll see how much personal and professional meddling they'll take without sending me back to Chicago on the next red-eye." They both laughed for the first time in their conversation.

Joanne changed course. "I should find Matt so we can order dinner before the show starts. I'll look for Marcus and Natalie in the audience and see if they'll meet with me for coffee."

"Sounds good. Now, go hang out with your son. Let's talk soon," said Emily as she hung up.

Matt was chatting with some customers at a front-row table as Joanne came out of the office. She waved at him. Matt quickly ended his conversation and walked over. "My cafe spies told me you were sipping wine on the deck. When I got there, I found an empty glass and your jacket. Knowing you, I figured you had taken a work call in my office."

"Yes, honey, I did have an important call. Let's get food so we can talk before the music starts."

"I thought we were taking dinner home."

"Liz is exhausted and has gone to bed already, so we can have a mother and son evening here."

"It's just what I need. You've probably felt the tension since you've been here. Liz and I could use a break. Also, I need some of your wisdom right now."

They chose a table in the back corner for privacy. When Colleen came to get their order, Matt introduced her as one of the original employees. Liz and Sophie had started the business hiring only friends, even though most of them had no restaurant experience. As the business grew, they branched out by hiring "friends of friends." Colleen went to college with Drew's best friend which got her the job. It helped that Colleen played guitar and sometimes filled in when Matt was unavailable to play with his band. Both Liz and Matt loved that the Cafe was an extended family where they could trust the team.

Partway through dinner, Matt said, "Mom, I need to talk to Nia Lee, the reggae band's lead singer, before I introduce the show. I'll be back soon. Don't eat my entire dinner while I'm gone."

Joanne laughed because the Foley family had a bad habit of taking tastes of each others' food without permission, and often more than just a taste.

"I'll try to control myself, Matt," replied Joanne as she reached over and took a huge bite of his Moroccan chicken with mushrooms and green olives.

"Right, Mom. Keep it up and there will be no Bailey's Irish Cream Cheesecake in your future!" Matt said laughing and shaking his finger at her.

After Matt left, Joanne scanned the room for Marcus and Natalie. She spotted them two rows up and started to walk over. They looked like they were engaged in an intense conversation. Joanne hesitated before tapping Natalie's shoulder.

"Hey guys! How are you doing?" They quickly stopped talking, smiled, and jumped up to hug her.

"We're good. Both on break from school. Marcus from teaching, me from counseling."

"How long are you here?" asked Marcus.

"A long weekend. I might extend it, though. We'll see."

"Good. We'll have time to get together then. To be honest, Joanne, we're worried about Matt. It's great timing that you're in town," Natalie confessed. "Can you join us?"

"Just for a minute. Matt's about to introduce the band. Thanks for being direct so I don't have to make up some fake excuse to see you. Do you have time tomorrow? Matt's biking with his cousin in the morning."

"We'd love that, Joanne," Marcus said. They exchanged cell phone numbers.

"I'll text you our address. Come for brunch at 11?" suggested Natalie.

"Perfect. I really need your help."

"We'll work on it in the morning. Promise. See you then," said Natalie.

Joanne rushed back to the table as Matt began walking up the steps to the stage. She didn't want to miss his introduction.

"Good evening, everyone. I'm Matt Foley and on behalf of Liz and me, welcome to the Shady Grove Cafe tonight." The audience clapped and Matt beamed, clearly enjoying his role as emcee. "Before I introduce the band and tell you highlights about upcoming shows, I want to remind you that the Shady Grove is a listening room. We ask there be no conversation during the performance. If you'd like to chat about how great the music or food is, we encourage you to head outside on the deck. And please no cell phones. Now help me welcome a Shady Grove Cafe favorite from Kingston, Jamaica: The Nia Lee Reggae Band!" The house was packed and the applause was deafening.

Either Matt or Liz made a similar introduction every night before shows began.

One reason for the Cafe's popularity with musicians

and patrons was the audience's complete attentiveness to the music. After first opening, Liz and Sophie had waited a few years before they got a beer and wine license. They didn't want people drinking so much they'd disturb the show. The Cafe had a solid reputation among musicians as a unique venue to play.

Matt went back to finish dinner with Joanne after the band was on stage. The audience loved Nia's original music and the band's melodic style. Then, towards the end of the last set, Nia brought the house down when she dedicated an original song to Matt's mom. It was, of course, his request. She introduced "Like a Hurricane," a song she had written years ago. It had been influenced by Maya Angelou's description of her own mother "as a hurricane in its perfect power."

Nia asked Joanne to raise her hand. "Matt told me this song reminded him of you, ever-changing and powerful."

Joanne nodded at the singer, acknowledging her kindness and squeezed Matt's hand. Listening to the song, Joanne was visibly moved by Matt's appreciation of her. Once it ended and the applause died down, Joanne was reminded that underneath Matt was good. She believed he had it in him to change.

Matt and Joanne got home after midnight and found Liz fast asleep. Joanne went to her room, texting Natalie and Marcus to confirm the time for a late morning brunch. She needed a good night's sleep.

X

After coffee the next morning, Matt attached his bike to the carrier on the back of his van. He was getting ready to drive to Cottage Grove to ride the Row River Trail with his cousin. Before he left, he went back into the house to put some coffee in a travel mug. When Joanne looked up from her newspaper, he said, "The ride is 17 miles and then we'll probably grab a beer. So, I won't be home until dinner."

"What a ride. I know it well. I love Oregon's covered bridges. The Dorena Dam and the Row River should be gorgeous today. We spent lots of time there with your father."

"I can't understand why you wouldn't jump on Liz's bike and come along. Offer is still open. Liz is working on the books today, so you'll have no one to hang out with. Now she's fast asleep after a restless night with the baby kicking like crazy."

"No, thanks. A quiet day sounds good. Anyway, I promised to make your favorite chicken schnitzel for dinner tonight."

"You're off the hook then."

Shortly after Matt left, Joanne headed out to Marcus and Natalie's. As she grabbed a bottle of champagne and orange juice from the refrigerator for mimosas, she left a note on the kitchen table about cooking dinner that night.

As they finished a vegetable frittata with cotija cheese, Joanne and Natalie showered Marcus with compliments on his culinary skills. Then, it was time to get down to business.

After Joanne reviewed the two renditions of "How Liz Broke Her Wrist," Marcus jumped in to defend Matt.

"I don't think Matt would deliberately hurt Liz. I'm not sure I would trust Emily's version. Matt told me she micromanages him because she's been at the Cafe longer. When he recently called her out on acting like she was his boss, they got into a major argument. Matt didn't intend to fire her, but in the heat of the moment, that's what he did. Emily doesn't trust his judgment on finances and she sure doesn't respect his authority. It's obvious to me that Matt's totally stressed out."

"Marcus, I do appreciate your loyalty, but I checked in with Emily, and talked with Ira, too. They were at the Cafe and witnessed what happened," replied Joanne.

"There's a good source for the truth about Matt," Marcus said sarcastically. "Ira still carries a torch for Liz and flirts with her all the time. Of course, Ira thinks Matt mistreats her. Kind of works for him."

Joanne remembered Marcus as easygoing. She wasn't sure how to respond and looked over at Natalie.

"This 'he said, she said' scenario is getting us nowhere. You know, Marcus, I normally agree with you. But, I've had a couple of conversations with Liz that make me believe Emily's and Ira's version. Liz has been upset and frightened by Matt recently. I've been supporting her, but it's not easy since I feel so close to both of them."

"Natalie, what's the deal here?" asked Marcus. "I know you've been talking to Liz a lot since her injury, but you didn't tell me she's afraid of Matt!"

"I'm sorry, Marcus. Liz would only tell me on the condition we kept it between us. And now, here I am violating her trust. But, I have no choice. By breaking my promise, we can help both of them." Natalie took his hand and squeezed it.

"Since I know about Matt's abusive father, I'm not completely surprised that he's acting like this," admitted Marcus with a shrug.

Joanne admired how Natalie and Marcus could have a

conflict, talk it out and find a resolution. They obviously trusted one another. The violence in Joanne's own marriage had a longer-term impact than she'd realized. It was time to see her therapist when she got back to Chicago. This was bringing up a lot of guilt and regret.

During the rest of the brunch, Joanne discussed how they could convince Matt to join a batterer intervention group. She shared Emily's research on groups.

"I don't have to tell you, Natalie, that Matt has to take responsibility for what he did to Liz. All of us should connect with him more. Groups work best when there's lots of support from family and friends. If he feels abandoned or ganged up on, he'll probably drop out," said Joanne.

With that warning, the three felt they had it covered. Joanne believed she could go back home on Monday night knowing Matt's friends would provide the backup he needed. They would call her if it wasn't working.

A part of Joanne believed this plan would work. Yet, another part of her couldn't help but wonder if her next flight back would be to visit her son in jail.

CHAPTER 21

When Emily arrived at Cafe Sofia to meet with Liz and Becca, she got some coffee and sat at her favorite table. An original rust and golden antique Italian tapestry hung on the wall. Tucked away, she was slightly secluded but with a window looking out onto the street. Perfect for privacy. Other customers would not be able to overhear them. She had called them together so Becca could share details about the Foley family.

Emily had gotten there early so she could study before Liz and Becca arrived. She treasured this found half-hour to catch up on reading for her Children, Youth and Families class. Just as she opened the text, her phone rang.

She looked at the caller ID and answered, "Hi, Becca. Hope you aren't calling to tell me you fell off your horse this morning. Are you in traction?"

Becca laughed. "Okay, that's it. I'm going to take you out to ride so you get why I love it so much."

"As long as I can wear protective gear that matches my turquoise boots."

"Always the fashion statement, Em. Listen, I want you to know what I learned about Molly. Since it's confidential, I can't discuss it in front of Liz. Katrina just saw her at the Domestic Violence Conference in Washington D.C. Remember her? That risky night in Cottage Grove?"

"You're kidding! What was Molly doing there?"

"Elana Cohen, the executive director of the Vancouver shelter, told me that Molly is now an advocacy volunteer. She helps women get restraining orders, find housing, and child-care. Elana says she's doing a great job and as a survivor all the residents trust her."

"I'm not surprised," Emily responded.

"Elana brought Molly to the conference to be on a survivor panel. The topic was 'What Happens After You Leave.' Since the travel budget was tight, a board member offered to pay Molly's expenses. But only if it was anonymous."

"Good for Molly! That's a big deal!" exclaimed Emily.

"Elana said that she's considering hiring Molly next year. She would be competitive for the Advocacy Coordinator job when the current one leaves. By then, Molly would be up to speed with the skills she needs."

"We definitely saw her strength in a crisis. What happened to Danny, her abuser?"

"He was convicted of a misdemeanor assault but got probation since it was his first offense. Because he didn't use the rifle in the assault, he dodged a felony conviction. He was also charged with criminal mischief, third-degree but got probation for that too. His uncle, a lawyer, worked out a payment plan for trashing the emergency room lobby in Cottage Grove. Danny is still living in Molly's Cottage Grove house."

"Did Katrina ask about Jason and Jenny?"

"Yes, both kids are doing really well."

"We knew it was dangerous to go to Cottage Grove that night, but we were right to break the rules."

"Yes, we were, but I wouldn't advise it as a regular practice. No choice when we're dealing with the Dannys of the world. We have to make some razor-thin judgment calls. In this case, it worked."

"Glad to hear Molly and the kids are doing so well," said Emily. "Good to get uplifting news for a change. Thanks for passing it along."

"Yep. You're right. Sometimes it's hard to remember that what we're doing matters. Can't wait to see you!" Becca blurted out affectionately as she hung up.

Liz arrived at Cafe Sofia a few minutes later and said to Emily, "I see you already have a cup of con leche. I'll order a pot of mint tea. I hope my baby appreciates the sacrifice."

When Liz came back with her tea, she put a plate with three healthy-looking muffins on the table. "I figured we could use some sustenance to get us through the conversation with Becca."

"I never turn down a good Morning Glory muffin," Emily said, moving the plate closer. "Plus, I have something to tell you before Becca gets here."

"Go ahead while I inhale a couple of these," Liz said with a grin.

"I should have told you before, but I'm dating Becca. As you know, she works at the shelter where I intern. And there is one more weird connection. She's Anne's older sister."

Liz looked shocked and then let out an incredulous

laugh. "Can things get any more bizarre and entangled? This could be a family drama binge-watch. How long have you known they're sisters?"

"About a month. I find myself caught in the middle between you and Matt these days. I was afraid this would make it worse."

"I understand."

"Becca came to the area to help her aunt recover from surgery. When she found out that Matt lived here, she decided to stick around. She had unfinished business with him about Anne. Then a job opened at Jill's Place, so she took it."

"Just so you know, I had an eye-opening talk with Joanne about her marriage to Quinn and about Anne. The good and the bad. She confirmed how dangerous Quinn is. I already guessed as much from my lovely time with him at the coast."

"Is it too much for you to meet Becca right now?" Emily asked in a concerned tone. "I could still call and postpone it."

"Strangely, this couldn't be a better time. I want to learn more about Anne. It's another part of Matt's past that's a big secret. I bet Becca has information about Quinn that will help too."

"She definitely does. Oh, here she comes!" Emily said. Her expression gave away how smitten she was with Becca. When Liz noticed, Emily blushed.

They watched Becca get off her bike and lock it to a parking meter.

As Becca approached the table, Emily said, "Hey Sweetie, this is Liz, my boss and good friend."

"Hi, Liz. I'm Becca."

Liz stood up to greet Becca, but lost her balance and caught herself on the edge of the table. When she winced in pain, they both stared awkwardly at her broken wrist. Recovering quickly, Liz said, "Technically, I guess Em's right about the boss thing, but I don't know how the Cafe could run without her."

"I know what you mean," Becca said, looking tenderly at Emily. "Our executive director says Em is a super intern and indispensable at the shelter, too. You have so much going on, Em. I'm surprised you have time to be in a relationship with me and sit around drinking coffee this morning."

"The relationship part is easy, Becca. Drinking coffee instead of studying is the big challenge." They all laughed as Becca went to get a cup of coffee.

When she returned, Liz said to her, "I would never have agreed to meet you if I didn't trust Emily. I know we have a connection through Matt. I just learned your sister was Matt's first wife."

"First, thanks for coming. Yes, Anne and Matt were married for a short time. I also know that you're trying to help a young woman who Quinn assaulted at the hotel."

"It's true. I do want to talk to you about that, but first I'd like to know more about Matt's and Anne's relationship. I think it would help me understand him better. He's a complicated soul these days."

Becca paused and began fiddling with her bracelet. "I know both sides of Matt. Even though I had misgivings in the beginning, he seemed committed to Anne once they got married. She seemed happy at first. Her life with him was full and exciting. She said Matt seemed more secure than he was during college. Then things went downhill fast during law school. He began to act possessive and jealous again. He harassed her at work and put her job in jeopardy. He became physical."

"Your version of Matt's and Anne's relationship sounds more dangerous than Joanne's."

"I'm sure Matt kept it from his mother," responded Becca with a look of disgust.

"After a couple of years of marriage, Anne complained that she was feeling low most of the time. No energy. She couldn't sleep and lost interest in hanging out with her friends. She rarely called me. She finally left him and moved away to a location I can't share with you. Anne was afraid Matt would find her and get violent again. Maybe even force her to come home. The first time he hurt her was at the school where she taught. He dragged her by the arm to their car after physically threatening her colleague, out of jealousy. Something else happened making it impossible for her to stay."

"What was it?" asked Liz.

Hesitating Becca turned to Emily, touching her hand. "I'm not sure what my sister would want me to do. Should I tell Liz everything?"

"Yes, I think Anne would want you to warn Liz," Emily replied, looking from one to the other.

"Okay," Becca said with a deep sigh. "Be prepared for something ugly. The worst part is what Quinn did to Anne. That's why she ultimately left Wisconsin."

"What did he do?" Liz asked, tapping her fingers against her tea cup.

"Quinn knew that Matt was at a law conference in Chicago. He went over to their house, knowing Anne would be alone," Becca said as she teared up. "I still cry about it after all this time. He raped her. She told me he acted as though the sex was consensual even though when he left, she was sobbing on the kitchen floor. The man is a psychopath!"

"What a pig!" Liz cried out. "Exactly what Quinn tried to do to Rachel at the hotel, only so much worse. Did your sister press charges?"

"No. Anne was too afraid. She believed Quinn was capable of anything, maybe even having her killed. Before she could get away, Matt continued to harass her constantly, trying to get her to reconcile. Anne applied for a restraining order against him, but Quinn convinced the judge, an old law school buddy, to deny it. Once that happened, Anne knew she didn't have a chance so she disappeared."

"She was smart to leave. Is she okay now?" Liz asked.

"Not so okay. But she's safe and far away from Wisconsin."

"That explains why Matt was so devastated when she left so suddenly. Did he know why?"

"I honestly think he never knew about the rape. I can't imagine how he would find out. Quinn will keep that secret forever."

"Did Quinn try to find her?"

"Anne and I assume he left her alone because of what she had against him. She could disclose the rape at any time."

"That's the worst piece of Foley family history I've heard so far. Just recently, I've heard a lot," said Liz.

"I guess you know the rest. Matt dropped out of law school and left the country for a couple of years to regroup. He told some mutual friends he felt abandoned by

Anne and his father."

"I knew about Matt's volunteer work at a non-profit in Leon, Nicaragua. It was one of the few things he told me about his past. He ran a small business training program to help people start their own businesses so they could become economically independent. It made me think we had similar values," Liz said.

"That's the other side of Matt," Emily chimed in. "He has a strong social conscience. He supports local causes, like Jill's Place. It's what I liked about him when he first came to the Cafe. Like his father, he has good and bad sides."

"I'm surprised to hear that you don't think Matt's all bad," Liz said.

"Of course I don't. We became fast friends in the beginning. I just don't like the way he's been treating you lately and how hard he is on staff."

"You never complained about him until recently. I can't read your mind, Em."

"Well, after the night of the Kofi Harper show, I couldn't be silent anymore. I was seeing all the danger signs."

"There are programs that can help Matt but that would be up to him. Right now, you need to figure out what you want to do, Liz," Becca said.

Liz looked up. "Nail Quinn, of course! How can we let him get away with assaulting Rachel, your sister, and other women we don't even know about?"

"Being involved could put you in danger," Becca pointed out as she leaned back in her chair to give Liz a chance to think. After a few minutes, she continued, "Since Matt has hurt you once, exposing his father won't bring out his kinder, more patient side."

Liz winced. Emily wished she hadn't told Becca about the Cafe incident. "I'd rather strategize about how to stop Quinn from becoming Wisconsin's next governor. I bet he'll abuse his power to hurt more women. I think we have a fighting chance to make him pay for what he's done, don't you?"

"I hope so. We should include Anne and Rachel in our group strategy session," Becca said. "I'll ask my sister when she could fly out here or at least Skype with us. After talking with us, she can decide if she would be willing to go public about what Quinn did to her. We'll see."

"What about Joanne?" Emily asked.

When Liz didn't respond, Becca looked at her intently. "What's your take on her? Could Joanne be trusted to keep this from Matt? It could be risky. If Matt found out, he could warn his father. If the scandal got exposed, he could take it out on you."

Liz interrupted. "But Joanne could tell us a lot about Quinn's violent history. Ade Coleman, Rachel's private investigator, already contacted her."

"Are you encouraging Joanne to cooperate?" Emily pressed.

"Not directly. Since Joanne already knows I'm playing an active role, all I've done is ask her to keep it from Matt."

"Is there any chance Matt would help us?" Emily asked.

"Not unless he knew about the rape. And we're not about to tell him. Had Matt known, he never would have helped Quinn in the hotel cover-up. Let's just move ahead with Rachel and Anne. I'll update Ade," said Liz.

"Good idea," Becca said. "We can check in tomorrow

after we make our calls to find a date when we all can meet." Emily and Liz nodded in agreement.

Liz slowly rose from her chair, stroking her belly. She grabbed her coat as she got ready to leave. "I hope I don't live to regret this."

CHAPTER 22

After spending her morning at Cafe Sofia, Emily headed to the University for a two-hour field placement seminar. She learned new approaches to parenting in crisis. It could help moms at the shelter be more tuned into the special needs of their children who had grown up in violent homes. Just looking at Matt, she could see the long-term effects all the way to adulthood.

At the seminar, Emily's questions touched on useful topics for all the students. Professor Harris used to be on the Jill's Place Board of Directors so knew how the shelter worked. She offered creative ways to bolster families' strengths. After class, Emily talked to her about 7-year-old Jason. She wanted to explore the research on halting the violence between generations. If there wasn't any, she was interested in doing her thesis on the topic. Her professor was fascinated and encouraged her to look into the topic further. Emily was so excited she had lost track of time and realized she had to rush home to change before her night shift at the Cafe.

When she arrived at work, Emily checked in with Ira about dinner specials for the night and staffing. They were short one server, but Ira had found someone to cover before the dinner rush.

Next, Emily went to the office to follow up on Liz's request. She had asked Emily to keep a close eye on the music expenses while she worked from home. About half-way through the Quickbooks program, Emily discovered some high rental fees for equipment and two deposits for concerts at venues outside the club. It cost four times more than had been budgeted for the month. Looking in the contracts folder, she found agreements for two big-name acts that were way out of the Cafe's price range. Matt must have secured these contracts without Liz and Drew's knowledge because they wouldn't have approved such a high financial risk.

Emily left a phone message for their accountant, Fran, to see if she knew about this. She didn't want to alarm Liz without knowing all the facts. Asking Matt to explain would only intensify the friction between them. She'd wait for Fran to call back.

During her early Cafe days, Emily learned there was another side to the Shady Grove their patrons never saw, the money side. Liz and Sophie used to joke with her about their responses to customers who asked about the financial health of their business during the Cafe's infancy. They were often questioned on nights when the show was half empty or sluggish mornings when the breakfast business just trickled in. Sometimes staff outnumbered customers. Liz and Sophie had a positive litany of responses to alleviate the worry of their patrons.

Before opening Shady Grove, they took a micro-business development class. They learned it was best to present the Cafe as successful. People wanted to support a thriving, not struggling business.

"Oh, it's the rain," Liz often used as an excuse for low attendance at a show. "These rain storms just scare people away. We get a slow night here and there, but overall we're doing just great. Thanks for asking!"

Since it rained about eight months of the year in Eugene, the customer would commonly nod with deep empathy and say things like, "Oregonians can be such wimps. I'm tough, though. I don't let anything get in the way of going out to hear good music."

"Good customers like you support us, rain or shine. That's what makes the Shady Grove so successful," Liz would add.

Sophie was not quite as diplomatic as Liz and often resorted to a touch of sarcasm when quizzed too frequently. One regular customer was particularly annoying. "If your business doesn't pick up soon, you'll probably raise your prices. While I'd hate to do it, I'd be forced to switch to The Amazing Grace Bistro, your competitor in Springfield."

"What a loss for us, but I'm sure that our friends Billie and Sylvia would welcome you with open arms. Should I call to alert them you're coming?" The customer laughed and quickly reassured Sophie that he was loyal to them until the end.

"The end's not near, my friend," Sophie said as she warmed up his coffee. "We're here to stay."

Because converting the old toy store into a cafe had cost more than anticipated, Liz and Sophie had to carefully watch their spending. After Sophie left, Liz trained Emily to manage the restaurant budget. She worked closely with Fran and the three met monthly to troubleshoot problems.

When Fran called back that afternoon, Emily told her about Matt's unusual expenses. Fran asked Emily to alert Drew so they could all decide how to approach Liz with the information.

Emily asked Drew to come to the Cafe after Matt had gone home. When Drew arrived, he unlocked the front door and headed back to the kitchen. It was midnight so the kitchen staff were tossing the trash out and getting ready to leave.

"Hey Em, I'm home," Drew shouted, going into the kitchen where Emily was checking the food inventory. She put down her iPad for a hug and they both laughed. Drew had played such a huge role in those early years that they referred to the Shady Grove as their second home. At that time, Drew had divided his time between his full-time EMT job and working at the Cafe.

"Want a Ninkasi Red Ale?" They served only locally brewed beers and she knew that the ale was Drew's all-time favorite.

"Do you really have to ask, Em?"

"No, Drew. I was just seeing if you had changed to drinking rosé like your lightweight sister did before her pregnancy."

"That will never happen. What's the deal? I don't often get summoned for a late-night beer with you. It's got to be about Matt. Do you want me to run him out of town? I'm happy to do it." He was laughing again, but his sarcasm tinged his humor.

Emily twisted the cap off her Helles Belles lager. "Yes,

please do. He's a complete pain in the neck!"

Drew went from light-hearted to serious in a split second. "Is that loser using my sister as a punching bag again?"

"Not that I'm aware of. This has to do with Matt and the Cafe finances."

"Not surprised. Matt seems to think he runs this place. What did you uncover? Is he stealing from us?"

"No, not that I can see. But, did you know that a couple of weeks back when I challenged Matt about overspending, he fired me on the spot. Liz re-hired me the next day and Matt is forcing himself to be civil and pretend that nothing happened."

"Em, what a fool he is! We trust your judgment more than anyone. I don't know how we would have kept afloat without you after Sophie left."

"Drew, I owe you, too. Who helped me when my parents threatened to disown me after I came out to them?"

"They needed to accept who you are and not turn their back on you. We knew they would come to their senses."

Drew and Liz had flown out to Brooklyn to intervene on Emily's behalf. They spent the weekend talking to her folks about how hard it was for their daughter to live as a closeted lesbian. They encouraged them to love and support Emily even when they didn't understand her life or her relationships. While it took months to work through it, they were back in her life now.

"Okay. Who is the better friend? Let's call it a draw. But is there more I should know about Matt?" Drew asked.

"I think there is. Matt has changed since Liz got pregnant. He acts like he has to control her and the Cafe at all times. He's overspending in a manic way to prove that only he can make the Cafe more lucrative. Last month, Matt overspent on music equipment and venues without you and Liz knowing."

"You're kidding! I won't let him ruin what we've built. I was furious when Matt tried to purchase the building next door to expand the music club. After only working at the Cafe for a few months, he did it without informing us. The only thing that stopped him was needing our two signatures to make it legal."

"I remember that crisis."

"We refused to sign until we got financial advice about the investment and the actual costs for an expansion. Matt, of course, never considered the details. I'll admit that he's had some good ideas, but no follow-through. And when one of his ideas happens to make sense, he expects everyone around him to make it happen. Then he takes all the credit."

Emily sighed in frustration. "After Matt and Liz got married, he thought it wasn't necessary to run things by the two of you. Instead of easing himself into an existing family business, he tried to take over. He wanted to be the brains of the operation. Liz has struggled to keep him in line."

"So, we agree, Em. Matt tries to manipulate us to get what he wants. He'll overspend first and apologize later when confronted."

Emily handed Drew a list. "Here's a summary of his latest spending with $16,000 over budget for the month."

"You've got to be kidding me. We can't afford this. What was he thinking?"

"Drew, I believe he's feeding his ego by acting like a

high-powered businessman. He has something to prove now that he's off the lawyer track. Anyway, I didn't go to Liz with this because I hate to stress her out any more than she already is. What should we do?"

"I'll tell Liz and then confront Matt." replied Drew. "Who knows? Maybe she'll want to join me."

"That's crazy! We both know he already broke her wrist because a band was late. Don't you think the two of you questioning his competence will set him off even more? And who will get the brunt of that after you leave?"

"Of course, you're right. I'll ask Fran to talk to Matt and keep Liz out of it for the time being. Fran has a good working relationship with him. In the meantime, I'll get Matt legally removed as a signer on our accounts, both bank and credit card. Liz and I are the only ones who can authorize signers. We added him when it became necessary through his growing role in the business. I'm sure I could remove him as a signer as easily. I'll ask Fran to look into it."

"This is a big deal. You're stripping his authority and basically demoting him. Doesn't it look like you're trying to push him out of the business? It could put Liz in danger again," Emily warned.

"You're right again. He'll probably flip out about it. My hands are tied until I know what Liz wants. I can't figure out if she's defending him because she still loves him or she's too scared not to."

"Could be both," speculated Emily.

"It's the problem with family businesses. Liz and I owned the Shady Grove Cafe before she married him. She told me she wanted to wait a couple of years before making him a legal partner. Because of her trust issues, she decided on a prenup with Matt. He would not co-own the building or be a legal partner. If they divorced, he could only benefit from profits since they married. Surprisingly, he agreed," Drew explained.

"Speaking of divorce, we both know Liz should leave him."

"The question is, does she?" asked Drew.

"Losing his wife and the business will be too much for him. His downward spirals tend to be fast and furious. Liz will need to hide out for a while if she decides to leave him," warned Emily.

"Makes sense. I'll ask Fran to discuss the finance questions with Matt so he'll think they're coming from her. I'll take out a bank loan to cover the overspending and for now Fran will lower Matt's spending limits."

"I'll go to Liz's tomorrow while Fran meets with Matt and take her to a safe place if needed."

"In the best scenario, she'll leave him. In the worst, she'll defend him."

"Either way, she's in danger."

CHAPTER 23

When Liz got home that afternoon from a checkup with her obstetrician, she grabbed her book, turned on her favorite Yo Yo Ma cello music and stretched out on the couch. Moments later, Matt stormed into the house, shouting angrily. "Where are you, Liz?"

Startled, Liz responded, "What are you yelling about? I'm in the living room."

Matt's face was beet red. "I ran into Fran today at the Cafe and she wants to meet tomorrow. She was vague about why, but it's obvious Emily complained to her about me being over budget. Emily is such a bitch. Who does she think she is? She has no right to tell me how to run my business. Well, it's no longer a problem. I fired her!" Turning his back on Liz, he walked into the kitchen, grabbed a beer out of the refrigerator and chugged it.

Damn, he fired her again, thought Liz. She got up from the couch and followed him into the kitchen. When Matt turned around and saw Liz's shocked and angry face, he seethed, "Whose side are you on? I'm the boss and once again Emily has the gall to question me. She's been angry with me since the Kofi Harper show."

"Matt, please. Just tell me what happened."

"What's the use? You'll just defend her!"

"We have a long history together. Remember Emily was one of the first employees I hired, years before I met you. She's a strong restaurant manager and hires great staff who stay on forever. Emily worked for low pay during the first year until Sophie and I got the Cafe financially stable. I couldn't trust any employee more." Liz spoke slowly to try to calm him.

"Well, too bad. I don't trust Emily! I want her out! You expect me to run the whole place while you're working from home and then you don't trust my decisions. It's easy for you to judge, sitting here with your feet up." He strode past her into the living room and dropped down into his recliner.

Liz went out to the deck to get away from him. She needed him to cool down. As she sat down on the Adirondack chair, Matt suddenly appeared and stood towering over her. Liz's stomach tightened and she felt nauseous. Here we go, she thought. He could go crazy on me again. The fear on her face was obvious. She began looking around for the best way out.

"You have no idea what it's like at the Cafe these days. I should fire all the employees that you've coddled for years and start over with my own crew."

"The Cafe is ours, not yours," she said in a firm tone, overcoming her fear. "What is this sudden need to completely control everything?"

"I'm simply trying to do my job. I refuse to let Emily,

who is supposed to be running the restaurant, tell me how to run the music! She actually questioned my decisions about equipment rental for upcoming shows."

"Emily ran the music club when I was traveling for a month and did a good job. She has some understanding of what it takes. You seem a little over the top about her questions."

"It's unbelievable! Emily challenged my decision to rent a special sound system for the Charlie Harlow Banks show. She thinks I've been doing a terrible job for the last two months since you turned the booking of the musicians over to me."

"Wait a second, Matt."

"No. You wait. I'm not done talking yet! I will not be accused of making poor decisions by someone who works for me. She has no right to judge me. I'm the boss, not Emily!"

Matt was talking faster and louder. They had disagreed about personnel before, but it had never risen to this intensity.

"Actually, I was the one who was concerned you were going overboard for the Harlow Banks show," Liz said. "These recent, last-minute demands from their tour manager aren't in our contract. I mentioned it to Emily the other day after Charlie's sound man, Frank called me. I don't think we should pay for these extras. If they want a pricey sound system, the band needs to cover the cost. I've dealt with them over similar issues in the past."

"Why didn't I know that? What else are you keeping from me?" he sneered.

"I'm not intentionally keeping anything from you. Stop being so paranoid. I firmly pushed back and reminded

Frank of our contract. And I remembered to mention it to Emily, but I should have included you. Anyway, Frank is reasonable. He's simply conveying what Charlie wants. You could suggest they pay for the cost of renting an outside sound system versus using ours. When you present that option, they'll probably just back off. It will work out in the end. It generally does."

Leaning over her, resting both hands on either side of her chair, Matt scoffed, "I don't need your know-it-all, condescending attitude."

Feeling trapped, Liz panicked and tried to get up. She felt his fingers digging into her shoulders. He shook her hard until she fell back into the chair. He stopped abruptly, startled.

Taking a deep breath and stepping back, Matt's voice returned to a normal tone. "Is it too much to ask that you back me up and not always side with Emily? You never support me, Liz. Not with Charlie's guy or with our staff. You choose Emily over me every time and I'm sick of it!"

"That's not what I'm doing!" Liz's heart was beating so fast that she felt dizzy.

"I've had it! Don't you dare let Emily manipulate us. We're not her puppets. You don't get it, do you?"

Liz was sweating and her heart was pounding. She thought she would faint. The baby, the baby. Trying to get up again, she pushed Matt away as hard as she could. He closed in, gripping her shoulders until she cried out in pain. She couldn't overpower him and finally gave up. A smile slowly crossed his face, one she had never seen before. Triumphant and disdainful. When she tried to pull away again, he shoved her back into the chair. For a moment, he put his hands tightly around her throat, then stopped and pulled away. She gasped for air.

"Stay where you are until I tell you to get up. Don't act like I hurt you! That was nothing. It's the only way to get you to listen."

"Stop, Matt. You're scaring me!"

"Shut up! I'm done with the way you run the Cafe! It's a business, not a rich girl's hobby."

Liz was terrified. She had to think fast. How could she get out of the house before Matt hurt her and the baby?

Matt turned away to see if the neighbors had heard the commotion from the deck. When he didn't see anyone at the windows or outside, he turned back to Liz.

"You're right," she said in a slow, extraordinarily soothing voice. "I don't know what it's like at the Cafe these days. Now it's larger and more complicated. I was just running a mom and pop place before the expansion."

Matt didn't take his eyes off of Liz. "Do you really mean that?"

"Of course, I do. I know you have a lot to handle these days."

It was an Oscar-winning performance. At least he fell for it. After staring at her for several more seconds, his shoulders relaxed, and he plopped into a chair. It was as though he'd released all his craziness in a frenzy and run out of steam.

The next few minutes were critical. Liz thought fast. How to get away from him? "Matt, let me make us lunch. You must be exhausted."

He looked at her sheepishly. "I got kind of crazy there for a minute. I didn't mean to. I didn't think you were listening to me. I want things to be okay with us." His voice was softer now, conciliatory.

"Maybe it's the stress of the Cafe. Let's take a break. I'll get us some sandwiches and we'll talk some more." Liz rose from the chair slowly, heading toward the kitchen. Her mind was racing and her body was shaking.

She wondered if she should walk out the door and hope he wouldn't catch her before she reached the car. Where were her purse and keys? She went into the kitchen. As she opened the refrigerator door, another plan came to mind.

She called out, "Matt, I have to go out to the garage for another loaf of bread from the freezer. I'll be right back."

She grabbed her phone to text Drew, "Matt hurt me @ home-help." She returned to the deck with an iced cinnamon coffee and assured Matt that the grilled cheese and avocado sandwiches were almost done and lunch was on the way. As Liz handed him the drink, Matt looked up with tears in his eyes.

"Liz, I don't know what just happened. I said things that are just not me. I didn't mean to scare you. Forgive me! I promise it will never happen again."

With great effort, Liz smiled at him. Her only thought was the baby. "I don't know what to say, Matt. The person who walked through the front door today was not the Matt I know."

Matt started crying, bending over, holding his head in his hands. "I'm so sorry. I'm so sorry. Forgive me."

Liz sat in the chair across the table from him and touched his hand. He looked up at her. "It's okay, Matt."

"Is it? My father always told me I'd never amount to anything. Maybe I'll end up being a horrible father, just like he is."

"Don't let your father determine the kind of parent

you'll be. And you have amounted to something. We run a thriving business together."

Matt looked surprised. "Easy for you to say. My father's not in your head."

"I don't completely understand all the pressure you're under with the baby coming. But we can figure out how to make things go more smoothly at the Cafe. And Matt, it's not all up to you. It's not your sole responsibility to manage our personal lives and our business."

"I am responsible. You still don't understand, Liz." Matt's voice started rising again.

"I managed my life and business before you came along."

"Yet, you let Drew control your life for years and that was just fine!" Matt shouted.

"It was a totally different situation. I was an adolescent when Drew basically became my parent. He was doing the best he could to keep our lives together."

They heard the front door open. Drew appeared on the deck and rushed over to Liz.

"What are you doing here?" Matt asked, looking bewildered and jumping to his feet.

"Responding to Liz's text for help."

"You texted him?" Matt shouted. "Why would you do that?"

Liz took a deep breath, looking at Matt for several seconds. "When you shoved me, held me down in the chair, and began to choke me, I was afraid for the baby."

Drew stepped toward Matt, balling up his hands, ready to protect Liz.

"No, Drew. More violence is not the answer," Liz commanded. "All I want is to get out of here."

Drew took Liz's hand and walked toward the door. "Grab your purse and phone, Liz. Let's go!"

Matt looked at Liz with contempt. "Drew to the rescue! You'll never be truly committed to me. How am I supposed to be a good husband and father if you run to your brother at the slightest conflict?"

"You call that slight? You hurt me and for all I know injured our baby. These days, most of the time I'm scared of you. It's like the night at the Cafe when you pushed me. Who are you, Matt? I don't know anymore."

"Why the hell are you bringing up your accident? Do we have to go over this again and again? Your fall had nothing to do with me." Matt was seething.

"How about what just happened? Did you have nothing to do with that either? You held me down in the chair and grabbed me by the throat. I saw a terrifying look on your face when I gave in. So pleased with yourself."

As she grabbed her purse and phone off the table, Matt shouted, "You're not leaving this house. Sit back down! You're my wife and pregnant with my child. You can't leave."

Then he leered at Drew. "Get the hell out of my house. You have no right to be here."

"Liz and I either leave together or I'm calling the police," Drew dared, glaring at Matt.

As Matt stepped toward him, Drew yelled to get his attention, "Back off, Matt! I refuse to fight you."

"Yeah, like you were so peaceful at Hector's Burritos," jeered Matt.

"My childhood wasn't violent like yours. What you saw at Hector's Burritos is not who I am. When I heard you'd hurt my sister, I was pushed over the edge. But no more.

We're out of here. Don't try to stop us!"

Liz looked alarmed, fearing what Matt might do next. Drew noticed her lips quivering to hold back her tears. She ran out the front door, turning to see if Matt was following. Nearly falling down the stairs, she grabbed Drew's hand. Crossing the wet gravel to his car, she climbed into the front seat before they sped away.

Once they had crossed the Ferry Street Bridge, Liz took a deep breath and started to cry. "I need help, Drew. How could I let this happen to me?"

"We'll get through this, Liz. We survived Mom and Dad dying within less than a year of each other. We've survived pain and loss like no other. We'll get through this, too."

"Our parents' deaths happened to us. We had no choice. My relationship with Matt was my decision and my fault. How can I ever trust my judgment again?" Liz began to sob.

"Don't blame yourself. Maybe talking to Emily about all this could help."

"I've talked to her before about Matt. She even tried to warn me that abuse often starts or gets worse during pregnancy."

Drew pulled up to his house. As he unlocked the door, he said, "I know you hate how judgmental I've been about Matt. I'll back off. Let me know how you want to deal with this."

Hugging Drew tightly, she said, "Don't blame yourself for any of this. You saw things I couldn't until now. You are the best brother and couldn't possibly support me any more than you already do."

She walked into the living room, sat on the couch and put her feet up on the ottoman. Taking out her cell phone, she called Emily who answered in an agitated voice. "So, you've heard about my firing from Fran?"

"No, from Matt. He ran into Fran at the Cafe today and she asked to meet with him tomorrow. He guessed it was about his overspending. He was furious when he got home and got violent with me again."

"Liz, I'm so sorry this happened. We planned when Fran met with him that one of us would be home with you in case he blew up."

"Not your fault! Matt wanted me to side with him about firing you. When I refused, he shook me and began to strangle me, but Drew got me out."

"Where are you now? Are you in a safe place? I'll come right over!"

"I'm at Drew's. You don't need to come, Em. After what just happened, I need some rest. Can we talk in the morning?"

"Of course. This time he was violent because you were trying to help me. But we both know he could have easily exploded about something else and hurt you again."

"Sadly, you're absolutely right. I hate to say it. How did my life get to be such a mess?" The tears kept coming.

"Liz, I'll stop by tomorrow," Emily offered. "Be sure to keep the doors locked and don't let Matt in, no matter what he says. Your leaving makes him more dangerous, not less."

"I feel safe with Drew and his German Shepard, Boris. That dog is a serious wall of protection. I just need to quit shaking and get some sleep."

Liz hung up and turned, looking around for Drew. She expected him to be lurking closeby. When she couldn't see him, she frantically called out, "Drew, you there?" She saw him come up the porch steps with Boris.

"You're safe with us, Liz. No one gets by Boris."

"I was a little freaked out because I didn't know where you were."

He sat next to her on the couch and said, "I was giving you privacy to talk to Emily. Did it help?"

"Yeah. She was totally there for me. My great epiphany is that it's time for me to stop leaning on you."

The next afternoon Liz was sitting in Drew's backyard sipping a cup of mint tea when her phone rang. Guessing it was Matt, she didn't want to answer. When she checked the caller ID, she saw it was Natalie. She's going to try to intervene, Liz thought. After another ring, she answered.

"Thanks for picking up, Liz. I would understand if you didn't want to talk to me or any friend of Matt's. He told us what happened. No doubt the sanitized version, but enough for us to understand why you're at Drew's."

"I don't really want to talk about it, Natalie. Why did you call?"

"Matt asked if he can stay with us so you can go home. We agreed if he promised not to contact you in any way."

"I would really like to go home, but I wouldn't feel safe there alone."

"Understood. In any case, we'll have Matt move here today. He blames everyone else for his problems and grows angrier by the day. He needs a batterer's group. Knowing the history with his father, Marcus and I will support getting him help."

"Thanks for understanding. Sorry I was so rude when I picked up."

"Don't worry about it. You're doing what you need to do to protect yourself."

"Am I? Then, why do I keep giving Matt another chance? Someday I'll find the courage to walk out the door for good. It's getting closer by the day."

CHAPTER 24

Emily rushed over to the shelter. She had just texted Becca that she needed to talk before her shift started. She parked her car two blocks from the shelter as was the policy. In case someone she knew recognized her car, they might figure out the confidential shelter's location. All staff and volunteers followed suit. Emily grabbed her backpack and power walked over to the shelter, hoping to get 15 minutes with Becca before the shift change.

Becca was drinking a cup of coffee on the patio when Emily arrived. A second cup, steaming, was waiting for her. "You're the best girlfriend ever," Emily said quietly. They kept their personal relationship private to keep things professional at work.

"Hey, Em. Tell me what's going on. It sounded urgent."

"I know I shouldn't feel this way, but I feel responsible for Matt hurting Liz again. They fought over his firing me and her overturning his decision. She called last night to tell me what happened. This time he terrorized her more than getting physical with her."

"So, he's escalating. Damn! I was hoping Liz would leave or he would get help before things exploded again."

"Well, she's left now. She's staying at Drew's but is pretty shaken."

"Don't blame yourself. It's Matt who is the abuser. Anything can trigger it."

"If only I hadn't called him on his overspending." Becca's phone rang.

"Sorry. I've got to grab this one. It's on my work line."

"Becca, this is Amy on the crisis line. I want to forward a call from Molly, an old client of yours from Vancouver. Can you take it?"

"Of course. I'll pick up line one. Thanks, Amy."

"Molly, you there?"

"Hey Becca: I'm glad you're in. You said to call you anytime. Still okay to do that?"

"Of course. I'm always glad to hear from you. What's up?"

"It's about Danny. I need your help. He's trying to get back in my life and I don't know what to do."

"You updated me last time that he got probation and he's still living at your old house. Does he want you to come back?"

"Maybe. He gets to have visits with Jenny now, so I have to see him sometimes."

"How often?"

"He comes to Vancouver twice a month. We meet at the courthouse where I give him Jenny for the weekend. Then back on Monday morning to pick her up."

"How's that working out?"

"I guess it's okay. I feel nervous when I'm with him, though."

"What makes you nervous?"

"He's being really nice to me and is paying child support now, so that helps. But I feel weird around him, like any minute he could start screaming at me. He never hurt Jenny so I'm not worried about that part."

"It's not easy to trust him after what happened. You had to move to another state to get away from him."

"He's buying me gifts and lots of toys for Jenny, and Jason, too. Jason won't take them. He hates Danny. He says he's not his dad so why does he have to keep his presents. He wonders why I let him see Jenny at all."

"Jason was old enough to understand what Danny did to you. He terrified Jason, too. It was a scary night when we went out to get you."

"I'm hanging on by a thread, Becca. I'm working at a fast-food restaurant and can barely make the rent. They just passed me over for assistant manager. I miss my house out in the country. It's too hard to do this alone."

"Starting out in a new city and being a single parent is tough stuff."

"No kidding. Danny looks like he's getting his life together. He even joined AA and is trying to stay sober. He told me he's cleaning up his act so I'll come back. He's working for a friend of his who's a contractor, so he's got steady work again."

"So, it sounds like you're still scared of him, but tempted to try again?"

"I don't know what to do, Becca. I love volunteering at the shelter here, but it doesn't pay the bills. I don't know how much longer I can keep doing this alone."

"Remember to use your support system there. Are you still seeing your old friend from high school?"

"Yeah, she's helping me with childcare to give me a break a couple of times a week. We usually hang out together one night on the weekends. But I'm tired all the time. Lonely, too."

Jenny was crying in the background. Jason called out: "Mom, I think Jenny's hungry. When's dinner?"

"Becca, I better go. Thanks for listening to me. Don't be mad that Danny is looking good to me again."

"I'm not mad. Just be careful and stay in touch. You've come a long way. You're a strong woman. Things will get easier as Vancouver becomes more like home to you. Give it time.

"Thanks, Becca, I'll try."

"Call any time. I mean it."

CHAPTER 25

Once Matt was settled at the Bernstein's house, Natalie brought up the idea of trying a batterer intervention group. He didn't believe that he was abusive and assured them that once the baby was born, everything would go back to normal. He argued that business pressures and Liz's pregnancy had strained their marriage. After they convinced him that Liz might leave if he didn't, Matt reluctantly agreed to find a group.

After dinner, Matt took a bike ride along the Willamette River to clear his head. Within a couple of miles, he felt calmer as he watched the clear water ripple over the rocks into deep pools. Maybe this batterer group idea wasn't the worst. He sure didn't want to go back to Wisconsin after another failed marriage.

After doing the research, he found what looked like the most tolerable group. It was on the outskirts of Eugene in Veneta, 30 minutes west. The location was important because he didn't want to run into anyone he knew.

The following Thursday, Matt was on his way to his first group. As he turned off Highway 126 onto Applegate Court, he found the Veneta Counseling Center, a two-story blue Victorian with yellow trim. He walked in and told the receptionist that he was there for the group.

"The batterer intervention group?" she asked.

Matt looked around before answering, "Uh-huh. I guess so."

"Just go through that door and you'll see Pete and Renee in the room on the left."

"Thanks," Matt replied with a slight nod. He hesitated before going in, but the thought of losing Liz and his daughter forced him to walk down the hall.

As he entered the room, a short, middle-aged man with a slightly graying beard stood up and said, "Welcome. I'm Pete. I'm glad you could make it. This is Renee, our co-facilitator."

"Hi, Pete. I'm Matt," he replied, looking around the room. Five other men were sitting and sipping coffee. He was relieved that no one looked familiar.

"Help yourself to a cup of coffee or a glass of water," Pete said.

Matt went over and grabbed some coffee while looking at the books on the shelf above. All self-help crap, he thought.

As he joined the circle, three more men came in. Matt watched Pete and Renee greet each of them. He was amused by how much Pete looked like a caricature of a shrink. Renee, on the other hand, was several inches taller than Pete and had the body of an athlete. Not what he expected her to be like.

Once they had settled in, Pete took the lead. "As I hope

you all know, our meeting today is an introduction to a 26-week group series. Renee and I are here to answer any questions you have. Let's start with introductions. Just to be clear, even during this introductory group, everything is confidential. So, just use your first names to protect everyone's privacy."

Each of the men introduced himself in equally brief and uneasy ways without looking around the room. Pete nodded and said, "Thank you. I used to meet with each participant individually before the first group but discovered that by everyone hearing the same thing at the same time, your expectations are clearer. Any questions before I give you my overview?"

The room was silent. Pete continued, "First, I want to make clear that this is not a counseling or therapy group. It is a class in which you can learn how to end abusive and violent behaviors. The goal is for you to understand how to have equal and healthy relationships."

Renee cast a glance around the group and said, "Pete, how about if we go around the circle first and hear from everyone about what brought them here." Matt was the last to share. He thought it was interesting that of nine men in the room, only he and one other had not been court mandated to attend. While wondering what they had done to end up in court, he recalled his mother's bruises and broken bones.

Matt said, "My wife blames me for a broken wrist when she slipped and fell during a chaotic moment at our business. I barely touched her. My best friends convinced me that I would lose her if I didn't come here. So, here I am." He noticed that three of the men began to chuckle.

"What's so funny?" Matt asked angrily.

"Oh, nothing. I've just heard that excuse before," Joe chided. "This is my second time in a group like this. It takes more than once for some of us to meet the bar set by the courts."

"Slow learner, huh?" Matt retorted.

"Okay. Okay," Pete said. "Keep in mind that being respectful is one of our group rules. You're here so you can each look at how your actions have hurt your relationships and how to have healthy ones. As you get to know and trust each other, please question each other respectfully. Joe, the remark that you made to Matt wasn't helpful. Because this is your second time around, you know how hard this is."

"Sorry," Joe said. "It's just that it's rare for men who aren't court-mandated to finish the group. You and the other guy who isn't forced to come will probably drop out and the rest of us will be stuck here. I'll give you one thing though. At least you have the brains to come here before you end up in court. That's something."

"Maybe I should just leave now," Matt responded, quickly discouraged.

Renee broke in. "You could give up right now but I can tell you it's impossible to stop being violent on your own. You think you can, but you can't. Trust me."

"It's true, Matt. After I finished the last session with these guys, I finally caught onto what this is all about."

"Thanks, Joe," Renee said, smiling at him and then at Matt. "It takes a lot of strength to decide to make such a huge change. You're definitely someone who is willing to take the risk."

"Yeah. Well, we'll see," Joe said, looking down at his lap.

"Actually, this exchange between Joe and Matt has been helpful. It gives you an idea of how our group works," Pete said. "We hope that you will be as honest as Joe has been. We'll give you information about different kinds of abusive behaviors but we won't be lecturing you. You'll spend most of the time talking with each other to draw your own conclusions."

Matt almost left but decided to stay so Natalie and Marcus would know that he gave it a chance and tell Liz. He sat back and looked at the other men. Some were still in their work clothes from the local lumber mill or a fast-food restaurant. Others obviously had come from offices.

After Pete finished describing how the group would work, he handed out the necessary paperwork. Matt filled out the forms but chose not to fill out an information release, designating a therapist, the courts, family or friends. He didn't want Liz or Marcus to be able to call Pete to check on how he was doing. Especially since he had no intention of coming back.

As he started to walk out, Renee came up to him. "I hope to see you next week. No one asked today, but I know the participants wonder why a woman is here. I survived and eventually left a violent relationship. Some participants find my perspective helpful."

Matt looked at her and thought of his mother. "How did you get out?" Matt asked before he could stop himself.

"My kids. First, I was afraid of losing our financial security. Then, I realized the emotional damage was much worse than not having a fancy house and a private school education."

"Sounds like my mom," Matt said, wondering why he kept responding when he knew he wasn't coming back.

"There are so many different stories. You will hear some of them in the group. Your understanding of what happened to your mom will make it much easier for you. Come back next week and give this another chance. You strike me as a guy who will figure this out."

"Huh, never thought of it that way. I can't relate to the batterer part. I feel like I've just been too hot-headed these days and have done some stupid things. I'm not the batterer or abuser you talk about in this group. Thanks for what you said about your own life. It helps."

"Maybe the way to look at the group is that you're working hard not to become a batterer," Renee responded.

As he got in his car, Matt stopped for a moment and let Renee's last remark sink in. He might consider coming back.

When Matt got back to the Cafe, he saw Marcus waiting for him at one of the tables in the back. As he approached, Marcus called out, "Hey, I got you a Black Butte Porter."

"I need to get to work, but I can sit for a minute. How's life?"

"Good. The big question is how was the group?"

"It was a little weird. It was a bunch of guys who were forced to be there by the courts. Some have been through the group more than once. These guys are doing really scary stuff. Not sure how well I fit in."

"Hmm...I'm glad that you went, though. You have such a good thing with Liz. Don't blow it," Marcus said.

"Well, I might try it again even though I think Liz and I could work things out ourselves. If only you could see the losers who are there. I'm not like them. Though some of them remind me of my father. Oddly, Renee, one of the facilitators, reminds me of my mom."

"Is that good or bad?" Marcus asked, taking a sip of his beer.

"It's good, mostly. But, I don't have time to talk about it now. Maybe tomorrow at breakfast, unless you're still awake when I get to your place tonight? Thanks for the beer." Matt got up and headed to the front desk to greet customers.

Marcus sighed and gulped down the rest of his beer. When he got to his car, he called Natalie "Hey Nat, I wouldn't put money on Matt sticking with the group."

"If he doesn't, I think that Liz should get out of town fast," Natalie replied.

CHAPTER 26

When Liz got the call from Natalie describing Matt's indifference to the batterers' group, she was relieved that she had already made plans to go to the coast for the weekend. The women who had been affected by Quinn's life of violence were gathering to connect and have a virtual meeting with Ade. The way the five women's lives overlapped had possibilities for both bonding and conflict.

Liz and Emily planned to arrive at the vacation rental in Yachats in time for lunch so they picked up shrimp salad sandwiches on the way. Leaving Eugene early, they had time to stop at their favorite viewpoint, Cape Perpetua, the highest point on the Oregon coast. The view to the north through the moss-covered evergreen trees was spectacular. They could see several beaches in the far distance. Waves were crashing on the sand in a pounding, rhythmic way that made Liz and Emily take deep breaths and relax into the pulse of the surf. When they looked west out onto the Pacific Ocean, the dark blue sky was framed by bright, wispy white clouds on the distant horizon. It was one of those magical days at the Oregon coast when the sun was shining and the breeze was soft.

As they drove down the narrow road from Perpetua and along Highway 101 to Yachats, Liz said, "I'm glad you talked me into coming for the weekend, Em. Although, I'm a little nervous about what to expect. Especially meeting Matt's first wife."

"Hard to know the etiquette around that! I get why you're nervous considering all that's happened with Matt. This entire weekend has the potential of being emotional and overwhelming."

"I'm glad that Becca arranged this gathering. It will give Anne, Rachel and me a chance–to talk about how Quinn has wreaked havoc in our lives." Liz shook her head as she contemplated her round belly.

"He seems a bit of an expert at it. That's for sure," Emily confirmed sarcastically.

Liz slowed and pulled off the highway into the parking lot at Devil's Churn. "Let's wait until the others arrive to dig into this more. It's the perfect day to just relax and appreciate where we are."

Emily jumped out of the car, yelling, "Let's get soaked!"

They stood by the edge of Devil's Churn where the powerful waves had carved a rugged inlet. A series of waves came toward them, crashing against the rocks, one after the other, spewing water up into the air. They jumped back laughing to avoid the soaking that Emily had predicted. After being mesmerized by the surging waves, they ran back to the car and drove along the winding roads of the high cliffs of Highway 101.

Thanks to Becca's directions, they found the house easily. One of the board members at Jill's Place owned it and allowed staff to use it several times a year. The owner had worked in a domestic violence program before becoming a lawyer and understood how exhausting the work was. She was well aware that the staff couldn't afford the luxury of a weekend at a beach house.

When Emily and Liz entered the house, they could see the beach and surf across three large spaces which included the open kitchen, dining room and living room. They looked at each other and laughed in amazement.

"I had no idea it would be this beautiful," Emily said. "Becca assured me it wasn't just a simple cabin at the ocean, but this? Good score!"

"Let's check it out," Liz said, walking through the cedar-beamed living and dining room. There were three bedrooms on the second floor, each with a view. With the bunk beds and a sleeping porch, the house could accommodate eight people. Since they had arrived first, they chose their bedrooms and unpacked. After eating their shrimp sandwiches, Liz laid down for a nap while Emily settled into a comfortable chair to read Kate Walbert's short novel, *His Favorites*. Since the *New York Times* review called it the first novel of the #MeToo movement, Emily thought it was timely for this weekend.

Becca and Anne arrived in the late afternoon with groceries. When Emily heard the car pull up, she ran out to greet them and gave Becca a long hug.

"Em, meet my sister, Anne. See the family resemblance?" Becca put her cheek against Anne's for full effect.

"You could definitely be picked out as sisters in a line-up should you ever decide to step over the line together,"

Emily said with a laugh.

Anne teasingly poked Becca's shoulder and said, "Great to meet you, Emily. Becca told me a lot about you on the way over. One foot at Jill's Place and the other at the Shady Grove Cafe."

"Never a dull moment," Emily responded, giving Becca a poke on her other shoulder. Emily and Anne laughed while Becca rolled her eyes.

"Welcome, welcome," Liz shouted from the upper deck.

As they came in, Liz walked down the stairs and directly over to Anne, holding out her hand. "I'm so glad you could make it, You're somewhat of a mystery woman to me."

"Well, I won't be after this weekend. Thanks for including me," Anne replied.

"Hey, Rachel just pulled up. Let's welcome her."

As Rachel got out of the car, she grumbled, "As usual, the traffic out of Portland was a mess. Sorry if I'm late."

"You're fine," Liz said. "Let me introduce you to this motley crew." They all laughed.

While Rachel was getting settled, Liz filled a glass with sparkling water and lime while the others poured glasses of wine. After going out on the deck to watch the sunset over the ocean, they made a fresh seafood dinner with salmon they picked up at the wharf. The chatter flowed easily as they got to know each other before delving into the hard conversation ahead.

As they sat down in the living room to deal with the numerous elephants in the room, Liz said, "First, thanks, Becca, for bringing us together."

"Glad to do it. We're fierce women with tough stories

to tell," replied Becca.

"The sound of the waves should keep us all grounded," added Emily.

"I love the size of this house. Chances are we'll each have moments when we need to get away and sort things out," said Liz.

"Becca is a born leader. She facilitated many family meetings when we were growing up, not to mention in her professional life," explained Anne. "Why don't you get us started?"

Becca looked over at the group, sprawled across two couches and an overstuffed chair. When they nodded in agreement, she began. "The first issue is Quinn Foley and how he has affected so many lives in this room."

Anne jumped in. "Quinn's sexual harassment and assault of women has to be stopped. He has abused women in his family, at work, and even in his social circle. Let's use the #MeToo movement to expose him." Nods again around the table.

"My ultimate goal is that he goes to prison for all he's done. This might not be realistic," Becca said.

"If nothing else, we could derail his chance to become governor," added Liz.

"Could we pull it off as a group? Or do we have too much going on in our personal lives to make something that big happen?" interjected Rachel.

"If I can speak for the group, we wouldn't all be here if we didn't want to take this on," responded Becca. A chorus of "Yeses" followed.

"Liz, since Matt is involved, how will this affect him if we go after his father?" asked Anne.

"I can only speculate. He could easily react violently to

whatever we come up with here."

"Like what?" asked Becca.

"We'd be challenging the deal he made for his father to keep Rachel quiet." Liz reasoned.

Rachel jumped in, "Don't forget Matt went to bat for me, to help get the best deal possible. The non-disclosure agreement stops me from getting Quinn for what he did."

Becca said, "We realize that, Rachel. Maybe we can prove to Matt how despicable Quinn is and he'll stop glorifying him. He'd realize that he doesn't need to repeat his father's mistakes. His choice."

"We certainly have evidence against Quinn," Anne said. "Ade is searching for more victims. We could ask our cousin if she would come forward after all this time. She could tell about Quinn sexually assaulting her during her sister's wedding five years ago. He invited her for drinks at an oceanfront bar and attacked her in a public place. When she began to scream for help, Quinn covered her mouth to silence her, but their server came out and stopped the assault."

"Your cousin could add to the others' testimony showing a pattern of assault over time," Emily said with a look of disgust.

When Becca saw agreement around the table, she said, "I'll call her. Like so many of Quinn's assaults, there was no physical evidence so she didn't pursue it."

"Now's the time to tell my Quinn horror story," Anne said. "Most of you already know that my father-in-law attacked me, but now you need to hear the details. It happened four years ago when Matt was at a law conference in Chicago. Quinn unexpectedly showed up at our apartment after having drinks with friends. It was right about the time I had decided to leave Matt because I was tired of him watching my every move. I was feeling more and more isolated. He was cutting me off from my friends, one by one. I could sense he was on the verge of physically hurting me again."

When Anne hesitated, Liz said, "I get it, Anne. If it's too much, you can stop."

"No. I want all of you to know the whole story. When I cracked open the door to tell Quinn it was too late for a visit, he started to taunt me. He went into a garbled, drunken tirade, 'I know you've always wanted to sleep with me. I've seen the way you look at me.' I was terrified. He managed to push past me to get inside. When he put his arms around me, I pushed him away and screamed, 'Get out!' When he wouldn't, I started yelling for help and pounding his chest, hoping the neighbors would hear. He grabbed me, threw me on the couch and raped me." Anne burst into tears. Continuing to sob, she said, "Afterwards, he actually referred to it as 'rough, passionate sex.'"

When she looked up, she saw only sympathetic eyes around her. Becca moved closer to her on the couch and hugged her tightly until she stopped crying.

Anne continued, "I can't tell you how guilty I feel for being silent for so long. I wonder how many more women he's assaulted since me."

"Survivors' guilt is the hardest thing to work through," cautioned Becca. "Rape victims do what they can to survive. You left town in fear of Quinn. You were also ready to leave Matt."

"I was trapped in a dangerous marriage. I had no choice but to leave and start over. It took me a long time to build a relationship with Evan."

Liz interrupted, jolted by Anne's story. "I need to stop. I have to sort out what I just heard. Can we wait until tomorrow to work more on the plan?"

"You're right. This has been an emotional day." Becca said.

CHAPTER 27

When Liz got up the next morning, Anne was drinking coffee and reading the *New York Times* on her iPad. Becca and Emily were out taking an early morning run on the beach. Rachel was taking a shower.

"How did you sleep, Anne?" asked Liz as she made herself a cup of tea.

As Anne walked over to the cupboard and emptied some granola into a small bowl, she said, "Not too well. Talking about Quinn pretty much drained the life out of me."

"He's worse than I ever imagined."

"I could barely get out of bed this morning. The last thing I need is to fall into a severe depression again."

"What a horrifying experience. I'm sorry, Anne."

"It was awful. I unraveled for a couple of years. Meeting you makes me feel guilty. I could have warned you about what you were getting yourself into by marrying Matt."

"I doubt that first wives have a whole lot to do with the second unless there are kids."

"We definitely have a weird kinship. My therapist would call it trauma bonding."

"Makes sense. We share the damage of the Foley family."

"Has Matt hurt you yet?"

"It's killing me that you already guessed. Is it that obvious?"

"Some things you said last night tipped me off. Like that if he found out about this meeting, he could get violent."

"Last night when you talked about being afraid of Matt, it shook me up. Since you know Matt more than anyone else, I could use some advice."

"Ask me anything."

After a long hesitation, Liz blurted it out, "Am I being stupid to stay with Matt? If he hurts me again, I could lose this baby!"

Anne responded slowly. "I want to help you. I don't think you can be involved in this while living with Matt."

"That's where I'm leaning. I've been reading online about domestic violence. So, I know when a woman leaves she's in the most danger. It's when we're most likely to be killed."

"It's terrifying to think that could happen to you. By the time I left Matt, it was too late to make the marriage work. I wasn't sure what he might do next. After what Quinn did to me, I had to get out fast!"

"I'm not sure what Matt is capable of. His need to control me is so strong. And it sounds like he was the same with you. He learned well from his father. It's hard to believe Matt could change anytime soon."

Anne waited a moment to make sure Liz had finished before responding. "If you're asking me if I think he will change, I can't answer that. I left because I didn't want to wait to find out. I'd go with your gut feeling. It's a good idea to live separately for now. Don't let him see you alone."

"That says a lot about how dangerous you think he is. I feel stupid for marrying a man who I barely knew. How long did it take you to realize you'd made a mistake?"

Anne stood up and began pacing. "I thought I'd blown it and picked the wrong guy about two years in. The emotional abuse got to me. The physical abuse was just beginning. Between Quinn and Matt, it's been hard for me to trust men. Evan can feel it. I can't seem to put those experiences behind me. Sometimes I'm afraid I'll never get over it."

Liz walked over to the window near Anne. The pacing stopped. They looked at each other and nodded, acknowledging their connection. "Do you mind?" Liz asked as she moved closer to Anne.

"No."

Liz put her arm gently around Anne's shoulder. They both began to cry.

Anne and Liz pulled apart when they heard Rachel coming down the stairs. At the same time, they heard a blast of laughter on the deck. Becca and Emily were about to come into the house, still breathing heavily from their run and glowing with exhilaration. Emily poked her head into the kitchen. "We're going to take a quick look at the tide pools before we come in for breakfast. Back in ten minutes."

"Coffee's on when you get back, you two lovebirds!" said Anne.

As they walked down to the beach, Emily's expression turned serious.

"You look gloomy all of a sudden. What's up?" asked Becca.

"We're about to do this heavy-duty meeting with Ade and the gang. We're bound to hit on the age-old question: why do battered women stay? I'm worried that Liz will feel ashamed for staying with Matt. Aren't you?"

Becca sighed. "Yeah. It's going to push buttons for Liz, and for Anne, too. I wish the question was: why do batterers hurt women they love?"

"So, why did Anne leave after a couple of years and it took Joanne well over a decade to divorce Quinn? I wonder if Liz can handle that conversation."

"Well Em, we can reassure her that leaving takes courage. We need to support her to make the decision that's right for her."

"She's likely to ask what's wrong with her. We can tell her what we've learned from doing the work. She's right to be afraid of what Matt will do if she goes."

"There are classic reasons why women stay. You've told me that Liz isn't the confident, take-charge woman that you once knew. The physical and emotional abuse have already taken their toll," Becca noted.

"And the baby coming is a built-in trap to stay for the sake of the family. I think Liz still loves him. Maybe she believes Matt can go back to being the man she fell in love with that first day at the Cafe," said Emily.

"Why don't you talk to Liz? Encourage her to leave the group if it's too much. She can talk to you privately if she needs to," added Becca as they strolled back to the beach house.

"One more thing. I have some surprising news from Molly."

"Please don't tell me she went back to Danny. Remember she had left him three or four times before we brought her to the shelter last year. I thought she was gone for good this time."

Becca walked toward a huge rock. "Let's stop and sit. It's a long story." Emily put her jacket on the wet rock. They huddled close together in the wind.

"For the past several months, Danny has been the perfect former abuser."

"Oh, like an extended honeymoon stage. Doing and saying all the right things."

"Exactly. So, Molly forced Jason to come along to drop Jenny off for the weekend with Danny. Jason made a scene. Holding tightly onto his mom, he told Danny to stay away from them."

"From the mouths of babes," Emily said.

"Danny screamed at Jason and tried to pull him away from his mother. Molly yelled at Danny to not touch her son. She told him she had a final answer for him. She would never go back to him, ever."

"Go, Molly!"

"Danny laughed at her. He told her he could care less. In fact, he would only be able to see Jenny once every couple of months, since his work was relocating him to Roseberg. His new girlfriend was moving there with him. Looking relieved, Molly told him that he needed to be out of her house by the end of the month because she had found a realtor and was selling it."

"I love this ending."

"It gets better. Molly has turned in her fast-food uniform because she got the Advocacy Coordinator job at the shelter. I think that gave her the strength to move on."

"Best of all, Jason got to witness his mother standing up to Danny and walking away. In light of this weekend at the coast, Molly's bravery gives me hope."

X

After a quick breakfast, the group sat around the dining room table and began to design a plan of action. They each took an aspect of the #MeToo movement to research, pulled out their laptops and went to work. Within two hours, they had made enough progress to regroup and report what they had discovered in time for the Zoom meeting with Ade.

When Ade joined the meeting, she began, "I'm so glad we're all here, Rachel. Thanks for the list of everyone here and their relationships to Quinn Foley. Why don't you each tell me your name?"

After introductions, Rachel said, "Ade, tell us what you've uncovered so far and what you need from us."

"I understand some of you are experts and others are survivors," Ade said. "During our investigation, we found more women who were assaulted. We aren't sure if all of them will testify against him. We have also found women and men who claim he is a strong activist lawyer who has done good work. They were shocked by the accusations. They could easily testify as character witnesses for him."

"No surprise," Becca said. "We know that many

abusive men are charismatic and admired. Quinn is no exception. It's true that he's done good work in the world to fight racism for people like Willie Wyatt. Thanks to Quinn, he got the settlement he deserved. It still doesn't diminish his long history of sexism and violence against women in his personal and work lives."

Ade described what she'd unearthed in her investigation, including women who had been assaulted and left their jobs quietly, without making any accusations. Others complained to Human Resources or to senior partners in their firms, but without results. Most were office support staff or law clerks who assumed they wouldn't be believed. Those higher up, the newer associates, were afraid it would hurt their careers.

"Ade, I have something else to tell you that only some of the women in this room know," Anne said in a quiet voice. "I'm willing to testify if it would strengthen this case."

"What is it?"

After a long hesitation, Anne blurted out, "I was raped by Quinn Foley, got pregnant, and had an abortion."

"Even after hearing this from so many women, it still breaks my heart," Ade said, looking earnestly at her through the screen. "Honestly, Anne, saying this to me, a total stranger, gives you some idea of how it might feel to say it in a courtroom. If you decide not to, I totally understand. Give it some serious thought."

"It has been a tough time," responded Anne. "The therapist I saw when I first moved to Montreal got me through the worst of it. Eventually, I couldn't stand to talk or think about it anymore, so I stopped seeing her. When Evan and I got together, I joined a support group because

I still was having trouble trusting men. Maybe going after Quinn will help me."

"It might. Some women who survive rape find confronting their abuser healing," Emily said.

Ade continued, "We need to find as many women as we can who have been assaulted by Judge Foley. I have alerted programs in Wisconsin to see if they would be willing to identify clients who were his victims. If their agency policy allows, I will ask them to contact the victims to find out if they are willing to talk with me."

"Can we help with that?" asked Emily.

"No, it should come from my agency. My staff will interview each of them. We'll start at the sexual assault program at the University of Wisconsin."

Becca jumped in, "Even though we didn't include Joanne at this gathering, she's offered to help in other ways. Should someone follow up with her to get names of other victims he assaulted during their marriage? Who knows what we'd find?"

"Good idea," Ade said. "I'll call Joanne. Our staff has already found nine other victims."

After an hour-long conversation, more items were added to the list. Becca would work with Liz and Anne to develop safety plans since they were worried about retribution from Matt and Quinn. Anne would contact the hospital medical records in Madison for her rape kit results and the abortion clinic for her medical records and DNA. They all agreed to send Ade an update within one week so she could create an agenda for their next conference call.

"It feels like we've moved the boulder a couple of inches today," said Becca.

"Just you wait and see. By the time Quinn faces his victims in court, we'll feel like we've moved it miles and miles," replied Ade.

CHAPTER 28

When Ade followed up, Joanne gave her a journal she had kept with names of Quinn's accusers. Each time Quinn came home annoyed by another complaint of harassment by a colleague or subordinate, Joanne documented it. She pretended to join in Quinn's frustration, convincing him that she shared his outrage at such unfair allegations.

Quinn believed these women were misinterpreting what was meant to be camaraderie. Men traditionally create friendships and long-term connections in the office that they rely on later in their professional lives. It wasn't his fault women misread his behavior as harassing. Joanne recalled some women demanded a transfer to a different lawyer in Quinn's firm or left the firm. Some left on the condition the firm provide positive references for potential employers.

By the time Ade Coleman completed her investigation, she had conducted in-depth interviews with Quinn's many victims. They included Anne and ten others from Quinn's workplaces. Joanne was a source for three of them.

When the Go Girls Investigations' lawyer reviewed Rachel's non-disclosure agreement, it was confirmed that no information about the hotel incident could be shared. Yet, Rachel remained involved in the "Get Quinn Project" and financially supported the investigation with some of her settlement funds.

Ade discovered that Quinn's assaults did not stop when he became a judge. From his current service in circuit court, Ade's team uncovered two young lawyers who had clerked for him and a paralegal who had all been assaulted.

When Ade's team completed their interviews, they discovered that Quinn's pattern of abuse involved getting the women alone while working late. He would touch them inappropriately, verbally harass them, or force himself on them. Most of the women felt that they had no choice. When they tried to fight him off, he threatened to get them fired or give a bad review if they reported him. For the ones who took the risk and filed complaints, Human Resources treated it as a "he said, she said" scenario. This resulted in no actions against him. Fortunately, some had kept copies of their complaints. Ade used this evidence in her report.

Some shared the details with family, friends or a counselor. Two of the women left the field completely because of the system's failure to respond. They were both willing to testify in court if needed. Ade suggested they sue for damages to cover their lost wages.

"We have written victim affidavits and complaints to HR as well as therapy notes released with permission. It's substantial evidence and highly believable," assured Ade.

Two approaches emerged, legal and political. The legal approach was for those assaults within the statute of limitations. These women were given names of attorneys who could aid them in civil suits or get the D.A. to file criminal charges where adequate evidence existed. The civil suits could recover damages for emotional trauma and/or lost wages.

The political strategy was to present the Foley Investigative Report to the Democratic Party of Wisconsin (DPW). The Party was interviewing candidates before selecting their final endorsement.

Ade assured the "Get Quinn Group" that sufficient evidence existed to convince the Party to drop Quinn and endorse his opponent, Isabella Sanchez. She had interned in Washington, D.C. for a prominent women's rights attorney and helped get national legislation passed. Sanchez was a strong choice since she had been Wisconsin's Attorney General for the past four years and was former vice-chair of the DPW.

Ade sent her report to Mary Berg, the DPW chair who was shocked their vetting process hadn't unearthed Quinn's long history of assault and harassment. In a subsequent meeting, she lectured the Cabinet that ignoring or hiding sexual allegations through payoffs and threats was over. Survivors of sexual violence had come forward in the entertainment industry, government, media, the Catholic Church, schools, and sports. They needed to endorse a candidate who was beyond reproach. Quinn would be under extreme scrutiny. Sanchez had a clean record and polls showed she had a good shot at unseating the incumbent conservative Republican.

Ade explained in a Q & A with the Cabinet that a recent

victim in Oregon was paid off, possibly with campaign funds as hush money to prevent her from coming forward. Through information from Liz, Ade easily verified Rachel's receipt of the money, substantiating the payment. She hired a forensic accountant to trace it back to the campaign.

When Ade completed her oral summary with the five members of the Cabinet, there was only one voice that strongly defended Quinn Foley's integrity and demanded more evidence. It was the First Vice-Chair of the DPW, Rick Matz, a law school classmate of Foley's. He mentioned his wife had stayed connected with Joanne Zimmer, Judge Foley's ex-wife who might be a source of information.

"Rick, please give her a call and report back to us tomorrow," Mary requested. "We need to inform Foley and Sanchez who we'll endorse by Tuesday. Will your history with Judge Foley be a barrier to your objectivity?"

"No, I simply want what's best for the Party. Since my relationship with Quinn is strictly professional these days, there should be no problem."

The board was eager to have Rick contact Joanne Zimmer. She was not only Quinn's ex-wife but also the director of a top women's legal advocacy center.

"If anyone else wants to contact Joanne, I'll step aside. I will say that based on my knowledge of Quinn, I assume the report is a sham, but I'll bring back whatever I uncover." No one accepted Rick's offer to take over the task.

After the special session ended, Rick returned to his office and phoned his wife.

"Olivia, do you have Joanne Zimmer's number? I need to check with her about some old history for the Party. I want to squelch some nasty rumors about Quinn."

"Come on, Rick. You and I both know that if it has anything to do with 'nasty' about your old friend, Quinn, it's probably true. You're definitely not Joanne's best friend, as I recall. Didn't Quinn ask you to advise him on the best approach to win joint custody of their son? He wanted to stop Joanne from moving to Chicago."

"I don't remember why Quinn gave up on the custody battle, Olivia," Rick said abruptly. He was tired and rubbing his temples.

"I do. He relented when she threatened to get a restraining order and charge him for assault. Honestly, Rick, do you think she'll be willing to talk to you? You sided with Quinn when he consistently denied his affairs and the violence in their marriage."

"I'm sure Joanne knew I was simply advising Quinn as a friend and nothing more. Quinn claimed Joanne wanted a divorce due to irreconcilable differences. I assumed his authoritarian style made the relationship unbearable for her. I don't believe his personal life informed his professional one. Anyway, that was all a long time ago."

"Don't be so sure," warned Olivia.

"Remember last summer? I worked with Joanne's advocacy center on a pro bono case where the victim was from Wisconsin and survived a near-death beating from her boyfriend. He held her captive for two days. Joanne wrote me an appreciative note when we won and the boyfriend ended up with a seven-year prison sentence."

"Your professional relationship might be fine, but Joanne will never forget how you crossed her. Fortunately, Quinn backed down so Joanne was able to move out of state without a custody battle. Her own domestic violence experience is perfect material for novels. Graphic, dangerous and life-threatening. Quinn controlled her every move. If you're really interested, I'll tell you the real Quinn and Joanne story over dinner. Good luck with your call. You'll need it. I'll text you her number."

"Thanks for the warning. I'll call Joanne before I meet you at 7:30 at the restaurant. I've got to take another call now. Bye."

Joanne was driving home when Rick's call came through on her speakers. "Hi Rick! What's up? You've caught me on my way home to change before giving a keynote at a fundraiser."

"I'll just need a few minutes of your time."

"If it's work, can I get back to you in the morning?"

"It's not work-related, Joanne. It's about the Democratic Party. I've been assigned to ask you some questions related to Quinn. Can we talk while you drive?"

"I'd rather pull over and call you back. I only have ten minutes to spare."

Joanne was furious by the time she called Rick back. Once she confirmed that the summary report was accurate, she laid into Rick, "You know better than anyone there was nothing false, exaggerated or vengeful on the part of the accusers."

"You're assuming that I know details about Quinn's private life."

"All I know is you ignored Quinn's brutality for years and continued your friendship with him. You did nothing to call Quinn out on his treatment of women in your office. That makes you complicit in my book. Show some integrity. Tell the committee you support the report and to drop the endorsement."

"Okay. I hear you, loud and clear. I looked the other way and I shouldn't have."

"Someone has got to stop him and you can be that someone, Rick!"

He had a lot to think over.

When Rick met Olivia for dinner, she gave him more detail on how harrowing life was for Joanne and her son. The fact that Matt was arrested for defending his mother with a knife convinced Rick that he had to act. When he got home, Rick called Quinn who immediately ignored his greeting. "Rick, I'm glad you phoned. I have a meeting with the DPW Executive Committee in two days and want your advice."

"I definitely have some advice for you, Quinn."

"Great! I knew that I could count on you. Tell me how I can get Lyle Oliver to challenge the accusations in the investigator's report. It's all lies and exaggerations anyway. I'm so sick of this!"

"What are you talking about, Quinn?"

"Don't play dumb with me, Rick. I have my sources. We've got to put the direct blame back on the 'supposed' victims. You've helped me in awkward situations like this before. I know you have the list of accusers with their complaints. It's the usual fake allegations professional men face these days, whether on the left or right. Now, I'm being targeted. Tell me I can count on you to back me up."

"You know that ethically I can't disclose that information, Quinn."

"Come on, Rick. We've been part of the same brotherhood since law school. Give me a break. I have to be prepared for this meeting so I can hold onto the Party's endorsement."

Now Rick was the one who was furious. He had been shocked by Olivia's gory details of Quinn's marriage. "Quinn, I won't help you lie and cover your ass. Too many of us have done that for years. Looks like it's finally caught up with you. You're on your own, buddy. I'm done."

"You'll be sorry when I'm governor, Rick. I'll have the power to pardon or commute sentences. I had planned to pardon your nephew, the one with the long drug trafficking sentence. You can forget about that!"

"Olivia was right. You're a loser! Your ambitious political career will take a dive after the Cabinet meets. Your days of power are numbered, Judge Foley!"

CHAPTER 29

When Becca got the group email from Ade about her presentation to the Democratic Party Cabinet, she phoned Liz.

"Did you see Ade's update? After she presented her final report to the Cabinet, they postponed who to endorse until Tuesday. If they choose Isabella Sanchez over Quinn, Matt might figure out that you're involved."

"Should I tell Matt the truth or just get out of here?"

"Your call!"

"If he hurts me, he hurts the baby."

"Then you've answered your own question. Yes. Leave right away to protect both of you. Should I come by and take you somewhere safe?"

"Marcus and Natalie are keeping an eye on Matt, but there's nothing to stop him from coming over here. Maybe I should go to Drew's again?"

"Nope. Drew's or Sophie's would be the first places he'd look. You need to go somewhere Matt wouldn't guess."

"There's Sophie's brother, Adam, who lives in Creswell. I'm sure he'd let me stay in the small cabin behind his house. He's a writer who uses the cabin for writer workshops so it's mostly empty. Adam is almost always home unless he's out fly fishing on the river. Besides, it's only fifteen minutes to the hospital from there. Since I'm due soon, I have to think about that. Best of all, Matt has never met Adam. He's pretty much a recluse. There's no way Matt would know where he lives."

"Sounds like you've discussed this possibility with Sophie before."

"I have, for obvious reasons."

"It's not just Matt I'd be afraid of. Quinn could send someone to keep you quiet and anyone else he suspects. He has a long history of silencing people," Becca warned.

Within half an hour, Liz asked Sophie to get Adam's okay.

"It's a go, Liz," Sophie confirmed.

"Could you drive me down to Adam's so I can leave my car in our driveway? Then Matt won't suspect I'm gone when he drives by."

By the time Liz had packed her "go to the hospital bag" along with other basic necessities, Sophie arrived and they headed out to the cabin.

The next several days went smoothly. Matt did text Liz to ask how she was doing. She let him know she was taking good care of herself and taking long walks for exercise. She told him she was in and out some nights, sometimes staying with friends. Emily and Ira agreed to a cover story about her whereabouts.

The following week, Liz went for a check-up at her obstetrician's near the University District. She thought about asking a friend to come along, but decided she didn't need to. She borrowed Adam's car and drove into town avoiding places where Matt was likely to be. As she left the clinic parking lot after the appointment, she turned right onto Hilyard Street and pulled over to call Sophie.

"I just saw a car that looked like Matt's, but maybe I'm just being paranoid. He's always at the Cafe this time of day."

"That's creepy. Keep moving and check your rearview mirror. I'll text Adam and make sure he's around when you get home. He's usually out for a run in the afternoons. If you think Matt's following you, don't go to Adam's. Go to the police department parking lot, lock your doors and call me back. If he tries to get in the car, lean hard on your horn!"

"Good plan. Thanks, Sophie."

Once Liz was confident that she wasn't being followed, she headed onto Interstate 5 toward Creswell, with a sigh of relief. This prenatal appointment had gone better than she expected considering her fall and her current level of stress. The doctor let her know everything was on track to give birth within the next five weeks.

When she got back to the cabin, she put on the kettle to make chamomile tea. Then she went back out to the car to get the doctor's summary. Stepping back inside she heard footsteps behind her. As she turned around to shut the door, Matt jammed it with his foot and stormed in.

Liz tried to remain calm but fear made her shout, "What are you doing here? You're freaking me out!" She moved quickly toward the back of the cabin.

"Wonder how I found you?" His stare was filled with rage. "All I want is to get some time alone together. But no, you refuse to see me. I remembered your doctor's appointment this week, so I called to confirm it. When I told the receptionist you're not tracking well these days, she told me the date and time."

Liz was terrified. He'd been stalking her! It never crossed her mind to alert her doctor's office not to release information to him. She had to think fast.

"Matt, you know I want things to work out. We decided to live separately until the baby comes," Liz said, trying to buy some time.

"Getting the locks changed at our house doesn't seem like a gesture of reconciliation. What are you doing out here in the middle of nowhere with our baby due? Are you living with some guy?"

"Of course not! I left our house because I needed a quiet place to rest. Just a short drive to the hospital."

"Why didn't you let me know? Your car is still in our driveway. Your game playing pisses me off."

"I'm not playing games. I just needed a change of scenery and some quiet," Liz said softly, looking down at her feet.

"I hate to break up your solitude, but I deserve an explanation. Why are you spreading false rumors about my father? Why are you determined to cause his political downfall?"

When Liz looked at him quizzically, he ranted, "Don't act dumb! Dad called last night and I got the brunt of it. The Democratic Party found out he's under investigation for a sexual assault in Oregon. Also, for using campaign funds to keep it quiet. The Party is endorsing Isabella Sanchez for governor. And for added humiliation, the front page of the *Madison Chronicle* reported others have come forward with sexual assault allegations."

Liz was speechless. Anything that came to mind would only infuriate Matt further. She started to cry. "Matt, I'm so sorry this happened. It must be horrible to have it all over the papers."

"Don't act like you care! Bet you any money your holier-than-thou friends are part of this smear campaign. I'm sure your pal, Rachel, is behind this. And what about you?"

"Of course not," Liz lied as convincingly as she could.

"Dad told the *Chronicle* his accusers came onto him to get ahead. He swore it was revenge by women he rejected."

Matt was sweating while pacing back and forth, blocking the front door. Liz had no way to escape.

"How hard for you." Liz was trying to sympathize in her calmest voice.

"Don't patronize me!" Matt shouted. "You're just like Mom. You only see Dad's bad side." He stood gasping and staring at her with contempt.

"Matt, you're not your father," Liz said, trying a different tactic, desperately wanting to get through to him. "You're a good man. You would never do the things he's done."

"You don't know anything about my father. Just exaggerations from my mom and lies from those women who are just out for blood."

Liz hesitated for a moment. Being the sympathetic wife wasn't working. Then, she simply lost it and revealed the ugliest thing about Quinn she could think of. "Matt, I know something about Anne. She didn't leave because of depression or because you married too young."

"What in the hell are you talking about? You don't know anything about Anne!"

"When I met her at the coast a month ago, she told me your father had raped her when you were out of town at a law conference. Anne left, fearing for her life. She was afraid of you, too, and made sure you wouldn't find her."

In three long strides, he was across the room, standing over her and screaming, "You liar!" He reached over and grabbed the back of her head. Pulling her hair, he whipped her head back and forth before yanking her to her feet. She lost her balance, folded over and fell to the floor, holding her stomach. When he kicked her in the back, she screamed, "Help, Adam! Help! Help me!"

Matt grabbed her arms, dragging her across the floor as she continued shrieking. He threw her on the couch, leaned over and put his hand over her mouth.

"Shut up or I'll kill you," he seethed. "I knew I couldn't trust you, Anne or my mother. You're all man-haters. You're jealous because we have power over you. The only way you can fight back is through lies."

In one last desperate move, Liz raised her arm up and drove her elbow into Matt's crotch. He yelled in pain and grabbed her neck just as Adam ran through the door.

"What the hell are you doing?" Adam shouted, grabbing Matt and flinging him to the floor. When Matt tried to get up, Adam kicked him on the side of his head. Matt lay on the floor moaning. His heading was pounding. His vision blurred.

Adam raced over to Liz, who was screaming in pain, and saw a puddle where her water broke and blood was all over the floor. He grabbed his cell and dialed 911 with one hand while cradling Liz in his other arm. "It's going to be okay," he whispered to her. "Just hang in there."

As soon as the 911 dispatcher answered, Adam said, "I have a pregnant woman here, due in five weeks. She's been badly beaten by her husband. Her water broke and there's blood in it. Send an ambulance to 27902 Elm in Creswell. I'll stay on the line."

"It's on the way. Is she conscious?" the dispatcher asked.

"Yes, she is, but in a lot of pain. Is there anything I should do? Her husband was strangling her and holding his hand over her mouth when I found them."

"Try not to move her in case she has broken bones, but enough so you can check her breathing. Ambulance and police are on the way! Does the husband have a weapon?"

Adam said he hadn't seen a weapon. He moved his arm slowly so Liz's neck was not bent and said, "Take a deep breath, Liz. Good. Now breathe slowly."

He could see movement out of the corner of his eye and looked over as Matt crawled out of the cabin. When he got to the door, Matt was writhing in pain and had to pull himself up by the frame. He gave Adam a look of sheer hatred. Since Adam couldn't leave Liz, he had no choice but to watch Matt slither out to his car and drive away just before the ambulance arrived.

The EMTs rushed in and immediately checked Liz's vital signs and gave her oxygen. Loading her on the gurney, they assured her they'd be at the hospital soon. The police arrived within minutes and got Matt's name and description from Adam.

"He left a few minutes ago in a blue Prius. No idea where he's headed," added Adam.

As the paramedics loaded Liz into the ambulance,

Adam called Sophie.

"Sophie, lucky you texted me to get back home. Matt had already beat the hell out of Liz by the time I got here. I'm following the ambulance to the hospital. Call the others."

"Oh no! I'll take care of it. Go!"

As the ambulance sped away, the sirens were wailing.

Sophie immediately called Drew, Ira, Becca, and Emily before taking off for the emergency room. Her mind went to the worst scenario. Would Liz and the baby make it?

✗

When Matt left Adam's, he pulled onto a side street, turned off the car and called Marcus. He was talking so hysterically that Marcus found him incomprehensible. When he tried to calm him down, Matt yelled, "Meet me at the emergency room," and hung up. Matt watched the ambulance get onto the freeway. With tires screeching, he made an erratic U-turn and just missed hitting the car behind him. He headed straight to the hospital.

By the time Drew got to the emergency room, Liz had been moved from the ambulance to a curtained exam room and connected to an IV with fluids to stabilize her. The doctor explained, "The assault was so serious that your sister's blood pressure is dropping to a dangerous level for her and the baby. Rather than check her into the emergency room, we'll take her directly to Labor and Delivery where we'll do a quick assessment to determine if we should perform a C-section immediately."

"Will they survive?" Drew asked, holding onto Liz's

hand, not wanting to let go.

"We'll do our best to save them," Dr. Cho responded.

✗

When the baby emerged, she was gasping. Being five weeks early, her lungs were not developed enough to breathe on her own. She was rushed to the NICU where nurses were able to stabilize her.

After Matt arrived, he sat in his car trying to sort out what had just happened and calm himself. After about five minutes, he was ready to walk into the emergency room. All it took was seeing Drew and Liz's friends standing at the intake desk for him to lose it. Rushing toward them, he screamed, "Get out of my way. It's my wife and my baby! I want to see them right now!"

Within seconds, two security guards surrounded Matt and restrained him while he tried to break free.

"Matt, stop it!" Marcus demanded, as he and Natalie rushed into the ER.

"Don't try to go back there to see Liz," Natalie pleaded.

"No one can keep me from Liz. I've had it with all of you."

As a police car pulled up in front of the emergency room door, Matt panicked. Harnessing his rage into all the strength he could muster, he broke loose from the security guards, punching one of them in the face, knocking him to the floor.

"Stop. Police! Put your hands up!" Matt froze. Two officers grabbed him, put his arms behind his back and handcuffed him.

"Are you Matt Foley?" demanded one of the officers.

"I won't talk without my lawyer!" Matt sneered, struggling as they dragged him out of the hospital and into the backseat of the police car. Everyone in the emergency room could hear Matt's piercing screams as the hospital doors closed. "Liz, I didn't mean it. Liz, I didn't mean it. I didn't mean it."

When Liz woke up after the C-section, she found herself in a hospital room with Drew and Sophie sitting by her bedside talking quietly. Before she could say anything, they said in unison, "The baby is fine."

She smiled at them through her drugged stupor. "Where is she?"

"In the NICU. The doctors said that the fetal distress called for an emergency C-section," Drew answered. "The baby will be here for a week or two."

"Can I go see her?"

"Not yet. Dr. Cho said that you might be strong enough by tomorrow," Drew said.

Sophie reached into her purse. "Here's some photos we took right after she was born. She looks just like her Mama!"

Tears came to Liz's eyes. "I'm so grateful she survived. I just wish that I could hold Sally now."

Drew smiled. "So, that's what you named my niece? Nice going."

"I figured naming her after Mom would keep her memory alive," Liz said, reaching out for Drew. He stood up and leaned over to gently kiss her forehead.

"I've been able to keep an eye on that baby girl of yours. Luckily, I'm on your medical release form so the surgeon could update me on your condition. She explained your vaginal bleeding showed just how severe the violence was this time," Drew said.

Just then her surgeon walked in and smiled at Liz. "You've been through a trauma today, but you made it! You and your baby are fighters, Ms. Lodde. I'm going to do a quick check to see how you're doing."

"Sure. Go ahead and poke around. I'm so grateful that you saved us." Liz broke into tears.

"You're lucky you got here in time. Ten more minutes and you wouldn't have survived the blood loss. Your pediatrician will have to keep a close watch on your baby during the first year. We know battering can cause birth defects and threaten the baby's healthy development. I'm hopeful your baby will be alright. Only time will tell."

Liz winced and said bitterly, "Nothing else I can do but wait and see."

"I have another surgery in fifteen minutes, but I'll stop by again in the morning. You need to send your visitors home and get some rest," she said kindly.

As the surgeon left, Liz turned to Drew and Sophie, "I wish I had never married Matt! He almost killed my baby." She began crying and couldn't stop.

Drew sat on the side of the bed with tears in his eyes. "Matt didn't succeed. You both survived. And that's all that matters."

EPILOGUE

Liz was sitting on the bench in her backyard. It had a plaque on it in memory of her parents. She smiled as she watched her three-year-old daughter, Sally, chasing their new goldendoodle puppy, Cricket, around the paths. She wished that her parents could have known their grand-daughter. Sally was rambunctious and curious about everything. She suddenly stopped chasing Cricket and sat down to pull dandelions out of the grass. Jumping up, she brought a bouquet of them to show Liz.

"Look at my flowers, Mommy!" she said, twirling around.

"They're beautiful," Liz said, smiling. "Can you find some more?"

Sally ran over to the pansies. Looking from the pink to the purple to the white, she tried to decide which one to pick. She settled on purple and tugged on it several times before it came loose.

"Purple flowers, Mommy," she said, running back and

handing them to Liz.

"Thank you so much. You know how much I love purple. You're so generous," Liz said, giving Sally a hug. "Do you want to sit on my lap and read for a while?"

Sally ran inside and chose the book *Hug* about a baby chimpanzee who is lost and says the word "hug" repeatedly to other animals. All the baby animals are being hugged by their mothers except for him. When his mother finds him, they reunite with a warm hug.

"Sometimes, it's a daddy who hugs the lost baby chimp," Sally's teacher told them reading the book aloud at her preschool. Sally's friend Charlie had two dads, something he proudly shared when he first joined the class. After Liz finished reading, Sally asked, "Where's my Daddy?"

Liz explained, "Your Daddy can't be here right now. He's far away. I showed you some pictures of him with your grandmother." Liz wondered if her response simply confused Sally.

Just then Cricket ran up and began licking Sally's face. She giggled and ran off to chase her into one of the garden beds. Liz watched and was relieved that Sally's attention span was so short. She knew harder questions about Sally's father would come in due time. But at least not today.

Liz thought about how lucky she was compared to three years ago. She looked over at the tiny house she had added in the corner of her backyard. Having Sophie and Pete living there with their nine-month old son removed some of the loneliness Liz felt after her marriage ended. With the help of her extended family and the tight-knit community at the Cafe, the shock of her life upheaval was fading. Enough time had passed so Liz no longer trembled when she flashed back on that last violent incident and how she nearly lost Sally.

After Matt was sentenced to five years in prison for assault, Liz had to rebuild her life as a domestic violence survivor and a single parent. Drew stepped up to be an extraordinary uncle. He spent as much time with Sally as his work allowed. He did everything from diaper changing to stroller rides in the park and accompanying Liz to Sally's doctor's appointments. He was a natural at comforting Sally when she was cranky or frightened.

Drew dropped the role of Liz's substitute father and accepted she was in charge of her own life. He watched Liz survive her abusive marriage and keep the business going while nurturing her fragile baby.

At the same time, Drew was available whenever Liz asked. Since she only worked part-time after Sally's birth, Drew went to the Cafe every few days to check on things and report back. Emily was now the music club manager after learning the ropes from Liz on concert promotions and booking performers. When Emily started working on her Master's thesis, she agreed to stay for one year or until Liz found someone to take her place. Ira was in charge of the restaurant, a promotion he deserved.

At Emily's suggestion, Liz was seeing a therapist who had expertise in domestic violence. Through counseling, Liz was learning to get past blaming herself for putting Sally's life and her own in danger. She was finally accepting that Matt, not her, was responsible.

Liz had learned how the ongoing stress and the repeated assaults had negative effects on her pregnancy. Having a preemie was one of them. Sally's pediatrician evaluated her regularly with this in mind. So far there were no indicators of cognitive or physical damage. Sally was a healthy and confident child who met all the developmental milestones.

✗

The criminal case against Quinn didn't move forward when Anne changed her mind and was unable to testify in court. Her rape disclosure to the women at the coast and the reality of reliving the horror in a courtroom triggered PTSD. Anne had become suicidal and required inpatient treatment when she returned to Montreal.

Becca spent a month with Anne while she was in psychiatric residential treatment and then helped her transition home. While Quinn didn't stand trial for raping Anne, he was facing multiple civil suits generated by women from his past. The not-so-honorable Judge Foley was no longer a judge and Isabella Sanchez became the next Governor of Wisconsin. Both Anne and Becca took some comfort in that.

Joanne came out from Chicago to visit Liz and Sally every three months or so. During these trips, she also saw Matt in prison. When Joanne informed Matt that Quinn's case was being dropped, she listened to his endless tirade.

Finally, she interrupted. "You're right, Matt. It's immoral that your Dad got off for what he did to Anne. He'll pay in other ways, financially and professionally."

"There's no way Anne could have stayed with me after what Dad did to her. Then, he goes and assaults Rachel and uses me to cover it up. No wonder Liz hates me."

"Liz couldn't figure out why you helped your Dad after

he had mistreated you for most of your life."

"I was a fool. Liz was right and I couldn't see it. Dad hurt both of us for years, Mom. Then he went on to brutally attack Anne. I've thought a lot about it while in prison. Anne wrote me a letter as part of her treatment. She reminded me that I had begun to act like Dad while we were still married. I couldn't stop myself. An example she gave was me grabbing her arm and forcing her into the car over some petty jealousy. She had to get away from me after the rape because she didn't trust me enough to confide what Dad did to her. Now we know she was right."

Joanne teared up. "It's true. Your father harmed you and people you loved."

Matt had recently learned that he would be released for good behavior after only three years of his five year sentence. His future relationship with his daughter had been weighing heavily on him. He looked at Joanne and sighed. "How do I deal with all this? How do I convince Liz that I can be a decent father?"

"Matt, the next few years will be hard. You have to take responsibility for what happened. You can't blame your father for everything. You have to turn this around."

"I'll do anything it takes to be in Sally's life. Can you convince Liz?"

"It's not up to me, Matt. Right now, I wouldn't advocate for it. You have to convince the courts and Liz you've changed. Maybe a batterer intervention group or counseling when you get out can help you get there. But it will take time."

Discouraged, Matt looked down and said, "I thought that group was a waste of time. I felt like I didn't belong there."

"After all that's happened, maybe you'll feel differently now."

"Maybe I should have stuck with the group. It might have prevented me from ending up in prison. Hard to know. If going back there can give me a chance to know Sally, then maybe it's what I'll have to do. Anything to be near her."

Joanne sighed with relief. "That's a good start! You know that you're luckier than most who leave prison. You have a place to live in Cottage Grove and some savings since Natalie and Marcus rented out the house for you."

"It's true. By renting out Camp Gramps, I didn't have to sell it," added Matt.

When Matt was released, Natalie and Marcus picked him up and drove him to Cottage Grove. He turned down their offer to go to their house for a home-cooked meal and spend the night. Solitude was something he needed desperately.

Joanne would come to visit in a few weeks. Matt wanted to adjust to being free before she arrived. When he called Pete to enroll in the Batterer Intervention Group, he explained his parole officer would need to approve his participation. Pete remembered Matt and was pleased to hear from him. He suggested Matt come to the next Thursday evening group. By the time Joanne came to visit, Matt had been to four batterer intervention sessions.

"Mom, I was surprised how different the group is for me now. I had to admit how violent I was. This time I was finally ready to face it."

As Matt described the group to Joanne over lunch, he started to laugh. "It's funny, but by the third session, I found myself lecturing a first-time member just like Joe had lectured me at my first group. I had claimed my wife blamed me for her broken wrist when I barely touched her. Joe and the rest of the group laughed at me. Joe told me it takes a long time to admit the truth about your violence. I never thought I'd say this, but I should have listened to him then."

"Well, you're listening now," Joanne replied.

"During the last few weeks, I've thought a lot about my future. One thing is for sure, it won't include Dad."

"I don't blame you. You have a lot to gain by changing who's in your life. I can think of something else you could do to show how serious you are. How about taking a parenting class? Liz would see how committed you are to being a good father."

"I wish I could be optimistic like you, Mom. I just don't know."

"Honey, I'm going over to see Sally later this afternoon. I'll take lots of pictures and videos. I may broach the idea of supervised visits with Liz further down the road. I'll only do it if she asks about you."

"That's fair."

"You know that Marcus and Natalie have been updating Liz on how you've been doing. The first couple of years she asked them not to mention you at all. She's been more open lately and knows about your early release."

Joanne hugged Matt tightly. It felt good to have him out in the world again. For the first time in years, she was more hopeful than worried.

When she got to Liz's, Joanne immediately headed to the yard. She smiled to herself as she guessed Sally would be in the garden picking flowers, on the swings, or chasing Cricket around a tree.

As soon as Joanne lifted the latch on the gate, Sally spotted her from the swing. "Hi, Jojo! Push me higher!"

"Yes, Missy. Anything you say!" Joanne had no boundaries when it came to Sally. She'd do anything for that little girl and Sally knew it.

Liz laughed at the exchange and saw Joanne's arms filled with books for Sally. "One of those books better be for me, Joanne."

"Of course, there's a book for you. *American Primitive,* more poetry by Mary Oliver. I know you love her work."

"Yes. Excellent choice. You may join me for a glass of wine for your efforts," Liz said as they both laughed.

They talked for about an hour, watching Sally play, being constantly interrupted by her requests to watch her swing, to come pick flowers or to be held on Jojos' lap. When Sally went next door to play with her neighbor, Liz sat quietly for a long time. Joanne waited.

"Let's talk about Matt. Natalie told me you were going out to see him today. I've had lots of conversations with Marcus and Natalie about him over the last months and even more since his release. So, I know what's going on."

"I'm relieved that you're willing to talk about him. My unwritten rule has been to let you bring him up. I know it's been challenging to continue our relationship after what happened. You know I love Matt and believe he can change. I'm forever grateful you've let me be an active part of Sally's life from the start."

"Joanne, I honestly don't know what I would have done without you. When I got home with my preemie baby, I was injured and traumatized by Matt's attack. A total mess, physically and emotionally. You took leave from work and stayed with me. You were juggling Sally and me, plus dealing with Matt's arrest and trial. You helped me survive. Sally ended up with the best grandmother ever."

"Stop. I'm running out of tears."

"I hit bottom after Sally was born. You did all you could to make me feel good about myself. And you still do."

"I know exactly how you feel. My sister, Eleanor, was my champion and supporter after I left Quinn. I couldn't have made it without her. I'm happy I could be that person for you. But, look at you now. You're strong and resilient. You've created a healthy family like the loving one you grew up in."

"And you helped me make that happen. You are the true matriarch of this family. My Mom would have loved you, Joanne."

"You just gave me the highest compliment of my life. Thanks, Lizzie."

"That's what Mom always called me."

"You told me that once. I hope it's okay that I used your family nickname."

"Absolutely!" They both burst into tears and hugged as they sat on the Sally and Peter bench.

"Enough mushiness. This seems to be an especially emotional day for us, Liz."

"It sure is. Are you ready for my breakthrough?"

"I think so."

"I started to see my therapist again about a month before Matt was released. She has helped me figure out a way for Sally to possibly get to know her Dad."

"Sounds hopeful. Tell me more."

"I've been working on forgiving Matt. It will be a long, long time, if ever."

"Maybe he could prove to you one day that he's worth forgiving."

"Be realistic, Joanne. You weren't able to forgive Quinn. You almost missed your son's first wedding because you didn't want to be in the same room with him."

"Point well taken. I can't help but look at things differently because we're talking about my son. I believe that Matt can be a better man than his father. Maybe prison woke him up. Quinn never made any attempts to change."

"I came up with this after a long conversation with Leah Jesse, my muralist friend you like so much."

"Funny. I just came across her work in *Juxtaposed*, the art magazine. She did a mural for the City of Barcelona that's gotten a lot of attention internationally. She's amazing. What did you two talk about?"

"I don't think I ever told you that Leah Jesse was adopted at birth. When I told her how conflicted I am about letting Matt into Sally's life, she shared something that made a lot of sense to me. When people ask her about her real parents, she explains the people who adopted her are her 'real parents', the ones who gave her love and support all her life. They taught her to believe in her dreams. But her birth family gave her a part of who she is, too. She got to know her birth mother through their open adoption."

"What about her birth father?"

"Because he was in prison for years, she didn't meet him until she was in her twenties. When they finally met, Leah Jesse understood who gave her the wild spirit that lives in her blood."

Liz hesitated and took a deep breath, "So, I applied Leah's story to Sally's situation. They're not identical, but both had incarcerated, biological fathers who neither knew growing up. It made me think about how crucial it is for Sally to at least meet Matt so she can understand where she comes from. But I have conditions Matt would have to meet in order to see her."

"This is a big deal. Go on."

"I ran this idea by my therapist, too. She told me to be cautious. First, I'd want Matt to complete six months of batterer intervention groups and the same for parenting classes. The Domestic Violence Legal Clinic advised me to have his parole office require an assessment to make sure that it's safe for Sally to be around him."

"That's more than reasonable. Matt was just talking to me this afternoon about parenting classes. He wants to be a good father."

"You have higher hopes than me. According to my therapist, it's a life-long process for a batterer to change. Right now, my trust level for Matt is at zero."

"Of course it is. Take it slow."

"I know you understand what I'm facing. Legally, it will be the court system and custody law that decides if and when it's time for Matt to see Sally. My lawyer told me that I can weigh in on this. It could take a year or more before I would recommend he be allowed to see her. The visit would have to be supervised."

When Sally came back from the neighbor's, she darted toward the bench. She found her Mom wiping her eyes and her grandma holding her.

"Where does it hurt, Mommy?" Sally asked as she crawled into Liz's lap.

"We were talking about a sad story from a long time ago. It made me cry."

"Are you better, Mommy? Did JoJo fix it?" Liz nodded, smiling at her innocence. Sally got off her lap, grabbed an almond cookie off the patio table and went to find Cricket.

"Joanne, will my life ever go back to normal?"

"I don't have a simple answer. I was depressed for the longest time. Just as things would get better, something would trigger memories of my terrifying life with Quinn. Violent episodes would flash before my eyes. I'd remember other moments reminding me how much I once loved him. That would set me back, too. I lost the life I once knew."

"But you created a new life. Maybe the rest will come later."

"I don't know. I've never been in a stable relationship since I left Quinn. Here and there, I met some decent men. I just couldn't commit. I hate to say it, but Quinn kind of ruined me."

"Prove Quinn wrong. You deserve to love again." Joanne wondered if Liz was actually talking about herself.

"Work, friends and family fill me up for now."

"That wasn't the pep talk I thought you would give me."

"It's all I've got, Liz. You'll find your way, just like I did."

Liz got up and walked slowly alongside the sunflower beds. She loved how they reached for the sky. On her gloomiest days, she gazed up at them, feeling hopeful. Liz smiled at her daughter doing cartwheels in front of the three pear trees near the back fence. Joanne strolled over to them as Sally finished her last cartwheel, falling to the ground giggling. They joined in as she began to sing her favorite childhood lullaby:

Shady Grove, my little love
Shady Grove, my darlin'
Shady Grove my little love,
I'm going back to Harlan.

ACKNOWLEDGEMENTS

Writing a novel as co-authors is no simple task. We began as friends and colleagues and transformed into writers blending two voices into one. And we're still standing. A miracle.

FROM EVELYN:
I'd like to thank Janet Anderson, my amazing spouse, for her unceasing encouragement as I spent hundreds of hours writing and editing this book, even when it meant time apart.

In memory of my older brother, Kit Anderton who did whatever he could to ensure that we would survive during the years of abuse. In appreciation of my loving younger sisters, Mary and Joan Anderton.

FROM PEARL:
I'm grateful to Bill Goldsmith, my loving husband, who believed that the best way to share what we learned doing domestic violence work was to write this novel. He listened carefully and always encouraged me to be creative and hold true to my values.

My daughter, Rachel Wolfe-Goldsmith, supported and

inspired me to take on a project that was creative and risk taking. She convinced us to drop the jargon of our profession, so the language of our novel engaged all readers.

Often one person is the greatest protector in an abusive and chaotic childhood. My big sister, Eleanor, was my person.

I so appreciate Beth Horikawa and Joanne Spiegel, my literary and longest time friends, for continuous encouragement.

FROM BOTH OF US:

An incredibly special thanks to our internal review team who read our numerous drafts. Charlie Price taught us to develop dialogue so our characters sounded like real people and gave our story more oomph. Kate Barkley's analysis of how institutions either help or create barriers added a realistic framework to the plot. Cherie Bynum's clinical understanding of survivors and batterers kept us true to their experiences.

We received a crash course on publishing from Fran Benson. We are grateful to both Fran and Andrea Fleck Clardy, who gave us important direction in our early chapters. We relied on Ben Spiegel, M.D. for accurate medical information about injuries and treatment in domestic violence incidents and to Hal Neth, J.D. for his legal knowledge. Barbara Pope's critique of our query letter was crucial to getting our book published.

We value our helpful team at Atmosphere Press: Nick Courtright, CEO; Megan Turner, Developmental Editor; Alex Kale, Managing Editor; Ronaldo Alves, Art Director; Evan Courtright, Digital Director; Cammie Finch, Publicity Director; Christina Garcia, Social Media Manager.

We are grateful to the National Domestic Violence Hotline, the National Coalition Against Domestic Violence, Oregon Coalition Against Domestic & Sexual Violence, and the Hope and Safety Alliance (formerly Womenspace). Their websites informed our novel by providing up to date information and best practices on domestic violence. Please see our Resource Page.

We are grateful to Womenspace for the experience and knowledge we gained during our years there. For us, it was an exceptional workplace with strong and nurturing staff and volunteers, operating 24 hours a day, 365 days a year. Domestic violence programs across the country save lives every single day.

We credit the women and children of Womenspace for teaching us the truth about domestic violence. We share their struggle for survival through this novel.

READING GUIDE
Discussion Questions

This reading group guide for *Walk Out the Door* provides a set of targeted questions to stimulate a lively discussion. It highlights topics to help you view the novel from different perspectives and generate unique insights from group members.

1. *Walk Out the Door* begins with a risky situation for Jill's Place staff. Becca and Emily drive to Molly's house in rural Oregon to bring her and her children to safety. Did anything trouble you about this incident? Since most shelters have strict policies about not going to homes, did they make the right call?

2. Liz and Molly have different domestic violence stories to tell. While Liz left early in her relationship, Molly went back four times before she left Danny for good. How did each respond to the violence they faced? What barriers prevented each of them from leaving their relationships? How did they lift those barriers?

3. Often children want the batterer to stop the violence, but not leave the family. How did 7-year-old Jason's reactions throughout the story help you understand what it's like to be a child in a domestic violence household? What do you think the long-term effects will be for Jason? What could Molly do to help her son recover from this trauma?

4. Abusive behaviors can be learned in families and through our culture. Why do some who grow up in domestic violence homes repeat what they learned as adults and others do not? We also know that people who batter have multiple sides to them. Describe the different sides of Matt. How did he engage people around him? What about him suggested he could be dangerous?

5. Sophie and Drew, among others, play key roles as Liz deals with her growing fears. Discuss the effectiveness of Liz's support system. How would you support a family member or friend in the same situation?

6. What went through your mind during Liz's fall at the Shady Grove Café? Why was it difficult for Liz to accept help from Emily and Drew? How did her experience at the emergency room affect her?

7. In Chapter 9, Liz reflects on the Café Incident: *"She went over to calm him down and the next thing she knew she had crashed against the wall behind the counter. The blurred memories of their argument replayed in Liz's mind. Her growing annoyance with Matt. His face turned red with rage. Her fall. Could he have pushed her intentionally? Would he do such a thing?"* Why was Liz second guessing herself on whether it was abuse or an accident?

8. In Chapter 18, Liz hears about the first generation of domestic violence in Matt's family, the story of Joanne and Quinn. How does learning about Matt's family history impact Liz's choices?

9. Often domestic violence advocates are asked why women stay. The more compelling question is what changes in their lives allow them to leave. Describe what drove Liz, Molly, Joanne, and Anne, our four survivors, to walk out the door for good?

10. Do you think Matt, Quinn, and Danny can change? Will they batter a new partner? Are they safe around their children? What do you think qualifies as "being safe" for children?

11. What added information and insights did you gain about domestic violence?

RESOURCE PAGE

✗ National Domestic Violence Hotline
Advocates are available at:
(800) 799-7233
www.TheHotline.org.

The National Domestic Violence Hotline (NDVH) is a 24-hour confidential service for survivors, victims and those affected by domestic violence, intimate partner violence and relationship abuse.

✗ National Coalition Against Domestic Violence
(303) 839-1852
ncadv.org

The National Coalition Against Domestic Violence (NCADV)'s mission is to lead, mobilize and raise our voices to support efforts that demand a change of conditions that lead to domestic violence such as patriarchy, privilege, racism, sexism, and classism. We are dedicated to supporting survivors and holding offenders accountable and supporting advocates.

✗ Oregon Coalition Against Domestic & Sexual Violence
(503) 230-1951
www.ocadsv.org

The Oregon Coalition Against Domestic and Sexual Violence (OCADSV) promotes equity and social change in order to end violence for all communities. We seek to transform society by engaging diverse voices, supporting the self-determination of survivors and providing leadership for advocacy efforts.

✗ Hope and Safety Alliance, Eugene, OR
(formerly Womenspace)
24-hour Crisis Line: **(541) 485-6513**
or **(800) 281-2800**
https://www.hopesafetyalliance.org/

Hope & Safety Alliance has been providing hope and safety to survivors of domestic and sexual violence for over 40 years. Each year we serve thousands of survivors and children from our urban and rural communities in Lane County.

Domestic violence does not discriminate on the basis of race, religion, politics, economic position, education, sexual orientation, gender identity or expression. Therefore, the Hope and Safety Alliance serves all survivors.

We believe everyone has the right to a life free from violence and fear of abuse.

ABOUT ATMOSPHERE PRESS

Atmosphere Press is an independent, full-service publisher for excellent books in all genres and for all audiences. Learn more about what we do at atmospherepress.com.

We encourage you to check out some of Atmosphere's latest releases, which are available at Amazon.com and via order from your local bookstore:

Shadows of Robyst, a novel by K. E. Maroudas

Dying to Live, a novel by Barbara Macpherson Reyelts

Looking for Lawson, a novel by Mark Kirby

Surrogate Colony, a novel by Boshra Rasti

Á Deux, a novel by Alexey L. Kovalev

What If It Were True, a novel by Eileen Wesel

Sunflowers Beneath the Snow, a novel by Teri M. Brown

Solitario: The Lonely One, a novel by John Manuel

The Fourth Wall, a novel by Scott Petty

ABOUT THE AUTHORS

Co-authors Pearl Wolfe and Evelyn Anderton recently completed their debut contemporary fiction novel, *Walk Out the Door*. They became colleagues and friends while at Womenspace, an agency working to end domestic violence in Eugene, Oregon. They each have over two decades of experience with issues related to violence against women. Both grew up in homes where domestic violence and child abuse were the norm, bringing an intimate perspective to their writing.

Both authors have a history as activists focused on domestic violence, homelessness, and poverty. Wolfe and Anderton are recipients of the City of Eugene "Human Rights Recognition Award" for their dedication to the empowerment of women through their work on domestic violence. Wolfe has a B.A. in Social Work from University of Wisconsin and an M.S. in Sociology from the University of Oregon. Anderton holds a B.A in English from UC Berkeley.

CPSIA information can be obtained
at www.ICGtesting.com
Printed in the USA
BVHW042258251022
650240BV00006BA/529

9 781639 883400